The Day They

Took My Uncle

and Other Stories

The Day They
Took My Uncle
And Other Stories

by LIONEL G. GARCIA

TCU Press
Fort Worth

Library of Congress Cataloging-in-Publication Data

Garcia, Lionel G.
    The day they took my uncle, and other stories / by Lionel G. Garcia.
    p.cm.
    ISBN 0-87565-235-2 (alk. paper)
    1. Texas, South--Social life and customs--Fiction. 2. Hispanic
Americans--Fiction I.
Title

PS3557.A71115 D3 2001
813'.54—dc 21
00-057716

Contents

Acknowledgements

The following short stories have appeared in the listed publications:

"The Wedding," *Cuentos Chicanos.* Albuquerque: University of New Mexico Press, 1984. Rewritten, 1996.

"The Day They Took My Uncle," *Americas Review,* 1984, and *Short Fiction By Hispanic Writers.* Edited by Nicolás Kanellos. Houston: Arte Publico Press, 1993.

"The Sergeant," *Americas Review,* 1987, and *Hispanic Literature of the United States.* Edited by Nicolás Kanellos. New York: HarperCollins, 1995. Rewritten, 1996.

"Mister Tyrone," *Texas Short Stories II,* Dallas: Browder Springs Publishing Company, 1999.

To the Texans

Introduction

Like most novelists, I began as a short-story writer. That was in the days when short stories were popular. Just about every magazine had at least one short story in it. Small literary magazines were everywhere. It was a good way to begin a writing career.

Some critics say that the short story is dead, gone the way of the literary novel. In the case of the short story, critics say it's not enough. In the case of the literary novel they argue that it's too much.

Personally, I love the short story. It can be the most thought-provoking, stimulating form of writing. In athletic terms, it is a sprint, and is as exciting. It begins and ends in a flash. A novel, conversely, is a marathon.

To the writer, and most importantly the reader, the short story brings gratification in a short period of time as opposed to the novel.

The effect of a short story is a suspended instant of humanity in which life is dissected and exposed for the world to see. It has in it a moment of time, a travesty of fate, a flash of emotions, the vagaries of life, a loss, a gain, everything.

It should leave the reader in a disturbed sense of feelings. It should make the reader think. The only thing close to it is a great poem.

No one should read a short story and be the same person afterwards. Put another way, the short story should change the way the reader looks at things—important or insignificant—forevermore.

Bernard Malamud, the great short-story writer, once wrote, "A short story is a way of indicating the complexity of life in a few pages, producing the surprise and effect of a profound knowledge in a short time."

The stories I have gathered here are a product of many years of writing. They are all different in many ways, like individuals, and like individuals they are to be taken at their value one at a time.

When asked which of his stories he liked the best, the great writer of short fiction and Nobel Laureate, Isaac Bashevis Singer, said that his stories were like his children, each one different and each one loved in a different way. There were no favorites, not consciously anyway.

Some of these stories have been published before, most of them have not simply because of the issue of first rights. The ones which have been published before, and which some readers might have read, have all been rewritten simply because I cannot leave a story alone.

I sincerely hope that you enjoy them.

Lionel Garcia
Seabrook, Texas

The Day They

Took My Uncle

and Other Stories

Alone

Constancia wondered if there was life beyond the fear of abandonment.

Married and divorced, middle-aged, and living in the sameness of her lonely life, she remembered she had asked her father why he worked every day and he had replied that there was nothing else for him to do.

"That's all there is," he said, wiping his hands of the grime.

Life's routine had absorbed him at an early age. He had become encased like a worm in a cocoon in a life whose dimensions dared not go beyond its webbing.

She feared the same fate beginning to fall on her. She went to work at the hospital and came home—back and forth—without a hint of change. She worked hard. She smiled a lot to hide the loneliness she felt. She was submerging herself more and more in helping others and abandoning all hope for herself. On Fridays she shopped for groceries, alone. Meals were the same, alone. When she lay down alone she had begun to hear her own heartbeat. At night she dreamed of snakes slithering out of her nostrils. In some dreams she had gone blind and she carried her eyes in her hands.

Constancia smoked her third cigarette waiting for Mr. Lea. He had promised to be there at ten in the morning to fix the leak in the kitchen sink. The water was collecting under the trailer. The dog that slept under the trailer had been enjoying the leak during the hot August. Constancia had seen the dog crawl out from under the trailer covered in the cool mud. She looked to the clock on the wall above the small refrigerator. Ten thirty. He was thirty minutes late, not like him at all

Once again Constancia went to the window in the trailer. She looked out toward the street, toward the church a block away. This time she heard the sound of the engine and then in a fraction of an instant, a block away, she saw a dark shiny car cross the space between the church and the old Catholic school. She followed the imaginary path of the car hidden by the church. And then she saw the car reappear. It was Mr. Lea, driving his car slowly. At the corner she saw him stop, look all around, signal a turn and then turn right. He came down one block and stopped completely at the sign. She could see him look cautiously both ways. He took an immediate left and he was parked by the trailer by the time she put out her cigarette. She walked to the living room at the front of the trailer to wait for him to knock. For some reason, she did not want him to think she had been waiting.

He knocked heavily. The old trailer shook. She took her time about going to the door, trying not to seem anxious.

She opened the door to see Mr. Lea.

Mr. Lea lowered his sights immediately when he saw her through the door. He had hated to come, to face her again. His bashfulness did not go with his large size. He looked painfully aware of his situation.

She tried to get the episode with Mr. Lea's wife out of her mind.

His large toolbox dangled from his left hand. "I'm sorry I'm late," he said in a heavy German accent and she opened the door for him.

She did not want to think about a man.

Mr. Lea wiped his shoes several times on the greeting mat

outside and then checked the soles to make sure he wasn't track-ing anything into the trailer.

"Being late's all right," she said. "I wasn't going anywhere anyway."

Mr. Lea insisted on apologizing. He said, "The car would not start. The battery was down. And it's only a year and seven months old. I bought it in April at the auto shop on Main."

Constancia led him toward the kitchen at the middle of the trailer. "That's all right," she said, not wanting to get into how many months it had been. Some of these things irritated her. "I had some things to do," she explained.

"You're not working today?" he asked. He had gone on to the kitchen and was talking from there. He placed his toolbox down in front of the sink and opened it, taking out several wrenches. He bent down in front of the sink. He was trying to bend down gracefully. He became embarrassed and knelt down instead. He opened the two valves under the sink and checked around the stems. They were not leaking.

She was standing at the door, lighting another cigarette, watching him work. Her husband had left her ten years ago. Slowly, day-to-day, she had lost interest in men but seeing Mr. Lea brought back memories of her married days, a man around the house. She felt a slight uncontrollable urge, something ill-defined, starting at the mind and sweeping through her body. Her images of Mr. Lea's wife made her feel ill at ease immedi-ately. How long had it been since a man did to her what he was doing to Mr. Lea's wife? She stood frozen at the car window watching them, enjoying the scene.

The muscular Mr. Lea was on his knees underneath the sink, half his body hidden. From there she heard his muffled voice.

"What?" she asked, broken from her reverie. "I couldn't under-stand." She had a glimpse of his back. She had to take another look and then when she saw him helpless under the sink she took one last look.

Mr. Lea backed out on his knees, felt the awkwardness of his position and promptly stood up. "The leak," he said in his thick accent, "it is right where the pipe comes into the floor. Right under there." He pointed his large finger underneath the sink.

"What does that all mean?" she asked. "All I want to know is can you fix it?"

"Yes," he replied, "but I'm going to have to go to the hardware store to get some of the material."

"Will you be back today, then?" she wanted to know. She had placed the burning cigarette in the ashtray on the counter.

Mr. Lea wiped his hands on his pants.

She noticed his discomfort. "You need money?" asked Constancia.

"Well, yes," he admitted, as though he was imposing on her. "I'm sorry," he added. "It's just that I haven't had that much work lately. And even then I haven't gotten paid. I used a lot of material the last job but no money."

"You're always too nice, Mr. Lea. Make them pay you," she said. She took the cigarette and placed it between her lips while she got some money out of her housecoat and counted it. After what had happened with Mr. Lea's wife she was glad to help him in any way.

"I try," he said, "but. . . ." Then he shrugged his shoulders to indicate that it was useless and said, "but they won't pay. They're saying I don't do such a good job."

"That's a lie," Constancia said. "You always do a good job. That's your problem. You're too conscientious. You take too long. Do too much extra. People take advantage of you. You go to fix a leak and then they complain about the toilet and you fix that for free and then they keep you all day doing other things, fixing doors, everything. It's not right. People are going to take advantage of you. Don't you see that?"

"Well," Mr. Lea replied, "what else can a man do? I'm just that way." The memory of his wife made him still more uncomfortable as he wondered if Constancia was thinking what he was thinking. He needed to leave.

In the afternoon Mr. Lea returned with his materials and with many misgivings. He parked at the side of the trailer this time under the tree so that he could put his threading machine in the shade.

Constancia called him in after a while. She had made coffee for him and toast and jelly. Mr. Lea said he was not hungry. Constancia knew he was but hated to eat in front of people. She insisted and he finally came inside. He was putting on his shirt when he stepped through the door. Constancia made him keep the shirt off. It was so hot. How could he stand the heat under the trailer?

"Just like the dog," said Mr. Lea, a faint smile coming to his face. He had thought his remark funny and Constancia laughed to make him feel more secure.

She watched him eat and he was so self-conscious that he stopped chewing when he noticed her stare. She was emboldened by her dominance over such a big man.

She was standing at the door smoking a cigarette. "Do you find life hard, Mr. Lea?" she asked. "I know it's been hard on you. It's been hard on me."

Mr. Lea nodded and said, "Yes, it has."

"But I have to admit that there are moments in life that are so precious that it makes it all worthwhile. Don't you think?" she asked of him.

Mr. Lea was trying to put his shirt on.

"When I think that all of us are going to have to die . . . what a shame," she said and Mr. Lea, having put on his shirt, began to eat slowly.

His silence caused her to feel more daring. "Are you ever lonely, Mr. Lea?" Constancia asked, taking the conversation one step farther. "Now that your wife is gone, I mean?"

Mr. Lea swallowed the toast. "Yes. . ." he managed to say, "sometimes I'm lonely."

"I'm sorry for what happened," she blurted out and then, in a repentant pose, looked down to the floor. After a decent silence she said, "I'm sorry. But you're such a decent man. I had to tell you. When I saw you in church praying I felt so sorry for you. I couldn't sleep thinking about you. I just couldn't help myself. But I am sorry. I'm sorry I did it. I'm sorry it happened. She was not any good. You understand that?"

"Someone would have to tell me someday," he said. "It just happened to be you."

"Do you resent me?" Constancia asked. "After all. You know what I mean. You understand that at first I tried to make like I didn't know what was happening."

"I know," Mr. Lea said. "It was kind of you."

"It put me in a bad light," she said. "I mean, I could see you and feel for you. I just had to tell you. I'm sorry if I hurt you."

"Don't feel sorry."

"Well, I'm glad that's out of the way. I knew you didn't want to come. To have to face me."

"I have a job to do. I need the work."

"Let's talk of something else," said Constancia, sighing. "Something good. For instance . . .

"Yes?"

"I'd like to have a friend. Someone just to talk to. I'd like to have a woman friend but it's hard for women to be friends. True friends, I mean. We're raised to compete for affection, you know. The minute you introduce a man into the friendship it goes to pot. And most men are different. They want something right away. They want to sleep with you."

Mr. Lea blushed. "No," he said quickly, meaning that it was not in his character.

"I know," Constancia said. "You are decent. A decent man. That's why I'm talking to you about friendship."

Mr. Lea spoke through his discomfort. He said, "There are many, many good men. Don't judge us all by what you have known."

"I guess you're right," Constancia agreed, sitting down next to him and putting out her cigarette. "After all that has happened, do you think we could be friends, Mr. Lea? Just friends?"

Mr. Lea could only smile. "I don't see why not, Constancia," he said.

"But just friends," Constancia insisted quickly.

"Just friends," Mr. Lea repeated, smiling at her.

Constancia became animated with pleasure. She said, rapidly, "We could go out together. Go places. Do you ever go to the movies?"

"No," Mr. Lea replied.

"Well," said Constancia, "we could go there. See a movie once in while. I mean, not every night or anything like that. But once in a while. Once a month. Just so that we know that we can. We can go to Corpus to the beach. I haven't been to the beach in so long. Do you think the water is still there?"

Mr. Lea laughed. "Sure," he said. Then he thought of the remark and he found it funny all over again. He laughed harder this time. "The water is there, Constancia," he said. "You say the funniest things."

Said Constancia, more emboldened than ever, "Do you think so? I really don't mean to. But I was thinking the other night. What is life anyway? I never go out. Never do anything. I'm so lonely. If I only had a friend. Just one friend. A true friend. Someone I can count on. Someone I can talk to. That would be great."

Mr. Lea had taken several sips of coffee by this time watching Constancia. He said, "I am your friend."

Constancia said, "Good. Then tonight I'm inviting you to dinner. What do you like to eat?"

"Potatoes and eggs," replied Mr. Lea.

"Good," Constancia said, "I'll cook potatoes and eggs."

Mr. Lea stood up and took the coffee cup and saucer to the sink. He gave out a little jerking laugh. The conversation had made him forget there was no water for the sink. He came back and bowed to Constancia. "Now," he said, "I must go back to work so that we can have water for tonight."

That afternoon Constancia could not help but look out through the window at Mr. Lea. He was threading pipe, burning okem, melting lead, going under the trailer, coming out, large beads of perspiration streaming down his back. She went to the front bedroom and picked her way through the closet. She found the old wedding dress in its box and carried it outside with her.

She said, "See, Mr. Lea. What do you think?"

Mr. Lea scratched his head and said, "I don't know. What is it?"

"My wedding dress. Isn't it pretty?" she asked, taking the dress out of the box, shaking it out in front of him.

The dress had yellowed through the years. The embroidery at the front had become unraveled in places and Constancia was trying to make it right by rolling the loose threads between her fingers.

"Now that we're friends, I just thought you'd like to see it," she said. "It's my favorite dress."

Mr. Lea smiled and agreed the dress was nice. Constancia noticed his confusion.

"Since we're friends," she explained, "I thought you might like to see it."

"Yes," he said and went back under the trailer.

She knew she had made a fool of herself. She went back inside carrying the dress over her shoulder. She threw the dress on the bed and sat on the edge. If he was offended then she was sorry but she was not about to apologize.

At five o'clock he knocked on the door and informed Constancia he had not finished. The pipe underground was rusted out and he would have to dig it out and replace it. He would need more money and more time. Constancia wanted him to go get ready for dinner. He could finish in the morning.

"Then I'll plug what I've done and turn the water back on," he said.

She said, "Let it leak. What's one more day?"

"I'll just plug the sink," he said.

"I won't use the sink," she said.

"You can use the sink," he said.

As soon as Mr. Lea left she went for groceries.

At six she took a long soaking bath while drinking wine. She was happy to have been bold enough, desperate enough, to approach Mr. Lea. She should have never shown him the dress. What must he have thought of her? Her loneliness had taken her to the point of desperation. She could think of nothing else to do except reward herself with another glass of wine and staying in the tub. She could hear the music from the radio. She was humming a tune along with it. Mr. Lea would be the perfect friend.

She got out of the tub and dried herself in front of the mirror. Her body was aging but she didn't look bad. She wrapped the large towel around her breasts and went over to the kitchen and took out two potatoes and peeled them. She took four eggs out of the refrigerator door to allow them to warm. She went into the bedroom and began to dress. She applied heavy make-up, took extra effort with her hair. She wanted to look good for Mr. Lea.

At seven, as he said he would, Mr. Lea knocked on the door

and she went to greet him. He admired the way she looked. He seemed to her a little bolder now that he found himself in a social role. He was dressed in an old suit with a clean white shirt. His tie was broad and florid and hung only halfway down his chest. She showed him in and sat him at the kitchen table. Constancia asked him if he drank and he said he did sometimes. She offered a glass of wine and he accepted. She poured some cold wine in a glass and set it in front of him. He tasted it and said he enjoyed the taste. Constancia was beginning to feel the wine and she made him toast to their new friendship.

Constancia began the meal, frying the potatoes first and then adding the eggs. She scrambled the mixture until it was done. She placed the meal on two plates and they started to eat. Constancia noticed Mr. Lea moving his food around the plate.

"Don't you like the food?" she asked.

"I've never eaten potatoes and eggs like this," he said. "All mixed up."

Constancia wanted everything to be perfect. She was sorry. She wanted to start over again. "It won't be any bother," she said to Mr. Lea.

"I'll eat them like this," he said. "I'm not particular. I don't know why I said what I said. Nervous, I guess. I should have eaten what was put in front of me and kept quiet. I'm very sorry if I insulted you."

But Constancia was determined not to ruin the evening. She fried potatoes, set them apart and then fried two eggs. Mr. Lea was satisfied but embarrassed that he had caused her so much work.

"It's not any work, see?" Constancia assured him, drinking some more wine. She poured Mr. Lea another glass and then began to eat.

They ate in silence, Mr. Lea afraid he was making too much noise with his chewing. Constancia wanted him to make all the noise he wanted.

"Chew your food well," she said. "Don't mind me. Look at me. Look at how I chew. When you're with friends you can chew all you want. Make all the noises you want."

She gave him and herself more wine. She needed louder music so she went and stepped up the volume on the radio. Mr. Lea was drinking the wine as fast as she could pour it. She opened another bottle and set it on the table. Mr. Lea could pour his own wine.

They finished the meal and Constancia set the dishes in the sink. She could not wash them, she said, laughing. He thought that was funny. The wine had made it funny. The water was on. She could wash dishes if she wanted to.

"But I don't want to," she said.

Constancia turned toward Mr. Lea, who was at the door, and she became conscious of the music at the same time. She felt like dancing. She walked toward him and as she was about to ask him to dance she heard the knock on the door. She hurried past Mr. Lea, who had gotten out of the way when he heard the knock. Mr. Lea went to the far end of the kitchen and sat down on a chair by the wall. He took a sip of wine. He heard the door open and Constancia talking to someone. The voices drifted through the trailer. It was a man. Gradually Constancia's voice became louder, more angered. The man's voice grew louder. Constancia was screaming at the end. The man finished by cursing her.

He heard Constancia say, "Yes, I have a man in here. What of it? It's none of your damn business. You can't come in here telling me what to do and who to see."

"I'll kill you some day," Mr. Lea heard the man say.

Constancia yelled back, "You don't have the guts to kill me. You damn coward."

Then there was silence and Mr. Lea got up and walked to the door to see if Constancia needed any help. He heard the door slam and she walked into the kitchen. She sat down heavily at the table and poured herself some more wine. She gulped that one down. Mr. Lea sat quietly next to her.

"What happened?" he asked. He was concerned for her. She was fuming.

"Nothing. Men," Constancia said very forcefully and Mr. Lea knew enough not to pursue the question about the man.

Constancia lit a cigarette and looked at Mr. Lea very intently and said, "Are we going to be friends or not?"

Mr. Lea answered, "Yes. For sure."

"Then," Constancia said, "why don't we dance?"

She stood up and extended her hand to him and he got up, bowed, and took her by the hand. They moved over to the living room and began to dance slowly. Constancia shoved the little coffee table at the center of the room with her foot to make room on the dance floor. She became more eager to be close to Mr. Lea. She could feel the warmth of his body and the warmth of the wine. Her mind was spinning. She got close enough to rest her head on his chest. "Like a good friend," she said, looking up to him.

Mr. Lea danced awkwardly, seeming to move one foot even before the other one was planted. He stumbled slightly and Constancia smiled at him.

"Why didn't you tell me you could dance?" she said. "You're a marvelous dancer."

Mr. Lea gained confidence, took steps in a more determined way, going in the direction that he wanted. He began to lead. Mr. Lea blushed and almost stumbled when he thought of what he was doing. They went by the little end table with the wine and Constancia picked up her glass and had a good drink. Mr. Lea drank from the same glass and emptied it. Constancia went into the kitchen, brought out another bottle of wine and poured some more into the glass. Mr. Lea took it and swallowed it all. Constancia was laughing at Mr. Lea. He was laughing at himself. Then she took the glass and filled it and drank it all. They danced closely. They heard a car outside. Mr. Lea stopped dancing.

"Don't stop," Constancia reassured him, "he won't be back tonight. He knows you're here."

"He could cause trouble," said Mr. Lea.

"Nah," she said, "he's a coward. If I were alone he would try something but not with you around."

Mr. Lea grabbed her by the waist and swung her around. Constancia felt an urge overtake her. She began to steer Mr. Lea toward the bedroom door. Mr. Lea noticed what she was doing and he began to resist. Constancia pushed harder, insisting on her way. She was taking him closer and closer to the bed.

Once she had him across the threshold his resistance gave way as she knew it would. He embraced her heavily. He kissed her and picked her up and took her to bed.

Constancia was a patient woman. She knew any false move would bring Mr. Lea back to reality. Slowly she began to undress him, talking pleasantly to him. She was calm and decent. When she asked him about the light he said he wanted the room dark. She reached over and turned the lamp off. Slowly she worked her way to completely devour him.

"This is for the pain I might have caused," she whispered after Mr. Lea was kissing her.

In the morning Mr. Lea was up before her and she could smell the coffee. Nothing could make her go to work today. She listened carefully for him inside the trailer and could not hear him. She covered herself. Then she heard the sawing going on outside. Mr. Lea was working. She got up, bathed very well and then went out to be with him.

When she came out with a cup of coffee for him he stopped work. "I'm fixing to turn the water off again," he said. He smiled at her, felt comfortable with her presence.

"I don't care," she said.

"I will finish today," he said, proudly.

"And then?" she asked. "What are you going to do?"

"Work," Mr. Lea said most definitely, as though there was not another answer.

"I mean about us," said Constancia. She had gone to be by the car under the shade of the tree.

"Well?" he asked, shrugging his shoulders.

Constancia smiled at him. She said, "How do you feel?"

Mr. Lea said, smiling, "A little tired."

"Do you have a headache?"

"Yes."

"I do too," said Constancia. "It's nice to have a headache. I can feel my brain. I hadn't felt my brain in so long."

"I can feel my brain too," said Mr. Lea, hitting his forehead hard with the palm of his large hand.

"Did you enjoy last night?" she asked him.

Mr. Lea blushed. "Yes," he said. He went under the trailer with a section of pipe.

"Well?" she asked, going to squat by the trailer. She was peering under.

"Well, what?" he answered.

"What about it? You and me?"

Mr. Lea stuck his head out from under the trailer. "What do you mean?" he asked.

"Well, I've been thinking it over. I think," Constancia said, "that you and I should be friends like that. Like last night. Not the other kind that only goes to the movies. Don't you? It's a lot more fun. And we're still friends. No one says we can't be friends."

"I have to agree," Mr. Lea said.

"And I think," Constancia said, "that you should move in with me. This job is going to take a long, long time."

"And your neighbors?" Mr. Lea asked.

Her answer was a shrug.

Mr. Lea came out from under the trailer. He didn't know quite what to do. He stood in his bare chest, a section of pipe in one hand and a wrench in the other. Constancia walked over to him and embraced him.

"That would be fine," he said.

"You see how life is?" Constancia said. "If I hadn't been so lonely I wouldn't be this happy."

The Emergency Room

The orderly slid the window open and peeked out from the receptionist's office into the huge waiting room full of people. The lady knitting had been there since morning. She was dressed in a faded black blouse with white buttons and a pale blue skirt with pleats all around the waistband. She wore her hair up in a bun and had wire-rimmed glasses. She had moved only a few places, sometimes giving over her place to someone else. The thought struck him that she must be there for the air conditioning. He had seen her eating her lunch at midday. At three she had taken some more food out of her hemp bag and had spread it on her lap to eat. From a large thermos bottle she had poured an endless supply of coffee. This would have been her *merienda*. She would leave as soon as the evening cooled the air outside. But then he saw her move up one place and he noticed that she put her foot up, above her head, to rest it on the back of the seat in front of her. The foot was bandaged with a bath towel. This brought up the possibility she was injured and the orderly was wrong. She smiled at the man next to her but he was not in any mood to smile. Someone had hit him on the right side of the face and it had swollen so that his eye, as big as an orange, had closed. The orderly tried to estimate the size of the crowd but when he couldn't, when he saw that the people stretched out in the hallway and beyond what he could see, he thought himself a fool trying to find an answer when there was clearly none. The noise—voices, the rustling of bodies, the coughing, sobs, moans, children crying, children shouting, children playing, the steady siren scream of ambulances coming and going—all served to make him feel hopeless, that the night would not end. It would not. From experience, these were the things that have no end. The lady knitting would have no end. She or someone like her would be there tomorrow in the same faded clothes. A symbol of waiting. He would have to turn his back and leave knowing that it had not ended, the misery and pain and subjugation had not ended. He would simply walk off at the end of his shift and he would not see it until the next day. And then he would be told of what had happened when he had not been there, not because some-one wanted him to know or that he was interested after all the years but in telling him that person vented the emotions that had built up during the late-night shift, a release of feelings which one cannot keep pent up. He would be sure to listen but he did not care anymore. He did not hear anymore. There were no more feelings in him to care about. He closed the sliding window to keep away from the crowd. Inside the receptionist's office he felt a relief from not seeing the people stacked waiting.

Nurse Johnson came into the office and handed him the list of patients. She asked him to call out the next name. He stepped out and yelled, at the top of his voice, *"Señora Beltrán? Señora Beltrán?"*

No one stepped forward. The orderly was looking at the row of people at the front where the patient would most likely be waiting. He said, again, *"Señora Beltrán?"*

He heard a man's voice from the hallway say, *"Esa se fué. Se cansó de tanto esperar."*

A black man came forward to the door and said, "Talk English man. We ain't in Mexico."

"She gone," the man said. "She tire of waiting. She said she go home to have baby."

Some wiseguy in the audience said, "She got pregnant here, man. She waited for nine months and she couldn't see no doctor."

"Everyone has to wait their turn," the orderly reminded them, stepping back into the refuge of the office. He was about to leave when he heard the urgent knocking on the receptionist's window. Grudgingly he went over and slid it open to find the small young man, his wife and two children. The man carried a child buried in a blanket. He seemed confused. The woman, very docile and subdued, could not bear to look him in the eye. The two children with them hid behind their mother's skirt.

He heard the words from the father and it stunned him. *"La niña. Parece que está muerta,"* he said.

"Un ratito, por favor," the orderly said. He closed the window and sat down. He looked at the time clock. He should have punched out thirty seconds ago. The doctor came in and sat down at the computer and put in some data and leaned back.

"Aren't you leaving?" the doctor said.

"Yes," he said. "Before I leave you should know that there's a dead child."

"Dead child? Where?"

"Right outside the window," the orderly said. "They just walked in. The father is carrying the child. There's a mother and two children with him."

"Are you sure the child is dead?" the doctor said. He could see through the frosted glass the silhouette of the man and the child in his arms and the woman.

"No," the orderly replied, "but that's what he said."

"I'm stacked," the doctor said. "I've got people in every damn room. Some have two people. I wish the relatives would stay home. Why do they have to bring all the family? Like it was an outing."

"Poor people enjoy each other's pain," the orderly said.

"I don't want to see the child," the doctor said. "There's three other doctors tonight. Give it to one of them. Or send it to the morgue. Let pathology handle it. If the kid is dead there's no sense in my seeing it."

"I've got to go. My shift is over. You get someone to handle it."

"Johnson can handle it. She'll be free soon. She speaks Spanish."

"Then give it to Johnson. Let her see the child to make sure it's dead and then you can sign the death certificate."

"I'm not signing shit," the doctor said. "What if they killed the child? Where would that put me?"

The knock on the window was urgent. The orderly went over and slid the opaque glass open. It was the same small young man. He wanted to know how much longer it would be to tell him if the child was dead.

"Nada mas un ratito," the orderly informed him and closed the window. "He wants someone to see the child."

"On your way out look for Johnson. Tell her to take care of it."

"What good would that do? You're not going to sign the death certificate."

"Listen, Joe, I can't sign the death certificate without an autopsy. I won't touch it. I can't afford one more mistake. I'll get canned. You know Barkley is after me. All I need is for this child to have been murdered and I sign the death certificate and Barkley finds out I screwed up and I'm gone."

"What about Dr. Rodriguez? Let Rodriguez handle it."

"I'd rather Johnson handle it."

"They'll trust Rodriguez. They won't trust Johnson."

"I've got Rodriguez in Room Three with a gunshot. He's sewing him up.

"Dr. Martinez."

"Martinez is in Four with a stab wound sewing him up. All the nurses are tied up. Johnson is going to be free in a moment."

"I'm leaving. My shift is up. I've got to get out of here. I've got to get away and get some fresh air. I can't take much more of this."

"You're quitting for good?"

"I'm thinking about it."

"And your retirement? You wouldn't give that up, would you?"

"I'm saying I'm thinking about it."

"Seriously?"

"Seriously. Doc, I can't take it anymore."

"And the dead child? You're going to leave the man standing there?"

"I'm off, I tell you. It's your baby. You said Johnson would take care of it."

"Joe, please. Do me a favor. You're right. They won't trust Johnson. They'll trust you. You're the best here."

"Yeah, but I'm not a doctor."

"Who cares? Just stay an extra ten minutes. Put them in my office. Check the baby out. For all we know it's not dead."

"I guess I can stay ten more minutes. I can take this for ten more minutes."

"I'll make it up to you, Joe."

"You always say that but you never do. You're a con artist, you know that?"

"I know that. Put the family in my office. Take a look at the child. Make sure it's dead. Explain the procedure. . . . You know that. What am I telling you for?"

The orderly went and slid open the window. He said, *"Venganse por esa puerta, por favor."*

The man took the infant cradled in the blanket and went to his left and opened the door leading into the hallway. The mother had the two children by the hands and she led them behind her husband. The orderly had come out of the receptionist's office and was waiting for them in the hallway.

"Siganme, por favor," he said and the man followed him down the hallway.

The orderly stopped at the doctor's office and turned the handle on the door and let himself in first. The light was on. At the back of the small office was the desk. He asked the family to come in and they all crowded in.

"Ponga la niña en el escritorio," he told the man.

The man placed the child on top of the desk. The orderly unwrapped the child slowly, hoping the child would move, hoping he could see the child breathe. As he unfolded the blanket covering the child he could see the pallid, morbid skin color. He felt the child as he continued to unwrap it. He felt the coldness, the stillness. By the time he exposed the little face he knew the child was dead. Its little mouth was open, its jaw slack, the eyes were partially open and dry and vacant. He had seen death many times and this was it.

"Está muerta?" the mother asked, leaning over the body.

The orderly could not see her two children hiding behind her skirt. *"Sí,"* he answered. *"Sí. Está muerta. Cuando se murió?"*

The man said, *"Pues hace unas cuantas horas. Había estado muy enferma. La llevamos con el doctor pero dijo que no era nada. Le dió una medicina y se la dimos y eso fué todo."*

The woman said, *"Ayer se puso mejor. Parecía que se había aliviado. Tomó leche."*

"Pero la depuso," the man said.

"Qué vamos hacer?" the woman asked.

The realization of the child's death was beginning to get to her. She began to cry and to stroke the child's head. *"Era tan buena,"* she said. *"Nunca los dió trabajo. Nunca lloró. Nunca se quejó. Fue muy linda mi niña."*

The orderly looked through the files in the desk and found the death certificate form. He sat down and placed the form into the typewriter. *"Qué edad tenía la niña?"*

The man looked at the woman for help. She said, *"Tenía tres años y cinco meses. Apenas comenzó a hablar bien."*

The man said, *"Tenía tiempo de que no comía bien. Se ponía la comida en la voca y no la mascaba."*

"Me puede decir el día que nació?" the orderly asked.

"Nacio el 30 de enero, mil novecientos noventa," the woman said. She turned around and took the children by the arm and brought them in front of her. The children leaned against her thighs and took her skirt and tried to wrap themselves in it.

"Como se llamaba la niña?"

"Beatrice. María Beatrice."

"Apellido?"

"Iturbe," the man said.

"Y sus nombres?"

"Faustino y Yolanda Iturbe."

"Su dirección?"

The man said, *"Dale la dirección."*

The woman took out a piece of paper from her purse and gave it to the orderly. After he had copied their address he asked, *"Y de donde son ustedes originalmente?"*

"De Guanajuato," the man said.

The woman said, *"Diós quiciera que estuvieramos ahí ahorita. Con nuestra familia."*

"Y nadie le pegó a esta niña? Nadie la atropello?"

"No señor," the man replied.

The woman said, *"Ni siquiera le atocamos un cabello a esta niña. A ninguno de nuestros niños se les pega."*

"Muy bien."

The orderly stepped out leaving the family with the dead child in the office. He spotted the doctor in one of the emergency rooms. The doctor was sewing up a black man who had been stabbed repeatedly in the back. In the room with the black man were several of his friends who had brought him in. The man was face down on the table, conscious, and talking to the doctor. He said, "So this motherfucker came at me with this little knife and I laughed at him. Shit! He cut my ass up in little pieces. I never saw the motherfucker before. Did you all get his name?"

The other blacks in the room shook their head. "No way," one of them said. "That little motherfucker was so fast we didn't know what he was doing. Bam. Bam. He got on your ass like flies on shit and the motherfucker was gone before we could axe him who he was."

"Like the Lone Ranger," said another one of his friends. "All the motherfucker left behind was your ass all cut up."

"That's for sure," said another partner. "That's that motherfucker's silver bullet."

"That's what you get for acting the foo'."

The man turned around to face his friends and said, "I was not acting the foo'. He was."

"Hell, Estrus," one of his friends said, "you act the foo' all the time."

"No time do I act the foo'."

The orderly asked the doctor to come out to the hallway.

"Is the child dead?" the doctor asked.

"Yes. A little girl. Three years and some months. No visible signs of trauma. I asked them and they claim they had gone to a doctor and he put her on medicine and told them to go home. The child looked like it got better but then it got worse and died. They claim never to have hit her. They have never hit any of their children."

"But how can we be sure?"

"You can't. You take their word for it. What else can you do?".

"We can do an autopsy."

"Why not sign the death certificate? Have the desk call the funeral home? Let them pick up the body and let the poor family go?"

"I can't, Joe. You know I can't."

"You said you'd make it up to me. I'm asking you. Let them go. They're clean."

"How can you be sure?"

"I've been doing this for years, doc. I know. Let them go."

"I can't, Joe. It's my ass. I can't afford one more mistake. Barkley will nail me. I just can't do it. I'll make it up to you some other way but not on this one."

"Okay. You tell me exactly what you want me to do."

"Tell them we need an autopsy. They have to leave the body here. The morgue will call them when the body is ready to be picked up. The way we usually do it, Joe. That's not too hard to do, is it?"

"You're the boss."

"Good. Just tell them what they need to do."

"And if they don't agree?"

"Tell them we call the police. Homicide. They wouldn't want that."

"You're going to call Homicide on this? Are you crazy?"

"No, I'm not crazy, Joe. I'm just covering my ass, that's all."

"Doc, how long have you been here?"

"Too fucking long. Why?"

"This is a child we're talking about here. Do you think that the parents—from Mexico, Catholics who believe God is coming and resurrecting us all from the grave—are going to agree to have their baby cut up and that they're going to bury only a shell of the baby? Do you think they will agree to that?"

"I don't care. We need an autopsy. I won't sign the death certificate without an autopsy."

"I'll get Dr. Rodriguez to sign it."

"Good. Let him do it. I won't."

The orderly took off down the hallway in search of Dr. Rodriguez. He found the doctor in an emergency room with a gunshot victim. He could not sign the certificate. It was not his case.

The orderly found Dr. Martinez in another emergency room sewing up a stab wound. He refused to sign the death certificate.

The other doctor on duty that night, Dr. Day, was busy with the outpatients and he would not sign the death certificate either.

The orderly returned to the office. The family was standing around the desk praying for the dead child.

"He said, *"Se requiere una autopsia. Saben lo que significa?"*

"Pues no."

"Tenemos que llevar el cuerpo con un patólogo para que él nos diga de que murió la niña. Sin una autopsia, no se puede firmar el certificado de muerte."

"Y qué es lo que le hacen a la niña?"

"Tienen que abrir el cuerpo para inspectar los organos. El cerebro. El corazón. El higado. Los riñones. Todo el cuerpo para ver de que murió."

The man said, *"No. Nosotros no queremos eso. Queremos llevarnos a la niña para enterrarla."*

"No se puede. En este país no se puede enterrar un cuerpo sin un certificado de muerte."

"No la podemos enterrar en el fondo del solar?"

"No. No se puede. Es encontra de la ley. Tenemos que tener una autopsia."

"Pues yo no quiero eso. Que la corten."

The woman, crying over the baby, had picked up the conversation. She said, *"Ay, Diós mío, no. Que no la corten a la pobrecita. Mi angelita."*

The orderly checked the clock on the wall. He was thirty minutes past his shift. He would be in the car and almost home by now. He left the family in the office and went to look for the doctor. He found him in Exam Room Fifteen, trying to stop a woman from crying. Her son was on a gurney, dead. He had been shot in the forehead. Another gang shooting in Mexican town. He had been the perfect son, she cried, but he had to join the gang in order to survive from day to day. She cried out, "Do you understand that he had to be in the gang, if not they would kill him?" She tried to hang on to the orderly, tried to cry her plight to him when he came in, but the orderly managed to get away from her. The orderly stepped out and the doctor followed.

"Well?" the doctor said.

"They won't go for an autopsy," the orderly said. "I told you. Not on a child. The parents won't allow it. You've got to sign the death certificate."

"Joe? Joe? I won't sign it. How many times do I have to tell you?"

"I'm desperate, doc. I need to get out of here before I go crazy. Before I blow up. I mean it. I can't take it anymore. Now, you've got one more chance coming, don't you? Barkley gave you one more chance, didn't he?"

"What are you talking about?"

"I'm calling in my chips then."

"I told you I'd make it up to you somehow but not now, Joe. This could be what does me in. I can't take the chance."

"Then I'm turning you in to Barkley."

"Are you serious, Joe? What for?"

"I'm in charge of drug inventory, right?"

"Yeah."

"We're missing methamphetamines. We're missing a lot of them. And I know you are the one taking them. Hell, maybe you're selling them."

"Joe, you can't prove that."

"I may not be able to prove it in court but if I go to Barkley and tell him I think it's you he'll believe me. That will be enough. You are out of here, doc. You're out of control."

"Don't do this to me, Joe."

"Now, I can cover methamphetamines and you can too. It's easy to keep robbing one bottle to put in another. But I know you're on them, doc."

"You sonofabitch. You're threatening me over this? Why is this so important to you? You've lost control, Joe. Go on home. I'll handle this now. I don't need your services any longer. You're fucking nuts. You know that?"

"You're calling homicide."

"Yes. I'm calling homicide."

"I'm not leaving then. You're crazy, you know that?"

"I'm crazy, Joe. You're crazy. That's why we're here. Do you think a sane man would do this?"

The dead man's extended family could be seen in the hallway coming toward them. The women were wailing. The men had stern looks on their faces, looks of revenge. There would be more killings. The doctor and the orderly got out of the way and let the family pass into the room. When they saw the body the wailing began in earnest. The men, for some reason, to show their anger, began to beat on the walls with their fists. The sound carried through the hallway like the marching beat of death.

The orderly went back to the office hoping that he could convince the family to have an autopsy done on the child. They would not agree.

The orderly said, finally, *"Entonces el doctor le tiene que hablar a la polecía."*

"Diós mío," the woman said, *"Porqué. Porqué la polecía?"*

The man said, *"No hemos hecho nada. Se murió la niña en los brazos de su madre."*

"El doctor no va a firmar el certificado de muerte sin una autopsia."

Then came the answer the orderly had dreaded.

The man said, speaking for the family, *"Entonces no queremos el cuerpo de la niña. Ustedes se pueden quedar con el cuerpo."*

The orderly said, *"No queremos el cuerpo nosotros tampoco. Haber que puedo hacer con el doctor."*

"Le agradecemos mucho, señor."

The orderly found the doctor embroiled in the family fight over the gang death of the young man. He was trying to be heard but the family had so much anger that the orderly feared for the doctor's safety. He went back to the receptionist's office and called Security. Two officers arrived in moments and he escorted them to Room Fifteen where the argument was still going. Security was able to quiet the family and they sat in the room with the body and began to pray the Rosary. The doctor was out in the hallway with the orderly.

The orderly said, "Can't you understand what it must be like to be in a strange country and have your child die?"

"No one invited them here," the doctor said. "They come on their own. You take your chances. And don't you think it's worse for them where they come from? Why do you think they're here?"

"They don't want the child."

"What do you mean, they don't want the child?"

"The body. They don't want the body if we're going to mutilate it."

We're not going to mutilate it, Joe. It's just an autopsy. They won't be able to tell the difference."

"I can't convince them, doc. If the child is cut that's mutilation to them. If we do an autopsy they don't want the body."

"Tell them I'm calling homicide."

"Okay. I'll tell them but they won't understand."

"I don't care if they understand or not. We're in a war zone here, Joe. I've farted around with them too long as it is. People are dying all over."

"Tell me about it. I've been doing this for twenty years. Every year it gets worse."

"Just hold them and call homicide."

"It's your show."

"Thank you, Joe."

"Don't mention it."

"You're not pissed off, are you? You're not turning me in, are you?"

"No. I'm not turning you in. God only knows who would replace you."

"Now you're talking sense, Joe. It could be worse. I could be worse."

By the time the orderly arrived at the office the family was gone. The orderly took the death certificate off the typewriter, tore it into pieces and threw it into the wastebasket.

As the family walked back to the Metro bus stop in the early morning drizzle, small brown raindrops barely pelting the worn out sidewalk in front of Hermann Hospital, the mother struggled behind, crying softly, not wanting to attract attention from the crowd in the streets, her two children following behind holding on to her skirt. She noticed through her tears that her small, frail husband—carrying the dead child buried in the blanket—had lost weight, that the denims he had bought at Fiesta Supermarket were too large and long for him, the waist gathered and puckered around him and she noticed for the first time that in his haste he had missed the belt loops in the back. A police car, its siren wailing, shot past them toward the hospital.

At that hour the heavy early morning Houston traffic was

beginning to shake the streets and foul the air. Trucks shooting off gray leaden puffs of exhaust and loaded with workers passed them at the bus stop, the men shouting obscenities at the waiting crowd. With the morning downdraft pressing heavily against the city, the air smelled acrid, horribly pungent and unbreathable, as if a giant had eaten sulfur and batteries and was belching on the city.

Nano Returns

Nano was sitting on the top step of the porch. He had placed his two heavy suitcases on either side of him and he was fanning himself with his stained fedora. The children could hear the click of his false teeth from afar. He would blame that on his loss of weight. He had his familiar dark wool suit on, a vest, a faded, old, dirty white shirt and a red and white tie, a selection from his assortment of clothes. His fedora, used as a fan a moment ago, was hanging from his right hand between his knees.

He did not look like the old Nano to the children. There was something about him. He looked sadder, more spent, older, more tired. His shoulders, always stooped from carrying his suitcases, were still lower today so that he looked like he had no form. He appeared to be thinking deeply and at the same time was swaying his head back and forth like a turtle, something the children had never seen him do before. They stopped several yards in front of him to see for themselves this transformation of their uncle. They looked at each other and they began to move their heads like Nano and then they began to giggle. The sound of the children disturbed his thoughts and his eyes opened wide as though he had been scared into the present.

He greeted the children as they came to greet him but not by name. He never once said their names. It was always "This one and that one" when he was telling Maria something they had done.

Maria had seen him coming from the kitchen when she checked the water in the bean pot. She had quickly taken the bean pot with her to the bathroom. There, the beans would be safe from Nano. She was sick of him, not wanting to cook for him, not wanting to watch him eat three people's portions in one sitting. She could hear the sounds of the high children's voices from the bathroom and then she could hear Nano's low voice. She could not tell what they were talking about. Very quietly, tiptoeing, she went over to the wall and placed her ear against it.

"No," Nano was saying, "the world is entirely different now. There is no civility. Do you children know what civility is?"

"No."

"Civility is when you treat everyone as well as you would like to be treated no matter the person's station. Do you children understand?"

"Yes."

"In the ranches nowadays the people are not civil. When I started selling clothes in the old days . . . Twenty years ago this year. My, how time goes by. It's hard to believe, isn't it? That I have been lugging those suitcases for twenty years? Before any of you had been born. Think of that. And I don't have anything to show for it. Look at my pockets. . . . Empty. It's hard to believe. You see, I had worked on the railroad. Helped build the railroad from Corpus Christi to Laredo. The old Tex-Mex like we still call it. That was work, my friends. You children don't know what work is. I've heard you complain when your mother Maria tells you to do the simplest of things. Let me tell you that taking the goat out and milking her is not work. That is recreation. How many children of this world would like to milk a goat? Think of that. But it was different then. I tired of the job. But you children know that. Your mother has told you so many times, I'm sure. Don't be like Nano. No future. No money. Selling clothes on consignment. Not even his clothes is he selling. I thought I had made the right decision. Left the hard work of the railroad to sell clothes through the ranches of South Texas. I have no remorse. I could have done things a little different. I know I would not have been so kindhearted with the people. Oh, I raised my family. We struggled. But everyone did. No one goes through this life without a struggle. You children remember that. Each one of you is going to have something happen to you. Something bad. Your life will never be how you wanted it to be. God never lets you. God is there waiting to bring something on you. You wait and see. . ."

The children snickered.

"You laugh at me."

"No."

"Oh, you were not laughing at me?"

"No."

"I thought you were. It appeared to me that you were laughing at me. You always do, you know."

"We don't laugh at you, Uncle."

"Yes, you do. I know you do. The indignities I have to go through just to come and see my cousin Maria. Is she here?"

"Let me see."

The eldest of the children, a girl, went inside and found the kitchen empty. That was a clue. Maria was hiding somewhere in the house. The child went into the living room and looked behind the sofa. No one. In the bedroom she looked under the bed. No one. She went to the closet. No one. Then she walked down the hallway. She tapped lightly on the bathroom door.

"Mama?" she said.

"What is it?" Maria whispered through the door.

The child whispered back. "Nano is here. What should we do?"

"I know he's here. I saw him. I don't want to see him. He will eat all the beans. He won't leave any for us."

"What do I tell him?"

"Tell him I'm gone."

"Where?"

"Tell him I went to Corpus to buy new glasses."

"What if he won't go away?"

"He'll go away when he knows I'm gone and there is no food on the stove. Be sure the stove is turned off. Take the tortillas and put them in the refrigerator. Cover up any food you find so he won't see it."

"What if he wants to go into the kitchen?"

"For God's sake don't let him. Block the door. Is everyone there?"

"Yes."

"Well, you have enough bodies to stop him from opening the door."

"But we don't want to. You said we should always respect our elders."

"Not Nano. Don't respect him. He will eat anything that he finds. . . . Do you want to eat today?"

"Yes."

"Do you want rice and beans and tortillas?"

"Yes."

"Well then, don't let him in."

"We'll try."

"Don't try child. Do it. Don't let him in."

"All right."

Maria could hear the child run back to the kitchen. She went to the wall and pressed her ear against it. She heard the child go out and the door close.

"My mother is not here," the child said.

Nano took the news by looking up the road. He had his hat on by now. The child winked at the other children. "How sad," said Nano. "I had gotten this ride from Robstown just to come see my cousin Maria. I heard she was going through life's struggles and I said to myself, 'I have to go see her. To talk to her. To tell her that she is not alone. To tell her of my and Angelica's tragedy. . . . If only I had the money to help. But I don't. As you can see by the clothes I wear and the shoes I wear. I am not a wealthy man. Just look at the old suitcases. Falling apart. I can't afford new ones. What for anyway? How much longer am I going to last? Someday someone will find me on the road, dead. The suitcases on top of me. Tragedy after tragedy takes its toll. . . . In the old days I could count on people at the ranches. If I came upon hard times they would buy from me to help me out. They would invite me to stay. If I was there during the meal I would be served and served properly and with the respect that a guest deserves. You have been to my house. Haven't I always treated all of you with respect?"

"Yes."

"There. You see. You agree with me. In the old days if nightfall came to me on the road I would be taken in for the night. . . . Today? I am glad that they don't run me over when they pass by. They shout obscenities at me. They call me "the glutton". I wish I knew what has come over the people. Something has changed them. . . . The Depression has changed them. Made them scared of life. Life is too short for you to be scared. . . . Well, you say Maria is gone?"

"Yes."

"Where has she gone?"

"To Corpus to buy new glasses. She couldn't see anymore."

"She was blind."

"We had to take her by the hand everywhere she went."

"May God Almighty bless her. Knowing what a wonderful person she is I know God will help her. With new glasses, she will be a different person. You'll see. Once more she'll be the old Maria. Cooking. Cooking. Always at the stove. She was born at the stove and she will die at the stove but she will be happy. . . . Maybe she left something for me to eat?"

"No. There is nothing to eat."

"Not a morsel? A small piece of something? I crave something sweet. An empanada?"

"No. There is nothing to eat.

"Not even one tortilla? Left over from the last meal?"

"Give him a tortilla," one of the younger children said.

The eldest got up and went into the kitchen, went into the refrigerator and brought a tortilla. She handed it to Nano who chewed it and swallowed it in one bite.

He took out his false teeth and licked them clean. Then he said, "Thank you for your kindness. I must be on my way. Does anyone know what time it is?"

The eldest went to the kitchen door and looked in at the clock on the wall. "It's almost five o'clock," she said.

"I have to be leaving. Maybe I can catch the bus to Laredo. This trip has been bad for me. Not that I didn't expect it. The last month has not been good for Angelica and me."

The children were surprised when Nano took out his hand-kerchief and began to wipe tears from his eyes.

"I wanted Maria to know. That is why I came by. It was not the food. I can live without food. I don't have to beg for food. I know you children think I take food from your mouth."

"No."

"Yes, you do. I know exactly what you think."

"No, we don't."

"I came this afternoon to tell Maria of our tragedy. Angelica's and mine. To share with my favorite cousin the struggles of life. If there is anyone I wanted to tell it was Maria."

"She is not here."

"I know. That is why I'm going to tell you what has happened. So that you can tell her. Listen carefully. . . . Our son Gil died. Twenty-seven years old. You cannot imagine the pain it has caused us. Angelica is not the same. I am not the same. I think about it all the time. I cannot get it out of my head. I think hard about it and hope that I am in a dream. But in the end, no amount of dreaming will change the truth. Gil is dead. You children remember Gil?"

"Yes."

"He was the thin one. The one who loved to eat. I'll never forget that one time he was eating so much that I took him outside on the porch and gave him a whole loaf of bread and I made him eat it all. He tried to vomit but I wouldn't let him. I thought that would cure him of the problem but it didn't. And then I realized that that was how he was and I left him alone after that. Angelica got angry with me for forcing him to eat the bread. I understand now how wrong I was. But all parents make mistakes. My father used to hit me for eating. It never changed me. I was always hungry. . . . Gil was always a happy child. Never one to brood or to cause us problems like Jose. Jose is the scoundrel of the family. But Gil was so innocent. So good. So good-hearted. Hey, if Gil saw a little bird on the ground he would pick it up and try to help it until the bird could fly on its own. Many a time he helped animals in distress. He loved people. He had married just two years ago. Left behind his wife and a little precious girl. You have no idea how much Angelica and I love the little one. God willing I will be with her tonight. But Gil died."

"How did he die?"

"A fever. He was fine on Monday. Went to work as usual and he felt a little bad on Monday afternoon. We saw him that night and he said he wasn't feeling good so he went to bed. We didn't think anything of it. But on Tuesday he had to leave work to go see the doctor. The doctor examines him and says that he has a fever and a slight cold. Well, it's going around so Gil goes home and goes to bed. By that night he has convulsions and we take him to the hospital. He gets worse and worse. The doctor keeps telling us it's nothing. A high fever of some sort. They pack the poor child in ice. The doctor says that by morning he will be fine. But in the morning he calls us into the office in the hospital and he tells us Gil is dead. He doesn't know what happened. . . . Gil worked for the chamber of commerce. Do you know what that is?"

"No."

"He had an important job. He didn't go to college like I wanted him to. And he could have gone there in Laredo. He could have gone to college. He was smart. Gil was smart. But he did fine. Had a good job. A good family. A little money. What else can a man want? I mean, to me that's everything." Nano wiped some more tears from his eyes. "Excuse me. I can't help but cry when I talk or think about him. I think about him all the time now. I loved him so much. I didn't know how much I loved him until I saw the casket going down into the ground. I let out a cry like a woman. I was so embarrassed. But Angelica said I did the right thing. I showed my emotions. My love for Gil. No one said a word about it afterwards. You know that men aren't supposed to cry. . . . We buried him in the Catholic cemetery, the one on Highway 44. We buried him next to our daughter, named Angelica also. She died of yellow fever as a child. I bet you children didn't know that."

"No."

"Well, why should you? Why bother your lives with something that happened so many years ago . . . Tell Maria that Angelica is heartbroken. I cannot console her. Gil was her favorite child. We now have only Jose left. The only one left out of three. Those are the struggles of life. You children will experience that in your life. . . . But I didn't come to eat. I had eaten before. Not much, but I had eaten some . . . Do you want to see my clothes?"

"Yes."

"Well, I'll open the suitcases for you. Here," he said, standing and cleaning his bottom with his handkerchief. Then he took the handkerchief and folded it into his hip pocket. He took one of the suitcases and opened it. It was full of clothes. The other one was full of shoes and boots. He said, "Look at these boots. Fine boots. Belong to a man in Laredo who uses them one year and then throws them out. Those are people with money, children. When you can afford to throw out a pair of boots every year. Look at the assortment of clothes I have. It's like a store."

He held up garment after garment for the children to see and feel. To them it was Christmas in July. Then he began to put everything back in its place. When he had everything the way he wanted it he closed both suitcases and set them up beside him. He was sitting down again, his fedora at the back of his head. He had the look on his face that the children had noticed when they first saw him. He was thinking of Gil. He began to sway his head like a turtle. He clicked his false teeth unconsciously over and over again. Finally, the scared look returned to his face and he took a deep breath and stood up. "Well," he said, "I've taken up a lot of your precious time. Tell Maria that Gil died. Tell her how he died and that we buried him in the cemetery on Highway 44. Tell her that if any of you ever pass by you can stop and pay your respects. Tell her that if you don't have time it's all right. A simple sign of the Cross will help him. But I'm sure he's in Heaven. Tell Maria we didn't tell her about it when it happened because we didn't want to bother her and Gonzalo. Angelica thought that I bother them enough when I stop to eat and sleep here. 'Why bother them more?' she said to me. And she's right. 'They'll want to come,' she said, 'and they don't have the money to be coming to Laredo.' It costs money to travel, you know. And I know I bother my cousin Maria and I understand if she doesn't want to see me. . . . "

He looked at his suitcases as though they were the burden of his life, his crucifix. He appeared undecided as to which one to pick up first, the heavier one with the shoes and boots or the lighter one with the clothes. He gave out another sigh and said, *"Dios mío."* He reached down for the heavier suitcase on his right and then the lighter one on his left. He balanced himself with the great weight of the two suitcases. He walked down the steps. When he was down he said, "I just thought I could come by and tell her that I understand her struggles in life, and to tell her about mine. To tell her Gil died."

As he left the yard and took to the street, the children could hear Maria crying in the bathroom. Later, at supper, she said, "If only he didn't eat so much."

The Day They
Took My Uncle

The day they took my uncle I was under the house playing with a little girlfriend older than me and she had shown me her most intimate of female parts. I was amazed, seeing it for the first time in the flesh, at how simple it was. At that age I would never have imagined it as I saw it that morning. How beautiful it was and again, how simple. A marvel of nature. How appropriate and functional. Afterwards, I could never get her, teaser that she was, to show it to me again. So the memory of it faded from me through the years and I was left with a blur, a blur much like the pictures of female pubices in the nudist colony magazines that I had a peek at as a child before I saw the real thing. I imagined that these magazine pictures had been true and that these female parts were constantly moving at a great rate of speed. How else could they create a blur on a photograph? But that was not what I had seen this morning. What I had seen was standing still. Two very small, very fleshy, delicate lips which the young girl opened for me to see still more pink lips inside. Were there even more inside of those? Did the thing end there or was it like the Morton Salt Girl? But she had not let me see. Before I could react, before I could touch it or smell it to embed the beauty of it in my mind, she had put her panties on and I had been educated. But that is another story.

My uncle Mercé was insane. He had been insane for many years and he was accepted as part of the family. Aside from my grandmother, no one had ever known him well.

His fits of insanity followed a certain routine. He would begin by walking about without a purpose, mumbling desperately. He would progress to grab his ears and yank at them violently as if trying to shake some diabolical voice from them. Then the worst part would come. He would start to curse in a loud voice. He cursed the town. He cursed the people. He named names, except the priest and the nuns. The priest and the nuns would be cursed by title. El Padre this . . . Las Monjas that. . . . Everyone else unlucky to be named had their names repeated over and over during the cursing. He remembered pasts that were better off left unsaid. Sometimes he dealt in minutiae so trivial that it caused us to laugh, like the time he cursed the nuns for not letting the children use the swings when the parochial school was out.

He was fine and we could control him as long as he stayed in the yard. But usually he didn't, despite our efforts to steer him, push him, within the boundaries of our yard. Recently he had begun to go to the mayor's house to curse him and his wife. For some reason known only to him, he insisted that the mayor was a sonofabitch, a bastard, in other words, in Spanish, an *hijo de la chingada madre,* which is very serious name-calling in the Hispanic culture, or any culture for that matter. But in the Hispanic culture it is demanded that everyone consider their mothers sacred, except the children, of course. No, the mayor's wife was not spared. Being there he took the opportunity to call her a *puta, hija de su chingada madre,* again, very rough language. Now he had insulted a mother and wife at the same time and the Hispanic rule applies double in that case. Then he named names of men she had been generous with, if you know what I mean. He shouted out standing on the mayor's front steps that the mayor's wife was giving it away to the mayor's nephew. What a *puta*. But the mayor's wife was a little old lady, all shriveled up who probably didn't even do it with the mayor much less with all the other men Mercé had accused. He ended the fit that day by calling her the foulest of names, names which I could not in good conscious put on paper. All I can say was that it concerned her most intimate of parts which I know did not look at all like the little girl's. I know what he said because I was with him that day.

For some reason I was his favorite person and he took me with him whenever he had the opportunity. By the age of five I had heard and could repeat every curse word known to man. He tried to do things for me. He would whittle away with his knife, occasionally having these fits, the knife in his yanking hand next to his ear, until he would finish some little wood carving for me. He was not a good whittler or anything else. He was good at drinking beer and causing the family trouble.

He was an alcoholic, which, according to my grandmother, was the indirect cause of his insanity. My grandmother believed he had been possessed when he drank the dregs of a bottle of beer laced with a special potion, a potion so powerful that it would cause insanity. According to my grandmother, the potion was meant for someone else, the husband of a woman with a lover. She was so sure of the scheme that she passed it on as the truth. It involved a woman wanting her husband out of the way without killing him. Insanity was the solution. The husband would be alive but would not be able to keep the wife from her lover. The two lovers, *sinvergüenzas,* could do whatever they did to their hearts' content in front of the husband. Through time, my grandmother thickened the plot. The potion became one that did not mix well with beer and it settled at the bottom of the bottle. The husband drank of the beer and found it to taste somewhat off. He left the half full bottle on the counter. Here came Mercé, the poor soul. Not a care in the world. He saw the bottle of beer on the counter with a few swallows of beer remaining. He drank it and went insane. But how did the potion work? My grandmother knew the answer to that too. "The potion," she would say, "kept his manhood from descending. And God forbid when a man's manhood does not descend. Why, he goes crazy. What you are seeing from Mercé is unde-scended manhood. He feels his manhood, tries to descend it and can't and he goes into his fit."

"And where is the manhood in a man?"

"In his brain . . . before it descends."

"And where does it descend to?"

"If you children don't know that then I could never explain it to where you would understand."

And that was the end of the conversation.

He lived by himself at the end of the block in the old unpaint-ed house that had belonged to his mother. In the morning he would come to our house. We would find him sitting at the kitchen steps whittling, waiting for us to eat so he could have the leftovers. By early afternoon he would be at the taverns drinking anything anyone would give him, the men hoping he would begin a fit to entertain them. No one knew who he would curse and that brought out the worst in the men. He would run around inside the tavern, knocking chairs and tables around, yanking at his ears, cursing at the top of his voice, the men yelling for him to keep on and on and on. Finally, when the fit was over he would sit down exhausted and someone would buy him a beer and they would laugh and he would laugh, a vacant laugh, not knowing what he was laughing about.

Sometimes, when he had a fit in town, the children would run behind, taunting us.

Whether he remembered what he did or not I never knew. I never asked him. In fact, after he was through with his fits I would try to change the subject, talk of something else, something less painful. That was what he preferred.

———•———

One day he took me by the hand and we went to get the milk cow that he had tied across from the mayor's house. As we came by the house I could feel a slight trembling starting in his hand. And suddenly, as if a demon had possessed him, he started cursing and running toward the mayor's house, dragging me along with him. He would not let go of me. He yanked his ears one at a time with his free hand. By now I was barely touching the ground as he swung me around on his rampage. He started with the mayor and cursed him and then he continued with the mayor's wife. I could see the lady, worried as she was and scared, peeping through a crack in the curtain, watching all this: A deranged man yanking at his ears holding a little boy by the hand and running, menacingly, toward her house.

———•———

It was embarrassing to some of us to have an uncle like this one around the family. Your friends had to be very tolerant. My sister didn't like him because she could never invite any of her playmates over.

One time a young man came uninvited to ask my sister about some school assignment and as he was walking to the front door my uncle started having a fit inside the house and ran out, bursting through the front door, screaming obscenities. My uncle ran right through the young man and knocked him down. The young man's books flew out of his hands. The young man got up fast and started running away, but everywhere he tried to run it seemed he'd run into my uncle. He never came back to see my sister. He left his books on the ground and my sister had to take them to school to return them to him. My sister said she had never been so embarrassed in her life. She was not able to explain Mercé to her satisfaction. The young man said that he would never call on a girl who had heard so many curse words in her young life. My sister cried that night, saying she would never get married as long as Mercé lived with us. As soon as she could, she left for college and never returned to stay. She married. Twice.

He didn't stay with us at night. He preferred to sleep in the old iron bed with the thin mattress in the unpainted house that had no electricity, no heat or water. Later on, when he became sick and right before he died, my grandmother moved him into the dining room that we never used and set up a small cot for him. It was interesting, as I was told, that in his last days the doctor told him he couldn't drink anymore unless he wanted to die. So he quit drinking and died within a week. What he died of no one knew and no one cared. That was the beauty of life in a small town. People died and that was that. There was no need for heavy medical expenses or lengthy hospital stays or exotic diagnostics. If a person got sick and then got well that was a cause for rejoicing. If a person got sick and died, well, they buried the body and everyone kept on living. So when Mercé died, he just died. Even the doctor was not particularly interested as to why a person had died. He was there to treat well people.

———•———

The mayor was not home when we were trampling his front yard but his wife told him about it and he became very angry and rightfully so. He had had enough from Mercé. That night the mayor came to call and talked to my grandmother and my mother and father and they assured the mayor that they would scold Mercé. Mercé, in the meantime, was at the tavern begging for beer and getting drunk and forgetting to bring home the cow.

———•———

My uncle had only one job to do. He was to take the cow to a pasture in the morning after milking her and then he was supposed to bring the cow back before sunset, milk her, feed her and put her up for the night. He was able to do the morning part of the job well and with consistency but bringing the cow back presented a problem for him. If he was in the middle of a fit he would forget what time it was or where he had pastured the cow, or whether he had already taken the cow home. Or if he was getting drunk, if someone was buying him beer, he didn't want to quit just to bring a cow home.

So very often, as we did that night when the mayor came to complain, my father and we children went to look for the patiently waiting cow to bring her home. We never knew for sure where my uncle had tied her that morning since the pasturing of the cow and the location was left entirely up to him. If he found a lush grassy place by the cemetery he tied her there. The next day he would tie her somewhere else. The cow was never at the same place on two successive days.

We would go look for the cow and my father would hold the lantern as we walked the dusty streets and when we thought we saw the huge bulk of the animal in the darkened field my father would take the lantern and raise it above his head to illuminate a larger area. And there she would be, in the dim light, chewing her cud placidly, as if she knew that eventually we would come to rescue her so that she could have a drink of water, so that we could relieve the discomfort of her full udder.

My father never got angry with Mercé. He would scold him lightly and in very gentle way. Mercé would look at him with his large sorrowful eyes and would promise to do anything my father wanted him to do. Then he would walk away, the halter rope in his hand, the cow walking slowly behind him. Sometimes he would start his fit at this time and let go of the cow and walk away, tugging at his ears and cursing at the sky. The cow would stop and look at him stoically as if she knew this was the cross she had to bear. She would wait patiently, chewing her cud, for him to complete his fit.

———•———

The following morning was a Saturday and he wanted me to go with him to stake the cow. He had a fit as we crossed Main Street in town. It was at the time of day when the old, unemployed men would gather around the post office door to exchange gossip. Everyone there heard him curse the mayor and his wife. Soon the word reached the mayor.

That night the mayor came to visit again. This time he brought the sheriff with him and the doctor. We children were allowed to stay in the room to hear what the men would say. Mercé, the mayor said, was getting worse. He had taken the cow by the post office and had cursed the mayor and his wife at the post office door and the old men there had heard him and had spread the news throughout the town. Not only was the mayor offended, he said, "But my wife and my political career are beyond repair." Things could not go on like this. My grandmother, who was Mercé's legal guardian, asked what else she could do?

"Nothing," the mayor said. "There is nothing else to do. Which is why I have brought representatives of the law and medical science with me tonight. And, I might add, there is another formal complaint. The priest and the Sisters of the Incarnate Word, the three who have remained holed up in the nunnery after the priest closed the school . . . why, they have all complained. Sheriff?"

The sheriff was standing at the door. He had just eaten a heavy meal and he had said that he did not want to risk indigestion by sitting down. He belched once very quietly, placing his fist to his mouth very delicately to suppress the noise, a thud-like sound like a beat of a tight drum coming from his upper chest. He said, "Excuse me. I'm full of gas."

"The opinion. The opinion," said the mayor, looking at the sheriff.

"The opinion," the sheriff said, "by legal experts is that a man of Mercé's mentality should not roam the streets cursing everyone he pleases. There are laws against such things. Defamation of character. Slander . . . that sort of thing."

The doctor was sitting at the table with the mayor and my grandmother and my parents. He was drinking a cup of coffee. He put the cup down and said, "Medically speaking, Mercé is a phenomenon. Not a good one, though. As you know, there are good and bad phenomenons. Unfortunately, Mercé is a bad phenomenon. His brain is not working properly. He is a menace to society."

"There you have it," the mayor said. "We all agree that Mercé should not be living with us."

"Where should he be?" my grandmother asked.

"In an insane asylum," said the mayor.

My grandmother gasped. "That would kill us all," she said.

———•———

The sheriff's car came slowly by the house, went slightly past it. From under the house we saw the sheriff straining to spot my uncle in the yard. He had come for Mercé. He went a little farther to be able to see the side of the house. He went a few yards more and then he stopped the car and backed up and parked in front of my grandmother's house next door. He got out, a formidable man, well over six feet tall with a large belly, his gun belt hidden by the bulge of fat in front. He carried a large long-barreled revolver and a pair of handcuffs was tucked under the belt at one side. We crawled to the side of the house to watch him. He knocked on my grandmother's door and no one answered. We could hear him shouting my grandmother's name. "Maria. Maria," he yelled as he knocked and no one came to the door. "I have come for Mercé."

My girlfriend and I watched as the sheriff got back into the car and backed it to the front of our house. He appeared more suspicious. He got out of the car looking all around. He closed the car door quietly and he came up the dirt path bordered by the lime-covered rocks. We had crawled to be under the porch. He walked toward us but he could not see us in the shade under the house. The sheriff walked up the stairs above us. He was standing on the porch and we could see him from underneath through the cracks on the floor. We watched as he adjusted his revolver and handcuffs before he knocked on the door. The whole house seemed to shake under his heavy fist. Dust fell on us below.

We heard the sounds of footsteps inside and it was my mother. She said, "Coming. Coming." The door opened. "Sheriff Manuel," my mother said, surprised. "I thought you were going to go next door to my mother's house."

"I did," he said, "but no one answered. I wanted to ask you if you know where Mercé is. I have come for him and I can't find him."

"I thought he was with my mother," she said.

"I don't think so," the sheriff said. "I haven't seen him. Unless he's inside."

"He might be," my mother said.

The sheriff said, "Well, I'm sorry to bother you."

"Have you seen the cow?" my mother asked. "If you see the cow you might find him nearby."

The sheriff said, "The cow is in the pen. The cow has not left this morning. I checked on that."

"Have you tried the taverns?" my mother said.

"No," the sheriff replied. "I am now. If you see your mother tell her I came and left."

"I will," my mother said.

The sheriff, his heavy boots sounding like thunder, walked off the porch, got in his car, slammed the door hard and took off in a cloud of dust. When he disappeared my grandmother ran from her house across the yard to our house. She came in and we could hear her talking to my mother. She had hidden Mercé in the little toolshed behind her house.

"Why did you do that?" my mother said.

"I don't know. I just did. I hid him. He's hiding there right now."

"But you promised the mayor and the sheriff and the doctor that you would have him ready to go."

"I know but I can't let him go. I love him too much. He means so much to me and the family. It will be the death of us."

"But he has to go."

"We could hide him for a few days. Maybe they won't bother him after that. Maybe the mayor will forgive him by then."

"He won't. We agreed he would go. I can't believe you're hiding him."

"If they don't forgive him then we can send him to San Antonio for a few months. Let the mayor change his mind. Let things pass. Let the town forgive him."

"They'll find him."

"We could move him right now. Take him to Alice to the bus station. Put him on the bus to San Antonio."

"Where will we get a car to take him?"

"We could call Gonzalo."

"What phone are you going to use?"

"We could go next door. Borrow the phone from Quina."

"And then what? What is Mercé going to do on the bus by himself? What will he do? What if he has a fit on the bus? He can't go on the bus."

"If we put him on the bus to San Antonio and tell him to behave he won't have a fit."

"You can't control his fits. Who will meet him at the bus station?"

"We can call your Aunt Herminia. She can be waiting for him at the bus station. She can take him for a few months."

"Herminia can't take him. She's old and can't take care of herself much less Mercé."

"Mercé can help her. Help her at home. Herminia has gardens. Mercé can tend the gardens. Maybe we can send her money to buy him a cow. Herminia needs milk for her bones. That is what her problem is. She never drinks milk. That would be the perfect solution. We send him on the bus. Herminia picks him up and takes him to her house. Mercé tends the garden and milks the cow. Your Aunt Herminia gets her health back. Your Aunt Herminia doesn't have to worry about a thing."

"Mercé can't help Herminia. If Mercé could help anyone why doesn't he do it here?"

"Because I spoil him. Don't you understand that he is the only thing left for me from the old family?"

"I can't help you," my mother said. "This is crazy. They will find him and take him. You can't hide someone like Mercé. It's impossible."

Within one hour the sheriff was back. This time he came like a bull. He drove up to my grandmother's house and slammed on the brakes and created a cloud of dust so big that the car disappeared in it momentarily. He emerged from the dust like an apparition, his hand on his revolver, running toward my grandmother's house. We had crawled to the side of the house to be able to see what he would do.

Mercé and I often went hunting but we never killed anything. He carried the rifle and I walked by his side wondering when he would start a fit. I knew when one was coming because he let me have the rifle. Then he would begin the walk around in circles, mumbling at first and then the yanking of the ears would start. Then the cursing would begin and off he would run into the brush where he would quickly disappear. Once in a while he would carry me to keep me from getting stuck by thorny seeds called goat-heads or devil heads. If I had already gotten into a patch he would kneel down and pluck the goat-heads off. He would spit on my foot and rub it. "It will soon be well," he would say. When we came to a rabbit I would almost scream with excitement, "There's one. Can you see it, Mercé? There. Right in front of us by the cactus. Can you see it? Can you see the rabbit?"

Mercé would look closely. He could see the rabbit. He would raise the rifle and point it at the little animal and then he would lower the rifle. "We'd better save him," he would say. "We'll kill him on the way back."

In the morning he had come to the window by where I slept and he had scratched on the screen to awaken me. Today was the day they would take him, he said. He didn't want to go. "But you have to go," I told him. "You can't hide from the law."

"I'll hide," he said and he thought for a moment. "I'll hide in the toolshed."

I felt sorry for him at the time. Sad. I wanted to cry. This would be the last day I would be with him. No more helping him take the cow on weekends and school vacation. No more knowing where the cow was pastured. No more useless hunting. But then I told him how fortunate he was that something would be done to make him well. "You will be cured, Mercé," I told him. "Someday you will come back and you will be like everyone else. Won't that be great? For the two of us to go to the movies? To go hunting and kill something for a change?"

He walked away from the window. I felt that the last time I would see him would be in the sheriff's car.

We could hear my mother running inside the house. Then we saw the sheriff run up my grandmother's porch and go inside the house without knocking. My mother had seen him and she ran out from our house to my grandmother's house. We followed my mother until she went inside. We could hear my grandmother pleading with the sheriff to let Mercé stay. Mercé could go live with our Aunt Herminia in San Antonio for a while. Herminia had gardens and Mercé could help Herminia with them. We would buy Mercé a cow in San Antonio. He would get well there. Then, if the mayor and the sheriff and the rest of the town wanted him back Mercé would return but not before then.

The sheriff apparently was not interested in my grandmother's plan. From the sounds coming from my grandmother's house he was going from room to room looking for Mercé.

In a short while the sheriff came out the back door followed by my grandmother and my mother. They followed the sheriff around the yard. The sheriff searched the yard and under the house. Then he stopped and he realized that Mercé was hiding in the toolshed. My grandmother saw the sheriff looking at the toolshed and she let out a scream. By now my mother had had a change of heart. She had to help my grandmother. My mother took the sheriff by the arm and tried to get him to go inside the house. The sheriff pushed her arm away and ran for the toolshed. My grandmother and mother ran after him.

The sheriff opened the door to the toolshed and rushed in. My grandmother and my mother stood at the door crying.

"Don't mistreat him," my grandmother cried. "He has not done anything wrong. Be careful with him."

My mother was holding my grandmother in her arms and she was crying. She said, "Please don't hurt Mercé. He's such an innocent soul."

"Poor Mercé," my grandmother cried, "his manhood never descended. If only his manhood had descended he would have been normal like us."

There was a great commotion coming from inside the toolshed. The sheriff was tossing things around digging for Mercé.

Then he found the old piece of carpet and he unrolled it. When he found it empty he threw it out through the door, and my grandmother and my mother thought it was Mercé so they screamed and tried to catch the carpet in the air.

Mercé had escaped. He was not in the toolshed. The sheriff came out tired and flustered. "Where is he?" he asked.

"He's not in there?" my grandmother said.

The sheriff was wiping the perspiration off his brow with his finger. "No," he said. "He's not in the toolshed."

"My God," my grandmother cried. "He's got to be there. I put him there."

Both my grandmother and my mother went in the toolshed to look for Mercé. The sheriff stood by the door in case they uncovered him under all the piles of junk. But they did not.

At the same time, when my girlfriend and I were the most involved in what was going on, I smelled the odor of Bull Durham tobacco and stale beer. I turned around and there was Mercé under the house with us. I had to look twice to make sure it was him. My girlfriend, who was afraid of Mercé, let out a scream. She crawled away from Mercé. He didn't want to go, he cried out. He wanted me to take him and hide him. There was nothing I could do except take him by the hand and we both crawled to the opposite side of the house. But then he went back from where we had come. He was watching the sheriff. And then it happened. Mercé began to mumble. He began to crawl aimlessly around under the house. He had begun a fit. My girlfriend was screaming. She crawled out from under the house and took off running for home. The sheriff turned around to face our house to see what the noise was. At that instant Mercé came out from under the house cursing the mayor. Immediately the sheriff saw Mercé and ran toward him. My grandmother and mother had heard Mercé. They came flying out of the toolshed, running behind the sheriff.

The sheriff stopped to check his handcuffs, and my grandmother and mother caught up with him. They jumped on his back and brought him to the ground. The three bodies were rolling on the dust. My grandmother was still trying to tell him that Mercé could stay with my Aunt Herminia. She was talking about the cow and Herminia's bones. My mother was trying to pin the sheriff down so that Mercé could run off. The sheriff managed to get away from them. Mercé was running in circles around the yard yanking at his ears. He was cursing the mayor's wife and the mayor's nephew. The sheriff was running behind Mercé. My grandmother and my mother were running behind the sheriff.

"We'll buy him a cow," my grandmother was explaining.

My mother was saying, "We can take him to San Antonio and he'll never be any trouble again."

The sheriff said, "I'm taking him like we said I would. To the insane asylum."

Mercé cut across the yard and shortened the distance between him and the sheriff. When they ran by the back steps my grandmother picked up a broom and she was hitting the sheriff on the back with it. Mercé stopped to curse someone else and the sheriff ran right into him, knocking him down. The sheriff fell on top of Mercé. My grandmother fell on top of the sheriff and my mother fell on top of my grandmother. All four were in a pile of bodies three feet high. Then they rolled over to one side as a group. The sheriff kept Mercé down. My grandmother and mother were on their feet. The sheriff reached for the handcuffs and my grandmother beat him on the head with the broom. My mother was trying to take the handcuffs away from the sheriff. But the sheriff was a huge man and the two women and the frail Mercé, whose manhood never descended, were no match for him. He finished handcuffing Mercé and had him sitting on the ground. The sheriff was dusting himself off with his hat. My grandmother and my mother were kneeling on the ground next to Mercé.

The sheriff said, "You women were almost the death of me. I should take both of you and put you in jail."

My grandmother said, "If you put us in jail you will never hear the end of it."

"That's what I'm afraid of," the sheriff said.

The sheriff went to the water faucet by the back door and rinsed off his face. He took a sip of water and gargled with it. He spat out the water and then he drank from the faucet.

"We tried," my grandmother said. "At least we tried. I would have felt bad if I hadn't."

"I knew you wouldn't give him up without a fight," the sheriff said.

My grandmother and my mother got up and helped Mercé up. They took him to the water faucet and let him drink. His fit was over and he was thirsty.

"Mercé," my grandmother said, "you have to go. There is nothing else that we can do. I only hope you would have behaved. Then you could have stayed with us."

My mother said, "He needs to go. Maybe someone can help him. You may come home someday all well and we will all be happy again."

They sat Mercé at the back stairs and they cleaned his face with their aprons. "Look at you," my grandmother said, "all dirty. What will they say when you get to the insane asylum? That I didn't take care of you? That's what they will say. And that's not true. . . . May God help you, Mercé. I don't know why he gave you this cross to bear but he did. Be good and behave. Then maybe they will let us see you."

Mercé was crying. He did not want to go. He fought the handcuffs for a while and then he gave up. My grandmother was wiping the tears from his eyes. She said, "I know you don't want to go. I don't want you to go. But there are people more important than you and me who say that you must go."

My mother said, sitting down by him, "Mercé, we will go see you. It's not like you will never see us again. It won't be like that. I promise you we will go. We will take the child with us and you can see him. You and he can pretend you are going hunting. It's not so bad. Herminia is in San Antonio. We will write to her and tell her you are in the insane asylum. She will be glad to visit you. You know how much you like Herminia. She has gardens, you know. Maybe you can go and visit her gardens. Maybe we can buy a cow and keep her there for you to walk around town. You will meet other people there. You will make friends."

"Friends, Mercé," my grandmother said. "Just think. You will make friends. You know you don't have friends here except for the child. You will meet women. And maybe . . . just maybe you can talk to them and little by little, day by day, your manhood will descend. And if your manhood descends then you will be normal like us. And you won't have all these fits and you won't have to curse."

The sheriff had recovered reasonably well and he was able to stand up. He said, "It's time to go."

My grandmother and my mother stood Mercé up. They began to walk him slowly toward the car.

My grandmother said to the sheriff, "Tell the doctors that his manhood never descended. That he drank a damn bottle of beer meant for someone else. That the potion in the beer affected him and his manhood never descended. It stayed in his brain. But they ought to know that. The doctors ought to be intelligent enough to know that happens. And when that happens, my God, you have a crazy man on your hands. Be sure and tell them that."

The sheriff was walking up front. He turned around and said, "I will."

"Don't forget," said my grandmother. "Don't get there and get all excited and forget. You know how you are. Look at the mess you caused around here. It'll take me days to clean up the mess you made. You could have come in here like a gentleman and asked for Mercé. But no. You have to be a bully. Just because you're big and strong. Just don't let me catch you being mean to Mercé."

"I would never be mean to Mercé," the sheriff said, huffing. "We have been friends for many years. Who has helped him bring the cow home for all these years?"

My grandmother said, stopping to reminisce, "The cow tied to the bumper. And with your lights flashing too. I'll miss that sight."

The sheriff opened the rear car door and guided Mercé in very gently. My grandmother stuck half her body into the car and gave Mercé a hug and a kiss. Then my mother hugged him and kissed him. My mother looked around for me and I hid away further under the shadows of the house. I did not want to cry in front of them. She called out over and over again until she found me under the house.

"What are you doing under the house?" my mother asked. "Come over here and say good-bye to Mercé."

I followed my mother and the sheriff opened the door for me. I went inside the car. Mercé was sitting in the middle of the backseat, his legs crossed at the ankles. I noticed he had no socks. He was leaning toward me waiting for me to hug him. He had filled the car with his smell of stale tobacco and old beer. I gave Mercé a hug. He rubbed his face against mine. He had not shaved and his beard hurt me. He tried to hug me but he couldn't, not with the handcuffs. He fought the handcuffs and began to cry, which made me cry.

My grandmother said, "I told you he would cry when he saw the child. He loves the child so much."

"The child can't be living with Mercé like this," the sheriff said.

"He's right," my mother said. "The child is hearing things he shouldn't be hearing living around Mercé."

Mercé let out a scream, which I'm sure was heard blocks

away. My grandmother began to cry in earnest, not the little tears she had been shedding up till now but the large tears, the ones which fell on the ground and stained the dust. My mother cried large tears also. They both began to pound their chest.

"How could we do this to him?" my grandmother wailed.

Mercé said to me, "Take care of the rifle and the knife. They belong to you now."

"I will," I said.

The sheriff took me by the arm and then closed the door. He got in the car and drove off. We could see Mercé's small head in the middle of the rear window. He was trying to look back at us.

———————

My grandmother and my mother cried every time they saw the cow, which was every day. The poor cow could never figure out what there was about her that made them cry. She would look at herself on either side, walk around in circles trying to catch herself, swishing her tail, slowly chew her cud, wondering what all the crying was about. Finally, she went dry from worry and my father sold her and the crying stopped. We children were happy. We were now going to buy milk from the store, milk that didn't taste like bitterweed.

———————

A year later we were even happier and normal again. Mercé was released and we went to pick him up. He was waiting at the front gate in his old khakis, his hat on, smoking his Bull Durham. From a distance we did not recognize him. He looked more like an Argentinean actor we had seen in the old movie house. But when he stood up we knew it was him. All we had to do was slow down for an instant and he jumped into the car. Not two blocks from the insane asylum he began his fit inside the car. He was still cursing the mayor and his wife. We sped off to see my Aunt Herminia, the one with the gardens. Never once during the visit to my Aunt Herminia was she told how close she came to having Mercé and a cow.

He returned uncured and ready to have more fits. He did, though, carry a little card in his billfold from the insane asylum, a testimonial to everyone's ignorance: He was not a menace to society or the enemy of the people. Neither he nor his cursing was to be taken seriously.

Mister Tyrone

Tyrone and his mother could see the huge articulated Metro bus from half a mile away making its way through the traffic, its top sticking above the rest of the vehicles. They could see the hot air blowing around it creating heat waves, distorting its shape. As it got closer they could hear the engine roar from a stop, spewing out black fumes. Slowly it came. Tyrone was at the curb leaning into the street. His mother asked him to come sit by her but he ignored her and began to run around the bus stop. He was shooting an imaginary pistol. Several people sitting with his mother were uncomfortable with his running and his mother sensed this and she got up and brought him by the arm and sat him down. He could hear the bus getting closer. A few more stops and it would arrive. Driving it would be his friend Gatemouth. He became excited and started to fidget. His mother squeezed his thigh and looked sternly at him.

"You behave like a man," she said.

Tyrone saw the other passengers staring at him and he lowered his eyes and said, "Yes, ma'am."

"Don't be doin' any foolishness on the bus. You hear? Don't be actin' the foo'."

His embarrassment grew even worse. It seemed all eyes were on him. "Yes," he answered.

"Yes, what?"

"Yes, ma'am."

"Don't be yessin' me. And don't be askin' Gatemouth for anythin', you hear?"

"Yes, ma'am."

"If I hear you acted crazy I'm agoin' to whup you and whup you good. You hear me?"

"Yes, ma'am."

"Where's your books?"

"I forgot 'em."

"Bof'um?"

"Yes, ma'am. Bof'um."

"Boy, I ought to whup you right here in front of all these people."

"I forgot."

"Forgot. Don't give me that story. You didn't bring it 'cause you didn't want to. You did that on purpose, Tyrone."

"No, I didn't. I forgot."

"Be quiet. I'll deal with you when we get home."

Tyrone leaned forward to get a better view of the street and he saw the bus one stop away. He was dangling his feet off the bench. He tried not to look at the others. For some reason he became very self-conscious. He began to squirm and he placed his locked hands between his legs to keep from fidgeting but his feet began to swing. His mother reached over and squeezed his thigh again.

"Chile'? You act like you got worms," she said. "You got worms or something?"

"No, ma'am," said Tyrone.

"Well then sit still."

He could see out of the corner of his eye that the white man sitting next to him was staring at him and his mother.

His mother said, trying to please the man, "Don't be

squirmin'. Sit still. You're botherin' the gentleman next to you."

"Yes, ma'am," Tyrone said. He looked at the man sitting next to him and the man quickly looked away.

The bus was on its way on their block. Tyrone could see it rocking along, Gatemouth behind the wheel.

"Don't be askin' Gatemouth for a hamburger either," his mother said. "He told me he bought you a hamburger last night. Don't be askin' for food. You got plenty of food at home."

"Yes, ma'am," said Tyrone.

"Yes, ma'am," his mother said, mimicking him. "That's all I hear from you. But you go ahead and do it anyway, don't you? Acting the foo'."

"Yes, ma'am," Tyrone said.

"Now here comes the bus and don't let me hear anythin' from Gatemouth about you e'cept what a good chile' you been."

"Yes, ma'am."

"Study in your head since you don't have no books. . . . Forgot your books. You know you is lying."

"Yes, ma'am," said Tyrone.

The bus stopped in front of Tyrone. His mother let everyone else on first and then took Tyrone by the hand and helped him up the stairs. Gatemouth was grinning at Tyrone. Tyrone was happy to see him.

"Tyrone," said Gatemouth, showing his large white teeth, "I do think you've grown an inch since I saw you last night. Man o' man. Whoeeee. Jessie, that Tyrone is growing fast. Like a weed. Pretty soon he's going to be playing for the Rockets. I do declare."

"Say hello to Mr. Jackson, Tyrone," his mother said putting the tokens in the slot.

"Hello, Gatemouth," Tyrone said.

"Mr. Jackson to you," said his mother, pulling on Tyrone's hand.

"Mr. Jackson," said Tyrone.

"Ah, he can call me Gatemouth," said Gatemouth. "Everybody else does."

"He's got to learn to respect his elders," Tyrone's mother said.

Gatemouth winked at Tyrone and Tyrone and his mother took the seat behind the driver. Gatemouth looked into the rearview mirror and waited for the traffic to clear. He pulled the bus off the curb. The bus swayed to one side and then leveled off. Tyrone could hear the roar of the huge rear engine.

Tyrone's mother leaned over to Gatemouth and said, "Don't be buyin' Tyrone no hamburgers, you hear? He's got food at home."

Tyrone looked to see if any of the other passengers had heard his mother. No one had heard and this relieved him. But he became self-conscious again, felt a flush come over his face, and he placed his little hands inside his thighs and began to swing his feet again. His mother squeezed his thigh and made him stop. She said, "I don't want any son of mine beggin' in the streets for food, you understan'?"

"Oh, Tyrone's not beggin'," said Gatemouth, his eyes fixed on the traffic around him. "I was hungry and I stopped for a hamburger. I bought one for Tyrone too. Right Tyrone?"

"Yes, sir."

"Well, don't be buyin' 'im any hamburger. He eats at home."

"Whatever you say," said Gatemouth.

The ride down South Main took twenty minutes. During this time Tyrone knelt at the window and looked out at the traffic, at the scenery on the way. Someday, he thought, he would come to Hermann Park and the Museum of Natural History and the planetarium and the zoo. Every day he admired the great hotels, the water fountains, the tree-lined Rice University, the medical center. Some days he wanted to be a doctor like the ones he would see in their white coats crossing the street in front of the bus when Gatemouth stopped to pick up and deliver passengers.

Shortly after the medical center he could see the difference. The buildings were not as pretty. The streets were not as clean. Farther on down it got worse. This is where his mother would get off and leave him alone with Gatemouth.

Tyrone's mother got up and straightened her dress. She said to Tyrone, "Now, you behave. I don't want to hear any bad things about you in the mornin'. You hear me?"

"Yes, ma'am," said Tyrone. He was looking down at his shoes, not wanting to look at his mother's face. He hated this part because he knew how much he would miss her. But then he would be with Gatemouth.

Gatemouth said, "Don't worry about Mr. Tyrone. He knows exactly how to behave."

His mother shook him by the shoulders and said, "And don't be askin' for no hamburger. You hear, young man?"

Tyrone said, "Yes, ma'am."

"Don't you worry, Jessie," said Gatemouth. "He don't ask for nothin'. He just sits there and he's a perfect little boy. Sure wish my chil'ren behaved like he does."

"Well, I should hope so," said his mother. She reached into her handbag and took out a quarter. She said, "This is for a phone call like I always give you. And like always, Gatemouth is keeping it for you. I expect it back when I see you in the morning, young man. Unless Gatemouth has to call me."

"Yes, ma'am," said Tyrone.

His mother kissed him on top of the head and got off the bus. When she was on the sidewalk, Gatemouth closed the door and took off. Tyrone ran to the opposite side to see his mother through the window. She was standing alone on the sidewalk under the streetlight pulling her dress down. He saw her take out her lipstick and apply some more on her lips. Tyrone watched her grow smaller in the distance as the bus sped off. She appeared to him as a lonely figure in the darkness lit by the solitary light. He could barely see her when she began to walk slowly toward the Loop.

"Well, there goes your mother," said Gatemouth. He and Tyrone were alone except for a wino who had gotten on the bus at a downtown stop. He too would ride the bus for a long time. "How you doing Tyrone?" Gatemouth asked, watching out for the wino through the rearview mirror.

"Fine," said Tyrone. He went over across the aisle to sit behind Gatemouth. He was afraid of the wino.

"Whatcha been up to?" Gatemouth asked.

"Nothin'," said Tyrone.

"Did you get to school?"

"Yeah. But I was too sleepy."

"So you didn't learn anything? You just slept?"

"Well, the teacher whupped me upside the head to wake me up but I was just too sleepy. She said I ain't learnin' nothin'. She wanted to know why I's so sleepy all the time."

"Did you tell her?"

"No, sir. That'd get my mom in trouble. And they take me away like they did before. I don't want to go live with strangers."

"You ought to sleep on the bus, man. There's no sense waitin' up for your mother. She don't get back on the bus till five in the mornin'. It's eight right now. If you go to sleep, by the time we pick up your mom you can sleep . . . Well, from eight to twelve is four hours. And then five. That makes it nine hours of sleep."

"But I can't sleep on the bus," said Tyrone. "The seats are too lumpy. And the bus moves too much. And there's too much noise."

"Yeah, you're right. But you ought to try to sleep. That way when you and your mom get home you can go to school."

"I don't like school."

"And you want to be a doctor? And you don't like school? Are you crazy? A doctor goes to school most of his life. And then some."

"I don't want to be a doctor now."

"Oh. You changed your mind? What do you want to be?"

"I don't know. Do I have to know?"

"No, you don't have to know. But it helps. If you can have a dream, Tyrone. You need a dream so that you can follow that dream. Make that dream a part of your life."

"What's your dream? To drive a bus?"

"No. That's not a dream. I have a dream."

"I didn't know that. What's your dream?"

"My dream is to play the guitar. That's why they call me Gatemouth. You know the famous guitar player they call Gatemouth Brown?"

"No."

"Well, I do. I heard him play the guitar once and I knew that was what I wanted to do. I wanted to stand up there on the stage and play the guitar just like he did."

"So you play the guitar?"

"No. Not like Gatemouth. Not right now. But I'm learnin'. I play every day come rain or shine. I practice my guitar. That's my dream, Tyrone. When my chil'ren are grown and me and the wife is all alone I'm goin' to set out to play the guitar. I'm goin' to stand on that stage and I'm goin' to play and the people are goin' to come to hear me and they're goin' to love the way I play. I'll be somebody important then."

"You don't think it's important to drive the bus?"

"Oh, no. Anyone can drive a bus. You don't want to do what everyone can do. I tell my chil'ren, 'Do somethin' no one else can do. Make yourself important.' That's what I tell 'em. Im-por-tant."

"Do they listen?"

"No. Just like I didn't listen when I was their age. I suppose bein' young makes you stupid."

"You think I'm stupid?"

"Oh, no, Tyrone. You're smart. But that don't count."

"Why not?"

Gatemouth slowed down at the intersection to see if anyone was waiting. There was no one. The light was green and he looked both ways and then gunned the engine, crossing the intersection.

"Like I was sayin'. Bein' smart don't count. It's livin' smart that counts. I know a lot of smart people in jail and prison. Too smart for their own good. They think they is smarter than the rest of us and they don't have to work. So they sell drugs. Do some pimpin'. . . ."

"Like my mom's boyfriend?"

"Well, forget about that, Tyrone. You're too young to be concerned with that. You shouldn't have to worry about your mama. Let's talk of somethin' else. . . . When we get to the end of the line and turn the bus around I'm goin' to let you sit on my lap and take the wheel for a little while. Kind of let you get the feel for drivin'. But I don't want you gettin' any ideas about drivin' a bus. You don't want to do that, Tyrone. That's not your dream. You want to be a doctor. Get educated. Make a lot of money. Live in a beautiful big house. You can invite me when I'm old and can't play the guitar anymore. Invite me to your house and I can sit with you and we can drink a cup of coffee out of a fancy cup with a saucer. I'll be proud of you Tyrone. Mister Tyrone. Drive a fancy car that you own outright. Not like some pushers and pimps who don't even have the down pay-ment and they go around driving Cadillacs and Lincolns. You don't be like them. If I hear that you turned out to be like that it would break my heart, Tyrone."

"I don't know what I want to be. An astronaut maybe."

"There you go. You can do it, Tyrone. You have the smarts. That's a good dream to have. I wanted my son to have a good dream but look at him. He don't want to go to school. He says, why go to school to wind up drivin' a bus. And when I tell him of my dream he laughs. They all laugh. Except me."

"Someday, Gatemouth, I'm goin' to see you on the stage playin' the guitar."

"Me and Gatemouth Brown. The two Gatemouths, they'll call us. I'll be sure to invite you, Tyrone. I sure will. They'll call you Mister Tyrone by then."

On the way back, Tyrone did not see his mother. The wino at the back of the bus began to moan. He was kicking at the seat in front of him and grabbing his sides in pain. Tyrone got up and went to stand by Gatemouth.

Gatemouth reached over with his right arm and held Tyrone close to him. He said, patting Tyrone gently, "Don't be afraid of no wino. He's dying."

Tyrone said, "I don't want to see him. I'm scared."

"Well keep your eyes lookin' ahead," said Gatemouth. "See? You don't want to wind up bein' no wino."

The wino began to vomit into the aisle and Gatemouth stopped the bus to try to get him off. But the wino clung to his seat with his hands like claws and he wrapped his feet around the base of the seat and refused to be thrown out. Gatemouth was no physical match for him so he gave up. He took some paper towels from under the driver's seat and he cleaned up the vomit as best he could. The wino stayed through the turnaround and staggered off at one of the downtown stops. As he got off he cursed Gatemouth, called him a motherfucking black nigger and Gatemouth said, "I love you too, man." And he shut the door so that the wino could not get back on to hurt him or Tyrone. The wino hit the door with his empty bottle of wine and shouted some more obscenities. He was trying to get the door open to get back in the bus. Gatemouth had to wait for the traffic to clear but then he pulled out in a roar of exhaust that left the wino gasping for air.

That left Gatemouth and Tyrone and a few night-riders until the turnaround at the other end.

At two in the morning they were alone. Gatemouth stopped the bus by the hamburger place and he and Tyrone got off to get something to eat.

"You want your usual hamburger, I suppose?" Gatemouth said.

Tyrone was standing next to him. "And fries," he said.

"And a Coke," said Gatemouth.

They took a seat and Gatemouth said, "You love hamburgers don't you?"

"Yes, sir," said Tyrone, his mouth full. "And fries."

"Well," said Gatemouth, "you have a dream and you make that dream come true and you can have all the hamburgers in the world. You can eat 'em three times a day. Four times a day. But you have to have a dream. Remember that, Tyrone. You have to have a dream. You're nothin' without a dream. . . . My chil'ren make fun of me for sayin' that but I know it's true. I guess I've told them so many times, like I have you, that they don't listen no more."

"I listen."

"Yeah, but you're smart, Tyrone. Where's your books? You haven't cracked your books all night."

"I forgot 'em."

"See, Tyrone. You can't forget your books. Books is knowledge." He reached over the table and hit Tyrone on top of the head with his knuckle. "That's for forgettin' your books. Man, you can't get nowhere without books. You got to study. Promise me you'll study." '

"I promise."

"Good. If you don't bring your books you're goin' to have to watch me eat my hamburger cause I ain't buyin' you one ever again. You understan'?"

"Yes, sir."

"Give me your head one more time. Let me hit you one more time."

Tyrone leaned his head across the table and Gatemouth tapped him gently on the head. "That's for forgettin' your books," he said, wagging a long black finger at him.

Going south again, the fog from the bay began to drift in and obscure the night. They saw Tyrone's mother standing at the corner under the light. She was leaning against the post talking to a man. Her bright red dress shone in the fog that surrounded her like a glistening shroud under the light. Tyrone had seen her first and was at the seat across the aisle by the window. He waved at her as the bus sped by and she waved back. He could see her talking to him and he said, "Yes, ma'am."

"Go to sleep, Mister Tyrone," said Gatemouth, maneuvering the bus through traffic. "Don't think about your mom. You go ahead and dream you some dreams."

Tyrone curled up in the seat behind Gatemouth. He said, resting his little head on his hand, "The wino called you a nigger."

"Somebody's goin' to call you a nigger all the time. You forget about that," said Gatemouth. "You go ahead and dream you some dreams. Go to sleep before my shift is up. No other bus driver is goin' to put up with you."

"Can I go home with you?" Tyrone asked. "Can I?"

Gatemouth gave out a little laugh and said, "I wish you

could. But you know your mama would kill us both. You go on and go to sleep and dream you some dreams, boy."

Girl

"So what am I doing here? Terri, you know what I'm doing. Getting drunk. That's what I'm doing. I just got rid of a guy. So I thought he might be interested. So I walk up to his table and sit down and start a conversation. This guy says to me, 'Get off my case, lady. You're old enough to be my mother.' He was real surprised when I slapped him. He gets up in a huff and tells me where to get off, and I say 'To hell with you buddy. You're the one that wanted to start something.'

'It's dark in here,' he says and picks up his beer and leaves like he got fooled by the dark and he thought I was young.

"I'm glad you came in, Terri. He was starting to get on my nerves, bragging about how much money he makes. He don't know what money is. Jew Dog had money. Now, that was money. He had so much money he bought me everything I asked for. He loved me, Terri. He really did, but he had a mother to take care of and his business."

"Are you married again?"

"Yeah. But not to Jew Dog. I married Friday. What day is today?"

"Saturday."

"Well, I got married yesterday."

"And who's the lucky man?"

"You're not going to believe this."

"Try me."

"I married Broken Dog again. For the third time."

"So where is Broken Dog?"

"In jail. Can't make bond. He doesn't have any money."

"How'd he get in jail? I mean, he just got married."

"Well, it's like this. We get married and we stop at his favorite bar. I don't like the place, you understand. It doesn't do anything for me. I don't like the music, the people stink, the beer is warm."

"And?"

"And we drink and we drink and then we start to go home. We're in the parking lot and Broken Dog says something to me that I don't appreciate and I take a swing at him. I miss and fall down. He jumps on top of me and who do you think drives up?"

"The cops."

"The fucking cops . . . How'd you know? The Pasadena police. Here is Broken Dog on top of me and it looks like he just knocked me down. The cops come out of the car and pull Broken Dog off me. I'm pissed off with the whole thing. The cops say they saw Broken Dog hitting me and that pisses me off more. You know me. I start to argue with them. They have Broken Dog over the hood of the police car. I'm fighting with one of the cops. They radio for help. When they're handcuffing me the other cop car drives up and they are angry. They were eating donuts somewhere when they got their call. You know loudmouth me. I tell them off. I say, 'What's a matter? You didn't get your fill of donuts?' Broken Dog is in the cop car. Now they ask Broken Dog to come out. Now they've got four cops and they can handle us. They search Broken Dog and on his rubber arm . . . You know he has a rubber arm, don't you?"

"No. I didn't know that."

"Well, Broken Dog has a rubber arm from where he lost the arm in that plant blast in Pasadena. That's all he got out of the blast. The rubber arm. The damn company acts like they were generous giving him the rubber arm. Like it was a privilege and Broken Dog ought to appreciate how generous they were . . . Well, on his rubber arm the dumb Broken Dog . . . You know how macho man he thinks he is. . . ."

"No, I don't. I've never met Broken Dog."

"You will, honey. You will. You'll fall in love with him when you see him. Rubber arm and all . . . Well, on his rubber arm he had pinned a joint. So they find that on him. One joint. Big deal. One of the cops is searching the car and he finds a 9 mm pistol under the front seat. He asks Broken Dog if he has a permit for the pistol and, of course, he doesn't. So they put the Breathalyzer to him and then to me. We're both drunk, honey. But we knew that. You don't act that way unless you're drunk. So now they have Broken Dog on . . . get this . . . assault and battery. That's on me. That's because they thought he was beating up on me. Public intoxication. Carrying a weapon. Possession of marijuana. Disturbing the peace. Resisting arrest. Me? They have me on public intoxication and disturbing the peace. Bail is one fifty on me. Broken Dog? He's got to stay in jail a couple more days. We'll come up with the money. My sister is good for the money. She always is."

"You're kind of stuck on Broken Dog, aren't you?"

"I've had a lot of others in between. I think I've screwed everyone in town. That wanted to get screwed. Let me put it that way."

"What's Broken Dog doing now?"

"I just told you. He's in jail."

"No. I mean, when he isn't in jail."

"Oh, same old thing. Selling jewelry. When he can. His arthritis really bothers him now. He ain't the man I married the first time. I can tell you that. He's more in Diaper Dog's class now."

"What happened to Diaper Dog?"

"Still playing with diapers, I guess. He was the biggest mess I ever married. I'll never forget the first time he took his pants off and he was wearing this diaper. I started to laugh and he starts to cry like a baby. He loved diapers. That's the only problem he had. Other than that he was a good man. I can't even remember being married to him except for the diapers. And he beat me a couple of times."

"Who'd you leave him for?"

"Trash Dog. Now Trash Dog was a man's man. His only trouble was that he loved his job more than me."

"Picking up trash?"

"You got it, Terri baby. He loved hanging on to the back of the trash truck, the wind in his dirty, greasy hair. He thought he was a pilot in one of those old planes you see in the movies. I'd drive right behind him in his old car just to see him howl like a hound dog. He was that happy. He was the best in bed too. I don't know if I ever told you that but he was. Of course, I'm not saying much. When you consider that after he beat me up and left me I married Denture Dog and then Jew Dog. Now Jew Dog was eighty years old and I didn't expect nothing out of him but money, honey. Turns out the man didn't have a dime to his name free and clear. I wound up having to support him."

"I thought you said he bought you everything you wanted."

"Yeah, but I didn't want for much."

"Too bad."

"Too bad? Do you know he had a mother? He was eighty years old and he was taking care of his mother. When does it end, dear Lord? She had all the money. Do you think she was going to turn loose of all that money on him? Not on your life."

"Where's Trash Dog now? Do you ever see him?"

"Oh, I see him once in a while. When I need to get laid or he needs a blow job. Just a quickie, that's all. He don't want me staying around. He's got all these sugar babes around, you know. He don't want no old hag hanging around the apartment cramping his style. You know what I mean?"

"I know exactly what you mean, girl. My ex don't talk to me. He won't even give me the time of day much less get me laid."

"You ought to get yourself a good lawyer. Scare the shit out of him. Is he giving you money?"

"No."

"That's where a good lawyer comes in. He ought to be giving you money."

"Is Trash Dog giving you money?"

"Are you kidding? I don't need money, Terri honey. I work. I don't want nobody giving me money and then telling me what to do. No way. No one tells me what to do."

"So who'd you leave to get married to Broken Dog?"

"I told you. Jew Dog. Jew Dog had a mother and a dog and he had to give her every penny he made so she could buy dog food. I had to help him out. I was selling jewelry. Doing damn well at it too. But you know how it is for a woman. I sold so much they didn't want to give me my commission. I'd be making more than the boss."

"Jack told me you got arrested."

"Which time are you talking about?"

"The DWI."

"DWI. Cops pull my ass over at three in the morning and ask me if I'd been drinking. What a question. What the fuck would I be doing at three in the morning if I hadn't been drinking? Delivering the paper? Anyways they put me in jail and in the morning they couldn't find the judge so they let me go with a warning. Didn't put it on my record. But you know I had to do a lot of favors for the police that time. You know what I mean?"

"Yes. I know what you mean."

"Don't be so tightass, Terri."

"I am not tightass."

"Yes, you are. Here, have a shot of Crown to go with your beer. That'll loosen you up. You do have a tight ass. I can tell just the way you answered right now. You don't like to get laid?"

"I like to get laid. I love it."

"Well, let's get aggressive here. Let's not act like the Bobbsey twins. Let them know you want it."

"So what about Denture Dog?"

"Oh, him. I think Denture Dog was older than Jew Dog. Didn't have a single tooth to his name. I thought a man his age would have something stashed away for the future but he didn't. He had a little house but that burned down. We stayed together three or four days. Had to leave Denture Dog."

"Too bad."

"Too bad? He took a shot at me. Missed me though."

"He shot you?"

"He shot at me, honey. There is a difference."

"He missed, you say?"

"Not quite. I got some buckshot in me on my chest. Around my tits. A little above my crotch."

"So he didn't exactly miss you."

"No and yes. I guess he could have killed me if he wanted to. But he loved me enough just to spray me like a hunting dog. Then he burned the house."

"He burned his own house?"

"Oh, yeah. He found some underwear of mine he didn't know I had and he goes crazy."

"Over underwear?"

"Yeah. He finds some underwear I had in a secret drawer and he goes crazy. He piles my teddies in the middle of the room and sets a match to them. Well, the rest is history. The house catches on fire. Went up in seconds. I break my fucking arm trying to get out of the house."

"You left him and got a divorce to marry . . . ?"

"I didn't divorce Denture Dog, honey. I don't divorce no one. I just get married."

"Who'd you marry then?"

"Broken Dog for the second time. Broken Dog needed me badly. He'd had the accident. He'd lost the arm. He couldn't walk. I just felt sorry for the man."

"And you don't know where Diaper Dog is?"

"Somebody told me he lives in Oklahoma. He's probably in prison somewhere and if he's not he ought to be. That man could turn violent. He beat me up so bad one time I couldn't see for a month. Blurred my vision. I went to live with my mother for a while like I always do. I always go back to my mother when things get rough for me. I don't know what I'd do without her. I know how much pain I've caused her and how embarrassed she is with me but I can't help it. I just won't take my medicine. The doctor says it's my brain. It's all messed up. I'm manic depressive. You know what that means?"

"No."

"Well, it means you have trouble."

"Why don't you take your medicine?"

"I don't need it. I'm not that bad. Oh, my mother begs me to take my medicine. My sister buys it for me. But I won't take it. I don't need medicine. I'm okay. You're okay. You read that book?"

"I heard of it."

"We're all okay. That's what the book says. It's just that some of us are a little different. I'm different than you. You're different than me. I figure that's what makes the world go round."

"Have you tried it with medicine?"

"Oh, yeah. I hated it. Everything is blah. No fun. Stay at home. Do nothing but watch TV. Who wants to live like that?"

"Why do you do the things you do?"

"I don't know why I do the things I do. God, sometimes

when I have the stomach to look back and see what I've done I think that I must have been crazy."

"Do you really think you do crazy things?"

"I do, Terri. I do crazy things."

"Lately?"

"Lately? What are you talking about? Just tonight. Before I got here. You wouldn't guess what I did. Not in a million years."

"I guess I couldn't."

"I stopped at the 7-11 to get cigarettes and the guy there and I started talking and he said how pretty I was. That's all he said. How pretty I was."

"So that's crazy?"

"No. But I gave him a blow job behind the counter."

"You gave a perfect stranger a blow job right there on the spot?"

"Yes. Don't make it sound like I'm a tramp or something. It's not the end of the world, you know. The sky didn't fall, did it?"

"But just to do it? Just like that?"

"Well, he said I was pretty. And then I liked the thrill of doing it right there. What if I get caught? What if this guy's wife walks in? I like the thrill. The excitement. Don't you see the excitement?"

"You're crazy. You did that?"

"Yeah, I did that. I know I'm crazy."

"But you just married Broken Dog yesterday."

"I know. I'm the one who told you. . . . I like dogs. Trash Dog had a dog that wouldn't quit. A Great Dane."

"That's an expensive dog."

"Well, it wasn't a real Great Dane. It was a cross. Had a lot of Great Dane in him though. Trash Dog loved him like he loved himself. Sometimes he'd take him on the trash truck with him. Whenever the driver let him. I still think I'm in love with Trash Dog. The way I talk about him and the way I carry on about him. Maybe this time it'll all work out with Broken Dog. I don't know. Tonight I need to get laid. Either here at the table or someplace. Anyplace. I don't care. I'm getting old though. It's harder and harder to get laid. That's why I love Trash Dog 'cause I can just walk in and get laid in a minute and I can be back with Broken Dog before sunrise. Have another beer, Terri. I got money for the both of us."

"Where'd you get money?"

"My mom gave it to me. And my sister. This is Broken Dog's bail money. We might as well have a good time with it. All he'd do when he came out would be to get in trouble again. Hell, he's safer in jail than anywhere else."

"You miss him?"

"Broken Dog? Are you kidding? Sure I miss him. He's my life. I couldn't live without Broken Dog. Believe me I've tried. It just don't work. And he's so forgiving. He won't mind me spending his bail money. He'll laugh when I tell him. He loves me, you know?"

The Wedding

His wife and I heard the old man cry out in the next room at the same time. She was standing by the stove warming up old coffee in a pan because she had insisted that I drink coffee with them. I was not in a hurry, although I had turned off at the wrong cattle guard and had come to this ranch by mistake. To complicate matters, when I had stood at the door asking her where I was she had asked my name and she had mistaken me for someone else, a cousin she had not seen in many years. Nothing I could do or say would convince her that I was not her cousin. She asked me in and I could not find a way to refuse.

But now someone else was with us in the house—the voice of the old man—and he was crying out for someone to help him. The wife made a face as if to tell me that I would not enjoy the old man being around. Well, I had not found the old woman good company either and I said that I would be leaving soon and she should tend to the old man, as badly as he was crying for help. She left the coffee boiling on the stove and went into the room where I assumed the old man was laboring with something. Then I heard the soft thuds followed by the moans. I could hear her saying something in a low voice so that I could not understand. Somehow she was muffling his voice. She had not let up on the old man and I could hear the small restrained whimpering. Suddenly I heard a crash and I was tempted to get up to see if I could help but before I could make up my mind I heard the woman speak out to me from the room. There was nothing to be concerned about, she said. The old man had fallen out of bed.

"He's fine," she followed. "This happens all the time. It's just that he's so thin and frail but he weighs so much. Like he's made of iron. His bones feel like iron."

"Please," I heard the old man plead, "I need help from this woman."

"Be quiet," she said. "If he hears you they'll take you away. Do you want someone to come and take you away?"

I heard a muffled, "No."

"Then shut up and take it like a man," she said, followed by more blows.

"But it hurts when you hit me," he said.

"I know it hurts," she said. "That's why I do it. What's the point of doing it if it doesn't hurt?"

"May God help me."

The wife came out cleaning her hands on her apron. She took a brick by the door and placed it between the end of the door and the door frame to hold it ajar. She walked past me and went to the stove. She turned it off and poured the boiling coffee and handed me a cup.

"Here," she said. "Coffee only. We don't have anything to eat with it. Unless you want crackers."

"No," I said, "I don't want anything to eat. I just got through eating in town."

I could hear the old man dragging a piece of furniture inside his room.

She noticed that I was interested in what the old man was doing. "Don't pay any attention to him," the wife said. "He's just getting a chair close to the door so that he can hear us. He loves to talk. If you get him going you will never shut him up. We used to go to the Mass on Sunday when the priest came but I had to quit taking him. He talked all during the Mass. The priest told me not to bring him back. And then all his friends left. He would not let them talk. So they left. So the priest himself left. Never came back. He left a message on the altar telling us all to go to hell."

"Who is he?" I heard the voice from the other room ask.

"It's none of your business," the wife replied. "It's my cousin and he doesn't want to talk to you."

"Your cousin? You have a thousand cousins and I know them all. Which one?"

"Leonel."

"Leonel is here? Why didn't you tell me?"

The wife went over and removed the brick to close the door. She said, through the door, "Don't be getting any ideas. You are not coming into the kitchen. You are staying in your room where you belong."

"Can you just open the door a little? Just to get some sunlight?"

The wife went and took the brick and again placed it between the door and the frame. "That's it," she said. "Not any more than that."

"Have you told Leonel that I've been sick?" he asked. "That I am not well?"

"No," she answered. "Why would I bother the man with your afflictions? Keep them to yourself. No one wants to hear about them." She turned to me and whispered. "Don't get him talking. Just ignore him. He's not sick. He's just lazy. His father went to bed at the age of forty. He said he was going to die soon but he lived until he was almost ninety. Spent all that time in bed. His wife running to his bedside feeding him, cleaning him. All those years. And he wouldn't die. Can you believe that? A man that would not die? Then the wife, this one's mother, died from work and the man got up. Went to the funeral like he had been walking around all this time. You can imagine what the relatives said. They wanted to kill him. After the funeral he went back to bed and his sister took care of him. And then she died and he went to her funeral and then back to bed. Five women his father killed. When I married him I saw what his father had done to his mother and all the other women and I promised I would never be treated like that. If he wants to die in bed let him. He's been in bed for twenty years, dying. But he won't die. I don't take care of him, not the way his mother slaved. I give him what I don't eat, what I don't drink. Let him die. Some days he says, 'Today I am sure I will die,' but he doesn't. He wakes up and asks me if he's dead. 'How can you be dead and be eating?' I ask him."

"Would it be possible to enter the room?" the old man asked.

"No," the wife replied. "You know very well you are not allowed out of your room." To me, she said, "The last time I allowed him out of his room I had a hard time putting him back. I had to take the whip to him and as frail as he is he fought me. But I was able to get him back in the room and I was able to close the door. Once I close the door he won't attempt to open it. It's like he's afraid to open the door. To see what is behind the door. It scares him. But once he gets out I have a hard time with him. He doesn't want to go back. He's like iron. You know iron?"

"Yes."

"Well, that's him. He's iron. He gets heavy when he gets into this room."

"Why do you hit him?" I asked.

She poured some more boiling coffee and said, "I don't hit him. He hits himself. I've never touched him. And may God strike me dead right here if I'm lying. I've never hit him. He hits himself."

"Why would a sane man hit himself?"

"Ah," she said, pointing a finger at me, "you've hit the nail on the head. He's not sane. Something happened to him to make him insane."

"What happened to him?"

"He was buried alive. . . . Look at him through the crack in the door. Can you see his eyes in the dark? See his eyes? You can see the light hitting his eyes and you can see the reflection from his eyes. They are the eyes of an insane man."

"How could he be buried alive in this day and age?"

She shrugged. "It's not as hard as it sounds. Not when he's been in bed all these years."

"I heard you hitting him."

"No, I tell you. That was him. He was hitting himself."

"She hits me," the old man said. "She's lying. She hits me. If you would open the door I could show you where she hits me. As God is my witness I'm telling you the truth."

"And he can never come out of his room?"

"Never. I will never allow him to come out of his room. That last time was enough for me."

"When I was a child," the old man said, "people were mean. They were angry. My father was always angry and so was my mother. Now people are not angry. And I don't know why. Why are people not angry anymore? What has happened during all this time?"

"I couldn't tell you," I said.

By now the coffee tasted very bitter and I was trying to drink it in small sips so that my mouth would not hold on to the bitterness. The man's voice was scaring me, carrying over from behind the door, resonating against the thin wood of the door like a low steady drum. When his wife had asked me to look through the door at his eyes I had seen them, a pair of small lights reflected from the kitchen, set in the cover of the darkness that was his room.

"He has something in his eyes, like a cloud," the wife said.

"But I see," the old man said. "What I don't see is why people are not angry anymore. When did that happen? I know my father was angry all the time and so was my mother. We would all stay away from them. I had wanted my mother to hold me once but she refused. She was that angry. We had mean people in those days."

"This is his way of starting," she said. "Be careful with him."

"There are many reasons for being angry," I said.

"Don't talk to him," she warned me. "You'll get him started."

"You are a wise man," he said. "Many reasons you say? But when I was a child we didn't know. You understand? Why were people so angry all the time?"

"I wouldn't know," I replied.

"Men would hit women. I never hit her."

"That's a lie and you know it," the wife shot back with so much hatred that it bothered me. "You know very well that you beat me every single day that you could. Until you became frail from staying in bed. Your fists were like iron balls falling on my head. I can still feel them at night."

"It is against the natural order to hit women," he said, continuing. "The man in the ranch next to us hits his wife. I can hear her screams during the night when I have a hard time sleeping."

"You never have a hard time sleeping."

"I can hear her cries all the way here. And the ranch is several miles. But in this territory the wind carries the sounds. You know that. We can hear a cow for miles around. Voices. We can hear voices. But you know that, don't you?"

"Yes. I was raised in the area."

"And now you're back. Back to stay. Everyone comes back."

"No. I live far from here now."

"Where do you live?" he asked.

"In Houston."

"Where is that?"

"A place very far from here."

"Are the people angry there?"

"Yes. I suppose you can say that."

"Why are you here then?"

"I came for my mother's funeral."

"Your mother died?"

"Yes."

"Was she angry?"

"No."

"My mother was angry all the time. . . . And you're not coming back?"

"No."

"This is the last time I will see you before I die?"

"That's very possible. I have no relatives here now so I don't intend to return for a while."

"I'll be dead by then. This is the last time I see you. How sad life is. That we can talk about it as if we were talking of the sun rising, the moon setting. My dying has become a known conclusion. No one seems to care about it anymore."

"That's what you get," the wife said.

"But I'm talking of hearing voices in this vast wilderness."

"That's because you're crazy. Your mother heard voices. She was crazy. Crazy for staying with your father for all those years until it killed her. No human could have stood what she did. Until she died from work. And then your father gets up to go to the funeral like he had been walking all those years. You should have heard the relatives. The only reason they didn't kill him and throw him in the same grave was because they didn't want him buried with his wife. One lifetime of that man was enough. Can you imagine living for all eternity with that man on top of you?"

"When I was a young man I attended a wedding. A beautiful wedding."

"Not ours, I'm sure."

"I was ten. There were three brothers, mean as rabid wolves and they delighted in creating trouble wherever they went. Never was a person at peace when they were around. One time they killed a calf in front of his owner and asked him what he was going to do about it. The poor man said, 'Nothing. The poor calf is dead. Take the meat if you want it.' But they didn't want the meat. They were offended. Did the man imply that they were hungry? Starving? Did they look like they were starving? The poor man said he meant no harm but the three brothers were insulted. They got off their horses and whipped the poor old man until blood came out of his eyes. You see, they wanted to teach him a lesson. No one insulted them."

"It's your fault," the wife said. "You got him started. She got up and left the room, went to the front room from where I had entered the house. I could see her sit down in an old beaten chair. She took out her rosary and began to pray. She raised the rosary toward me when she noticed I was watching her. She said, "So that he dies soon."

I glanced back at the door from where the old man's voice was coming. I heard the chair move twice in short hops. He was coming closer to the door.

The wife noticed my concern and said, "Be careful. He might come through the door. Be prepared for the worst if he does."

". . . . The poor man tried to leave but they tore his clothes off. Beat him to the ground until blood came from his eyes. These three were relentless. Once they took it on themselves to hate a man they would not let up until they killed him. Just one word, one gesture and the man would be the target of so much humiliation and in time they would kill him. So one day, a short time before his daughter's wedding, they spotted the man in town buying supplies. They approached him and reminded him that he had insulted them. They wanted something from the poor man. The man offered them money, whatever, but the more he offered them the more insulted they felt. They took the man to the street in front of the grocery store and beat him until blood came out of his eyes. The man's sons were in town that day and they found their father in the street, bloodied, and he told them that the same three men had beaten him. Now the sons had been fit to be tied the first time it happened but the mother had prevailed on them and so had the father. Why fight with these three brothers? The deed was done. Why aggravate the situation? Why bring on a feud that could last for lifetimes? Could cost many lives? Needless agony? But now? What about now? For sons to see their father in the street bloodied and almost dead? The sons looked for the three brothers but they had fled. They took their poor father home and tended to him. Once again the mother's wisdom prevailed. Why start a feud so close to their sister's wedding? Why ruin the wedding? After so much planning?"

"I told you you wouldn't be able to shut him up," the wife said from the front room. "I tell you I'm sick of hearing his voice. The reason I don't keep a killing rifle around is that I would kill him. Oh, I keep a twenty-two but that's for rats and rabbits. You couldn't kill him with a twenty-two. The bullets bounce off his skull like an old pig."

"You've tried to kill him, then?"

"Oh, yes. Many times. But I can't. I would need a deer rifle. A thirty-thirty. Something of that caliber."

The old man had not stopped. I picked up his story when the woman went back to her rosary. ". . . was beautiful," he said. "The wedding, I mean. It was beautiful. It was a Sunday. When people were married on Sunday. Now the priest won't marry you on Sunday. The priest won't even come to say Mass. Can you believe that? The priest left a message on the altar when he left never to return. He wanted us to go to hell, he said. Are you married?"

"No."

"I thought you had married. Didn't we go to your wedding? Didn't you get married in Corpus Christi? In that big church?"

The wife couldn't keep from interrupting. She said, "You haven't been to Corpus Christi in forty years. This man is in his twenties. Now just count and see if you could have been to his wedding."

"I went to a wedding in Corpus once. Beautiful wedding. Lots of food and drink. I never drank, you understand."

"You are a liar," the wife said. "You drank all the time. You were a drunkard. You spent all your youth drunk. You don't remember your own children's names you were so drunk."

"I don't have children."

"You have children," she said. "You have three children. None of which love you. They all hate you for what you were and what you have become. You are a source of shame for them. How could they love someone like you? A drunken coward who beat his wife without mercy?"

". . . *la canicula*. The dog days of summer. It was the middle of the morning and already it was hot. The men, of course, wanted to remove their wool coats and ties it was so hot but the women did not allow them. The women were in the house, all seated in a circle around the parlor all dressed up and a more beautiful scene you could not imagine. The bride and her mother were hiding in the back room. The groom was outside with his comrades, drinking nervously. The men had killed a calf the evening before and dressed it and they had built great fires and they had taken the coals and stacked them in ground pits and they roasted the complete calf all night long. By the morning the meat was falling off the bones and the men had stripped the bones clean and had placed the barbecue in great kettles dug into the hot ground. The men had baked large loaves of bread on top of the great kettles. Inside the house the women had cooked the beans and the potatoes. What can I tell you. The food was prepared and abundant. You have never eaten until you eat at a ranch wedding. The priest arrived and you can imagine what a commotion his arrival caused. The men were at the gate to greet him reverently. The men wanted him to stay outside and drink with them. The women came outside to greet him. They wanted him to come inside with them. The priest obliged by having one drink with the men and then excused himself to go inside with the women. In the meantime some of the men had taken the priest's things from the wagon and were setting up the small altar under the mesquite by the horse pen. My friends and I were playing beyond the ranch house where the clump of mesquites began. We played a game where we would hide and then someone went to look for us. The longer one hid the more interesting the game grew. One time I hid for three days and my parents didn't miss me once. The others left me alone in the wilderness for those three days. Finally I had to give myself up and by that time the game had ended and there was no one there for me to surrender to. But that was life. Simple life in those days although the people were angry. Do you suppose the simplicity made them angry? No? I don't think so . . . I wonder if I could come into the room to shake your hand?"

The wife was listening closely and she got up and went to the door and said, "If you come through this door I'll kill you. I have a knife in the kitchen that will kill you." She turned to me and said, "If he tries to come through the door shove him back as hard as you can because once he gets into the room he gathers strength and he weighs more than iron. But don't be scared. It's just that he might try something. You never know with him. A coward is unpredictable. You never know. He might kill me before I kill him. He can be that strong. Like an ox. Like a mule. I told you how much trouble I had getting him back into his room the last time he escaped. I had to take the whip to him and even then I had such a difficult time. . . . If you don't behave I'm going to take the brick away from the door and lock it again. Do you want me to do that?"

"No."

"Well, then behave. Don't you know you're scaring our guest? What kind of man are you anyway? Scaring our guest."

". . . . We were in the middle of August and the canicula when even the wind burns your face, the type of weather we had when we blazed the road from San Diego to Freer. It was so hot then that the snakes would hide under the hollow roots of the older trees. All we had to do was go to the old tree and throw gasoline at the trunk and the snakes would roll out in a tangled mess, some so angry that they would strike at each other and would fight to the death locked body to body. Some were so angry that they would bite themselves, kill themselves in anger. We would take a shovel or a grubbing hoe or an ax and kill them. But the more we killed the more there seemed to be. It was like the tale that has no ending. . . . The wedding was beautiful. All morning long people had arrived—on horseback and wagons and even one car. Who brought the car?"

The wife said, "There were no cars in 1900. The first car we ever saw was in 1913 or 1914, somewhere around that time."

"The wedding took place at eleven o'clock that morning. After the ceremony we ate barbecue. The father of the bride— Antonio was his name—said that this was the proudest day of his life. To see his daughter married and beginning a new life. Bringing new life into his life. . . . You understand that as children we were not allowed in the wedding ceremony. We were observers and we were fed last. We took our plates to the woods to eat. As we ate we could hear the sounds of the crowd, the laughter as they ate and drank. We were happy also. . . . And then it happened. Our happiness was short-lived. Why were people so angry? Why couldn't they leave others in peace? The three brothers appeared. From the woods we could see them approaching on horseback, trampling across the field of corn, riding toward the house. They had come to disrupt the wedding. I remember that Antonio's sons names were Adolfo and Octavio. The two men who had been drinking with them and helping prepare the barbecue were Juan Garcia and Julian Garcia. The troublemakers, the mean brothers were Juvencio and . . . I can't remember the others' names."

"Eusebio and Carlos," said the wife.

"Eusebio and Carlos," the old man repeated.

I heard the chair slide over the floor. The woman said, "Don't you get any closer. He's trying to get out. Don't let him out." She came from the next room and went to the door and removed the brick and slammed the door shut. "I warned you," she said. "You were trying to get out."

"I want to see his face up close," the old man said.

"No you don't," she said. "You want to get out so that you can attack us. Do you have the rifle?"

"No. I don't have the rifle."

"Did you get the rifle? Is that what this is all about? You have the rifle hidden in your room?"

"No. I don't have the rifle."

She said to me, "Be careful. He lies. He may have the rifle and he knows how to use it. If he tries to get out you better run. For God's sake don't try to fight him. He's like iron once he gets into the room. Do you know how to use a whip?"

"No," I replied. "I haven't used a whip in many years."

"Well, there you have it," she said. "It's better for you to run."

"I think I should be leaving," I said, looking at my wristwatch. "I'm expected somewhere else. The friend I came to see must be worried."

The voice, more muffled with the door closed, said, "Don't go. I won't try to get out of the room. Let me finish the story. Do you want to come closer? So that you can hear me?"

"Don't go any closer," the wife said. "God only knows what his intentions are." She went by the stove and put a pan of water on the burner and said, "This is to boil water in case he gets out. We'll throw it at him." She went to sit down to her rosary. She pointed the rosary at me and smiled. "He wants you to get closer so that he can jump on you. But the door is closed. You should be safe. But don't get any closer. You never know what a coward will do."

The old man said, "I was very brave once. When I was young I was the bravest man. I could ride two horses side by side at one time. One foot on one saddle and the other on another saddle. They used to call me *el maromero*. I could rope a bull and hold him with the lariat in my teeth."

"All lies," the wife said.

"Juvencio and Eusebio and Carlos Gonzales. How the mind remembers. Juvencio rode to the table where the wedding party was eating. His two brothers remained behind him by the house. The people were startled to see the horseman for the first time. Antonio jumped up when he saw the man, his old attacker. Then they looked around and saw the other two by the house. This was an obvious threat. The wind was blowing in my direction and I could hear every word as if I had been standing next to the table. 'What do you men want?' Antonio asked.

"Juvencio said, 'We received word of the wedding and we were told that we were not invited. It bothers us that we were insulted by not being invited. We are neighbors, after all.'

"Antonio hushed the crowd at the table and said, 'My family has forgotten what you did to me and we have nothing to talk about. You were not invited to the wedding and I ask you in the most courteous way to leave.'

"The priest got up to intercede. He spoke eloquently of the spirit of brotherhood. Love of fellow man. The love of husband and wife. The Ten Commandments. The men at the table were standing. The bride was being led quickly away. The women were carrying her to the house. The priest followed. The groom, Pablo Garcia, came to stand by his father-in-law. I could see very plainly from behind the mesquites. Pablo took several steps toward Juvencio. The two mean brothers galloped their horses to the wedding table and trampled it, the horses hooves shattering the plates, the cups, the glasses, everything. It was two against three. You see, Antonio's two sons had gone into the house to get their weapons. They came out running. Not only were they armed, they had brought pistols for their father and brother-in-law. Now it was four against three.

"Antonio said, and I can hear his words now, 'There will be no blood shed at my daughter's wedding. There will be no violence. This is a day for celebration and joy.'

"From here on my mind is very vague, as if I had seen this in a dream, the events unreal . . . I suddenly heard a shot. By the time I looked up all I could see was a puff of smoke rising from the barrel of a pistol held by one of the three mean brothers. The unarmed guests ran as any sane person would. My first instinct, from afar, was to see who had fallen. No one. Then I realized the shot had been fired into the air. Juvencio dismounted. He pushed Antonio backward and I could see the old man trying to resist him. Again Juvencio pushed him back. 'Let them fight,' said one of the mean brothers. 'Let it be the two of them in a fair fight.' But how could it be fair? Juvencio was years younger and stronger. The father didn't have a chance. 'Anyone interferes has me to deal with', said the mean brother. . . . Juvencio struck Antonio on the head and the poor man fell to his knees. Blood began to flow from his head. He had been hit with some type of instrument. Immediately I saw that it was a long barreled pistol, the type the Rangers used in the old days. God help you if a Ranger hit you on the head with a pistol such as that one. The barrel was thicker than my thumb. The sons, seeing their father bleeding, could not restrain themselves. How would you like to see your father bleeding? Struck on the head with the barrel of a pistol thicker than my thumb? His enemy standing over him ready to shoot? The sons opened fire. The confusion was great. I cannot begin to tell you the quickness with which all events took place after the first shots were fired. It was as if everyone was prepared beforehand to begin shooting at once. Juvencio fell dead immediately. Shot at point-blank range in the heart by Antonio. He fell but not before firing several shots into Antonio's heart. Antonio too was dead before he touched the ground. Now everything becomes a blur. A hundred and one things were going on at the same time. The action was fierce. So many shots were fired that no one could have kept track. The women were in the house yelling and screaming for their husbands. Most of the guests had fled into the woods. They could see the carnage unfold before their very eyes. They were powerless. The priest ran out to stop the killing. It seems to me that Pablo Garcia, the groom, was the next to fall. There was no cause to kill him. Newly married. Just starting his life with Antonio's daughter. He fell by the side of his father-in-law. The remaining mean brothers—Eusebio and Carlos—were exchanging shots point-blank with Adolfo and Octavio. It was anyone's guess who would fall next. The women broke through the door and were running toward the fight. The brothers, Juan and Julian Garcia, who had come to help with the barbecue, were unarmed and they did not have a chance to defend themselves. Both fell dead. Still the shooting at point-blank continued. When it was over, after an eternity of seconds, there were eight men killed. I had seen the death of eight men in the matter of seconds. What had begun as a day of anticipation for me had ended in tragedy. The priest was scurrying around giving the last rites to each one. Dead were Antonio Briones, the father of the bride and Adolfo, his son. Octavio, his other son, survived through the grace of God. He was maimed for life. Pablo

Garcia, the groom, dead. Killed defending his father-in-law's honor. The bride, in her once-white dress, was kneeling among the dead, covered in blood, turning from her father to her husband, trying to ease the death of each one, not knowing which one was the most important—her father or her husband. The three horrible brothers were dead. That's six. And the defenseless brothers who helped with the food, the Garcia brothers, Juan and Julian. Eight dead in less than one minute. . . . Do you understand what I mean when I say that life is worthless? That your life depends on the anger of others? Those were the days when people were angry. Why were they angry? What was in them to be angry? . . . We had not seen the end. Then came the most horrible deaths of all. The bride was on her hands and knees, covered in blood, screaming for God to help her. She began to frantically scratch around the ground as though she were trying to grab something. She found what she was looking for. She took her father's pistol, put it to her head and pulled the trigger. I could see the burst from the pistol, the recoil, and then instantly the spray of brains emerged from where the bullet came out. The priest had seen her put the pistol to her head and he had tried to rush over to stop her. But he was too late. The mother, seeing her daughter dead, took up her son's pistol, stood up and screamed so loud that I can still hear her at night, as if the scream will not die but will always travel through our territory looking for a place to end and rest. She fired the pistol into her head and again I saw the exact repetition of what I had seen with her daughter, the recoil . . . the spray of brains. . . . You can imagine what the episode did to me. I ran through the brush. I ran and I ran. I didn't care where I ran as long as I ran away. Ran to get away from what I had seen. In time I ran in an ever-decreasing circle as one does when disoriented, so that I came to where I started. By now the ten bodies were covered with sheets inside the corral, the priest praying over them.

"Are you through?" the wife asked, getting up.

"Just a few more words," he said.

The wife walked past me and to the door and opened it slightly and placed the brick between the door and the door jamb.

"When I was a child," he said, "my father would take us to a small lake near where I was born. . . . Excuse me while I wipe a tear from my eyes. . . . And on the surface of the lake you could see the salt as it collected and floated to the shore. We would go there and pack salt and in the winter we would kill the ducks that had migrated from God knows where. We would take the dead birds and wash the lice off them in the salt water, skin them, feathers and all, and clean them to take home. My father loved the tails. He ate them raw. He would chew the tail off the ducks just like one chews the end off a loaf of bread. My brothers and I, we would laugh and feel like gagging, but mostly we would laugh because my father was angry and we did not know what he would do from one moment to the next. No one knew why the lake was salty, but you could float an egg in it. We bathed in it during the summer, but we were never allowed to go to the deep end. Someone had told my father that it was very deep, perhaps one hundred feet and that was where all the salt was coming from, from the center of the earth. Later on in my older years when I was operated on in my head for a tumor I dreamed after the operation that we were cutting large slabs of salt and loading them on the mule-drawn wagons and it seemed the dream went on forever, the salt went on forever like my father's anger, like the tale that has no end. But those were the good days when I was new and I could take the anger. Now all my days are the same. They run into each other where night and day are one and I have nothing to live for except remorse. Don't think that I don't want to die. I do. But no man can will his own death. God knows I've tried. If only they had killed me too. Eleven dead. That would have been too much."

The wife went into the room with the old man and I could hear her moving him out of the chair. "Get up," she said and I could hear the muffled blows and his cries again.

"Please don't hit me," he said.

"Do you need to go to the bathroom?" she asked him.

"No," I heard him reply. "Maybe tomorrow I can tell him about the snakes?"

"No," the wife replied. "You can't. He won't be here. He's leaving as soon as I put you to bed. What do you have here?"

"Nothing."

"Where is the rifle?"

"I could tell him about the snakes."

"You have talked enough for two days. Now, shut up and go to bed. Let me have the rifle. You have it hidden in the bed. I can feel it."

I could hear her going through his things and then she came out with the rifle and said, "He's going to sleep now. When he awakens he will not remember talking to you. You see the rifle? He was going to kill us." She took the magazine out and showed me the bullets. "He had it loaded and ready to use. We would have had to kill him first. If not, he would have killed us both."

I refused any more boiled coffee and told her I had to leave. I had taken more of her time than I had intended. She wanted me to stay a while longer. But I wanted out. She walked me to the car.

"Don't be afraid of him," she said. "If you're afraid of him then you are afraid of everything."

When I arrived at my friend's ranch I told him of the old man and his wife. He seemed unduly curious, asking me question after question. He stopped for a while and then asked me if I had been drinking?

"Only boiled coffee from South Texas," I replied.

He asked me again which cattle guard I had turned on and he described the ranch exactly as it had been.

He said, "You must be mistaken about where you were. I know the woman who lives at that ranch. I admit I haven't seen her in years but she lives alone. I haven't seen her since her husband died. I saw her bury him in the backyard."

We talked about it for a while and we came to the conclusion that I had been at the wrong ranch. But still, in my mind I knew I was right and so did my friend because at one point he asked himself, "If he did not go to that ranch where was he?" He seemed distracted for the whole evening as I was too. In fact, the visit turned out to be nothing more than superficial small talk with the thought of the old woman and man bothering us in the back of our minds.

Returning that night I stopped at the cattle guard I had turned on by mistake and I looked to my right through the open car window. Several cows were bunched together for protection by the side of the cattle guard. I felt a strong breeze and I could see the eerie lantern light flickering on in the front room of the house as it sat in the dark on a clearing on a knoll surrounded by trees. I could see the frightening, moving shadows of the woman living inside. I did not linger on the scene.

Uncle Willy

He was a scrawny ten and his sister, with the same build, spindle legs, was nine and they had never seen their mother so excited. In the afternoon, when she got the phone call she sent them out to the chicken coop to get the hen. When they brought the hen to the kitchen door she came out and with one hand grabbed the hen's neck and with the other grabbed both the hen's feet. She stretched the hen across her leg and pulled the hen apart. The hen was dead in an instant. She cleaned the hen at the spigot outside the house, running water on the inside and outside until the dead hen looked clean, smooth, and limp. The children watched her dry the hen off on her apron. Then they went inside where she laid the hen on the counter. Here is where the children watched her cut the head off easily since the head had separated from the neck. She took the head and threw it out in the yard for the dog. She took out some old bread, crumbled it and made stuffing with raisins and peanuts and apples and sage.

It was Saturday and their Uncle Willy was coming. They had never met Uncle Willy, their mother's only brother. He had called from Beaumont. He was passing through and thought he ought to call before showing up. He didn't like surprises and just knew no one else did.

Their father came in from work at four in the afternoon. His shift ended at twelve and he had been drinking beer with his buddies after work so he wouldn't be in any mood for hearing about Uncle Willy. Their mother didn't tell him Uncle Willy was coming but when he smelled the roasting hen he knew something was up. Their mother would never roast a hen for him. So he tried to get the hen out of the oven to check it out but the mother wouldn't let him. He got so angry that he left to go pick up where he left off with his buddies without knowing Uncle Willy was coming.

Their mother cleaned house after their father was gone while they played outside and watched for Uncle Willy. They stopped playing with every car that went by and they ran to the street and waved. It could have been Uncle Willy. But it wasn't. What they didn't know, nor did their mother, was that Uncle Willy didn't own a car. Uncle Willy didn't own shit.

At nightfall the children stayed out as their mother had told them. They didn't want Uncle Willy passing by and not having anyone waiting for him.

Finally, it was too much to wait and the mother called them in and they ate jelly sandwiches because the hen looked too pretty to cut and mess up without Uncle Willy being there. Then it was back outside to play and wait. Their mother sat on the porch on the swing, one eye on them and one eye on Uncle Willy. She had lit a cigarette and was drinking bourbon and Coke fretting about the directions she had given her brother. It was out of the way, out of town, but they had lived there now three years and the people knew them. The guy at the filling station at the corner with the highway knew them and where they lived. Surely Willy would ask directions there if he were lost.

Shortly after midnight, when Texas law made the bars stop serving beer, their father drove in and went inside without a word. He took the hen out of the warm oven and tore a piece off it and ate it. Their mother could see him through the window but she did not say a word. This was not the time to start a quarrel. There would be hell enough to pay when their father found out Uncle Willy was coming. Let him have the hen, the whole hen if he wants it. She could make Uncle Willy a sandwich. Unless Uncle Willy had changed through the years, he had not been a particular eater. He ate what you put in front of him.

They heard their father stumble in the kitchen and fall, taking the hen with him. Part of the dressing, the part that had not fit into the hen and was spread around the hen, remained on the floor. He was just too drunk to pick it up piece by piece.

After their father was in bed their mother called to them. "Time to come in," she said. "I guess your Uncle Willy isn't coming."

The children undressed and went to bed together. They cuddled side by side and held their hands together and said the prayers their grandmother had taught them. They were tired after staying up so late waiting for Uncle Willy. They fell asleep almost immediately in each other's arms.

In the middle of the night they were awakened by the sounds of low voices and the light shining from under the door. The boy checked the clock by the bed. It was four in the morning. Uncle Willy had arrived. They got up to see Uncle Willy.

He was sitting at the table, the carcass of the hen in front of him picked clean. He had a beer in his hand. He was smallish, not big at all as the children had expected. His face was long and thin and his close-set eyes did not look tired for such a late hour. He wore a denim shirt and denim pants which fit large and a plain black belt with a plain steel buckle and heavy dark boots. The whole outfit looked new but dirty, that never-been-washed look. He had a small fedora hat at the back of his head. He had not shaved in several days. The children noticed something about his mouth—the thin lips puckered: he had no teeth. He had a long nose and big ears. He had a highly visible jagged scar that ran from the left ear all the way down the neck and disappeared under his shirt collar. He did not look at all like their mother. Their mother was blonde and he was dark with an abundance of hair. Their mother had a small nose and was beautiful, or so they thought. On his other hand he was smoking a cigarette. The children waited at the door not wanting to make the first move.

"This is your Uncle Willy," their mother said. "Come and say hello to him. Shake his hand."

"So these are the heirs?" said Uncle Willy, smiling at them. He had a scary smile, a cross between good and evil. A most uncomfortable feeling for the children. The children were scared to approach him. "You might as well know what I've been telling your mother," he said. He took a drag on his cigarette and let the smoke come out of his nose. He took some beer. "How long's it been since I saw you, Sis?"

"It's going to be twenty years," she said. "Since when Mom died."

"Time does fly. Yes, sir. Time flies when you're having fun."

"There ain't no need to tell the children, Willy," the mother said. "They're too young to understand anyway."

"They ought to know. I mean, what's a family for? You know me, Sis. I was never one to hold anything back from the family . . . both good or bad. Of course, the bad has gone overboard all my life. You see, children, I was always in the middle of trouble. Trouble was my middle name. I never once looked for it. I guarantee that. But it came to me. I tell you, trouble looked for me and landed right square in my lap. . . ."

"That's enough, Willy," their mother said. "It's time for them to go back to sleep."

"I come from prison," Uncle Willy blurted out. "Your mom doesn't want you to know. But I do. There ain't no shame in coming from prison as I see it. You know why you go to prison?"

The children shook their head.

"They tell me it's to pay my debt to society. What society? Where is the society? Do you children see any society around here?"

The children were paralyzed in fear.

"Every damn time I've gone to prison I find a lot of innocent people in there. At least they tell me they're innocent. Who's to believe? It's not a good place to be. I don't like prison any more than the next man. But you got to pay for doing the crime. I knew it was wrong. Hell, I've known it's been wrong forever but I can't help it. You children come on over and give your Uncle Willy a hug."

The children hesitated but their mother said, "Come over and give your Uncle Willy a hug. You two act like your scared of him. There's nothing to be scared of. He's family. He won't bite your head off."

Uncle Willy laughed that wicked, toothless laugh of his. He said, "I'll bite those little heads off if you're not careful. If you don't give me a hug." Then he gave them his smile and sent shudders through their little thin bodies.

First the boy and then the girl went over and with their arms limp at their side allowed Uncle Willy to hug them.

"Now, that's family," he said, grinning some more. "You know me, Sis. I've always loved the family. It makes me want to cry every time I think of it but you know I could have been a better son. I know I worried Mom and Dad a lot. I shouldn't've done it. But hell," he said and he took a drink of beer and a drag from his cigarette, "I was young. What was I to know? Hell, Sis, when you're young you do foolish things. And then you develop a reputation and anything that happens in town is your fault. Like I never sneaked in and stole from the movie house. That was Comer. Comer did that but I got the blame. Well, I went with him but I stayed outside. That's not the same as doing the crime. That's the first time I went to correction school. And I didn't even do the crime. But then again you figure the odds. I didn't pay for a lot of stuff I did do. So it evens out. I guess you could say that. It evens out in the end. Right, Sis?"

"Right."

"That stuff evens out. There's no two ways about it. It evens out. Life makes it even out. I never thought about it like that but it evens out. Funny the way things work out. You see, Dexter went to jail for robbing the filling station and Dexter didn't do it. It was me. But Dexter didn't say anything. He kept his mouth shut because Dexter had done so many other things he didn't pay for that he was afraid that if he squealed on me I would squeal on him. That's the way it goes. But I can tell you . . ." He took a drink and a puff. He gave his sister a stare. "Twenty years? It's been twenty years? God how time flies when you're having fun. I was saying . . . I can tell you that I have sat in prison thinking about all the things I've done and I can see where I broke Papa's and Mama's heart. Wonderful people. Churchgoing people. Remember how we always had to find the Baptist church as soon as we moved into town? How we had to go see the preacher? Remember, Sis?"

"I remember. Poor Mom and Dad."

Willy lowered his head like he was praying and said, "Poor people. They didn't deserve the son they got. I know that and you know that."

"They loved you, Willy. I can vouch for that."

"That's what made it harder for me when I sat in prison thinking about them. Thank God they died young. Maybe I helped kill them. I don't know. What do you think?"

"No, Willy. That's the way life is. It's not your fault they died young. When you stop to think about it, all of their family died young . . . their brothers and sisters and their parents. They just weren't a long-living family."

"That don't speak well for us, does it, Sis?"

"No. . . . You children go on to sleep. It's late. Tomorrow you can talk to your Uncle Willy."

The children walked away past the door, to the hallway and went into their bedroom. They spoke quietly in bed. They agreed that Uncle Willy was scary. Neither of them wanted to talk to Uncle Willy in the morning. He smelled like vomit.

They were about to say their prayers again when they were scared by the door opening very slowly. At first they could not see with the light from the hallway blinding them. It was their mother and Uncle Willy. Uncle Willy needed to sleep on the bed and the children would have to sleep on the kitchen floor. The children took their quilts with them. Uncle Willy fell into the bed and began to snore. Their mother closed the door gently and told them not to make any noise.

But noise there would be. Lots of it.

They heard their father get up and walk through the hallway to the bathroom. On his way back to bed he decided he need-ed a glass of water and he came into the kitchen and saw the children on the floor. He wanted to know what was going on? Their mother tried to explain that Uncle Willy had come in unexpectedly but their father then realized that the roasted hen had been for that no good sonofabitch Willy. Then he under-stood that Willy had taken the children's bed. He was angry and becoming uncontrollable. Willy got up when he heard the com-motion. He thought he was welcomed in the house but their father told him he was not. If he had known Willy was coming he would have waited up for him just to run him off. Willy was drunk now and the father was still drunk. In this state, Willy said something about their father owing him money from twenty years ago and that's why he didn't want Willy coming around.

That made their father angrier. His face turned red. They could see the veins in his neck bulge, his hands made into fists. He never owed any man nothing. The two were close to each other and neither of them was backing away. The children had run into their bedroom to hide. Their mother was trying desperately to stop any fight, first siding with her husband and then with Uncle Willy. Back and forth she tried to reason with them. More words were exchanged, curse words, personal insults, words which had festered from twenty years ago. But it was to be. Their father struck first, knowing that whoever gets in the first punch has the advantage. He hit Uncle Willy while Uncle Willy was arguing with his sister. Uncle Willy fell to the floor with a tremendous thud, shaking the small house, but he was not out. He got up ready for more. Their father had thought one punch would do it. Now he had an ex-con on his hands. No telling how many fights Uncle Willy had been in. And fights with convicts like himself. Hardened men who do not care for their lives. They exchanged punches, wild swings that did not mean anything. The fight could have continued like this forever and no one was going to get hurt. Exhaustion was the problem rather than the punches. But their mother panicked and called the police. The fight—the two men rolling on the floor weakly hitting at each other—was still going on when the police arrived and took them to jail. Their mother got the children out of bed and followed the police car. Both were booked for disturbing the peace. An hour later the night judge let them go on fifty dollars bail which their mother paid.

From here they took their father home.

Uncle Willy's case was different. He could not stay. They drove Uncle Willy to the edge of town to the first train intersection after the depot and waited. By now the children were asleep in the backseat. Their mother and Uncle Willy could hear the distant train. Overhead the sky was clear; the morning was coming in silent and cold. Willy said, "I don't think I've ever seen so many stars in my life. You think that means anything?"

His sister let out a sigh and said, "No. Nothing in particular. It's been starry for the last week or so. The children and I have been sitting on the porch counting stars, making believe we are what we're not. What we would like to be."

"Wishing on a star," said Willy. He took out a cigarette and pushed the lighter. He waited a few seconds and took the lighter out of the socket and placed it to the cigarette. A few puffs and he had the cigarette going. "I could see the stars from the prison window. I never thought to wish on a star. Maybe I should have."

His sister lit her own cigarette. She said, "It wouldn't do any good. It's all make-believe. The only reason I do it is for the children. They enjoy making believe."

The train engine went by slowly. Willy put his hand on the door handle. He lifted up and the door unlatched. "Well, Sis, I got to go," he said. "The train is here. Can't be missing the train."

"Here," she said, taking off her jacket, "you need this."

He took the jacket and said, "Thanks."

"Write if you can," his sister said. "Let us know where you're living . . . What you're doing."

"I will."

"I mean it, Willy. Drop me a line. Let me know how you're getting along."

"I will. I'll drop you a line as soon as I get on my feet . . . as soon as I get a chance. You know I don't get a chance very often. I'm a busy man."

"Well, you stay busy and stay out of trouble. You hear?"

"Yeah. I don't know how it happens, Sis. But you know how it is. Trouble just follows me. Trouble is my middle name. I can't seem to get away from it."

"Try. Try real hard, Willy."

"You know I will."

His sister reached into her purse and pulled out a five-dollar bill. She handed it to him and said, "Here. Take this. It'll help you out a little. That's all I can afford right now. You know how expensive children are."

"Thanks," her brother said, taking the money and putting it inside his shoe.

"Don't be getting into any more fights. You hear? Whenever you're going to get into a fight think of Mom and Dad. How much they loved you."

"I never thought of that," he said. "I'll do it next time. And tell Joe I didn't mean anything with what happened tonight. I like Joe. I don't know why he doesn't like me."

"The two of you were drunk. That's all."

"Anyway, tell Joe there's no hard feelings. OK?"

"I'll be sure to tell him what you said."

"In this life you've got to fight. What's a man going to do? Back down?"

He pushed the door open and swung his legs out, giving her his back. Watching him gave her a nauseous feeling of the most intense pity. He leaned forward to let his feet touch the ground and he stood up, out of the car. He closed the door and leaned on the window, looking at the train and then looking at his sister. "You sure have grown a lot in twenty years," he said. "You're a good-looking woman and you can take that to the bank and cash it."

"Thanks," she said. "Be careful getting on the train. You're not young anymore."

The children were awakened by the noise and rumble of the train. They were sitting up, their chins pressed to the back of the front seat, watching the train go by slowly.

Uncle Willy gave them his wicked smile but by now they were

too tired to be afraid. He said, "Good-bye, Helen. Take good care of the kids, will you? You know what I mean?"

"Yes. I know," she answered. "I will."

"See you in twenty years," he said, tipping his fedora.

Uncle Willy walked away in a hurry. He stood at the crossroads waiting to time the next boxcar, the red railroad crossing light bouncing off and on. When he had the timing right he ran alongside the train and hopped on. He waved back, standing at the open door.

Mammogram

Good morn.
Good Morning.
I am here for mamma . . . mamma . . . gramma.
Your name?
My name Consuelo.
Last name?
Last name García.
Do you have an address?
Sí. 13005 Hogan. La Hogan.
Zip?
77008.
Married?
Jes.
Husband?
Leopoldo García.
Same address?
Jes.
Do you have a social security number?
No.
Does your husband have a social security number?
Jes.
Do you know his number?
No.

Have a seat please. You will be called in a short while.

Buenos días.
Good morning.
I sit here?
Yes. You can sit here.
You here for mamma too?
Yes. I am here for a mammogram.
Me too. Too.
Well, we seem to be in the same boat this morning.
Jes. They say my *chiches* no good?
I couldn't say. I don't understand.
My *chiches*. Here. Right here.
I'm sure they know what you are here for. I am sure someone referred you here, otherwise you would not be here.
You marry?
Yes, I am married. Happily, I might add.
You children?
Yes. Three. A son and two daughters.
Me too. But I have trouble all time.
If you don't mind I would rather read the magazine.
I don't read.
I gather.
Your *chiches* bad also?
I don't understand. I am busy reading my magazine. Here, why don't you look at these pictures.
You marry happy?
Yes. I am happily married.
Me no. My *hombre* shit on me.
I beg your pardon. He does what?
My *hombre* shit on me.
I would rather not know about it. If you don't mind.
He shit on me all times.

I said I did not want to hear about this. Nurse? Nurse?

Yes, ma'am.

Could you sit me somewere else?

I'm afraid not. You have to sit in assigned seats. That way we can keep track of who's next. Sorry.

You O.K. here. My *hombre* man go out with woman. Muncho woman. He shit on me.

Oh. I understand now. He cheats on you.

Jes. I say him. You shit on me, me going to shit on you.

And what did he say?

He say I shit on him he kill me.

Well, you're here so I gather that you did not cheat on him.

Verdad. Very true. I no shit on him. No good for children.

But he continues to cheat on you.

Jes. He shit on me all time.

That's not very nice of him.

Me know. I say you no shit on me no more and he laugh.

And what did you do? Surely you cannot condone his cheating.

Oh, he use *condon* all times.

I don't understand.

He use *condon* like you say. With me. With all woman.

What did I say?

Condon. You say use *condon.*

I am sorry but I do not follow your conversation. You seem to be getting on my nerves.

He cloth like *mojado.*

I don't know, lady. I don't quite understand.

He cloth black jeans. How you say *sombrero?* Hat. *Camisa blanca. Botas.*

He must look very nice.

No. He look bad. He too short. Fat. You *esposo*—you man short, fat?

No. Actually he is very tall and lean.

Lean? What lean?

Thin.

Tin?

Yes, thin.

So he no shit on you?

No. He doesn't shit . . . I mean he doesn't cheat on me.

How you know? He no use *condon*?

He does not condone cheating in any form.

My *hombre condones* for everyone.

Mrs. Johnson?

Yes.

Will you come this way?

Yes, thank you.

Adios.

Good-bye.

I pray your *chiches* are good.

Thank you. And remember. Don't condone his cheating.

He *condones*. No worry, he always shit on me.

West Texas Cowboys

Chigger, one of the Adams boys, the tall skinny one, was looking up to the top of the sheer side of the hill waiting for Dexter, his bigger brother. Chigger had sent him climbing up from the other side, opposite the road where the hill worked its way in a more gentle slope to the pasture below. At last he saw Dexter come trudging to the edge of the cliff. Dexter waved down at Chigger, laughing. He threw his hat up in the air and then ran after it and caught it. He teetered at the edge, acting as though he were going to fall.

"It's windy up here," he yelled down to Chigger.

Chigger said, "Quit your messing around and tell me what you see."

Chigger was standing outside the pickup truck, one foot on the front bumper. He was smoking a cigarette and chewing on an old brown toothpick he had found in the ashtray.

They were laying fence for Mr. Henderson on the Henderson Ranch. The trick was to set a fence post on top of the rocky hill.

Dexter yelled down at Chigger to come up the hill the way he had. Chigger said, "I ain't walking up no damn hill just to see what you found. Tell me what you see."

"It's rock," Dexter yelled down. "We can't put no fence post here unless we dynamite the hill."

"Well, we'll dynamite the hill," Chigger yelled up to Dexter. "Grumpy gave us the dynamite. We might as well use the stuff."

"I don't think Grumpy intended for us to use it to dig a post-hole," Dexter yelled down to Chigger.

"Don't make no difference. We got a hole to dig. We can't dig the hole. We dynamite the hill."

"Bring the dynamite up."

"Jesus. You went all the way up there without any dynamite?"

"How was I to know the hill was solid rock? You tell me that."

"All right," said Chigger and he went to the back of the truck and opened the box of dynamite sticks. "How many you want?" he yelled up to Dexter.

Dexter studied the area, measured it with his boot and said, "Bring two and a fuse."

Chigger took two sticks and a cut-off section of fuse and went around the back of the hill to retrace Dexter's steps. When he got to the top he sat down, his feet dangling from the edge of the hill facing the road. "Why the hell does Old Man Henderson want a fence here? I mean, he owns all the land around. Why put a fence here?"

"Old Man Henderson can put up a fence any damn place he wants. It's his ranch. He can crisscross the whole goddam place if he wants to. He's got the money."

"I know he owns the place," Chigger said. "Still, I can't figure out why he wants a fence where you can't put up a fence? Why not put up a fence over there where we can get to it? Where we can dig a hole without dynamite?"

"I don't know," said Dexter. "Just give me the dynamite and the fuse. Old Man Henderson is going to do whatever he damn pleases. So let's make him a hole right here on top of the hill."

Chigger handed over the dynamite and the fuse. He was looking down toward the bunkhouse a good half mile away. He could see Jackson Grumbles, Grumpy to everyone, coming out of the bunkhouse. He was talking to Sweet Tooth and Big Jake and Little Jake. Palmer, another ranch hand, walked out, spitting tobacco. He could see Cornelius Whitaker off to one side under the hood of his truck.

"I can see Grumpy and the guys," Chigger said. "Something is going on."

"Nothing's going on except the hole I'm fixing to make here," said Dexter. He had taken the pick and broken up about a foot of limestone. He placed the two sticks of dynamite inside the hole and set the fuse. He lit a cigarette and with it he lit the fuse. He said to Chigger, "Are you going to sit there like a damn fool or are you going to run?"

Chigger saw the smoke coming out of the hole and he got up and ran after Dexter. When they reached the bottom of the hill they cowered behind a huge rock and waited for the explosion. It came. The ground moved. The noise was like an artillery shell going off. They looked up and saw large pieces of rock flying in the air. They covered up. All around them large pieces of rock began to fall. They crawled closer under the rock for protection. Even the rock they were under got hit by a large boulder that disintegrated on impact and sent smaller pieces ricocheting all around them. They saw the pick, which they had forgotten, fly through the air and land about a hundred yards away. They heard the metallic sound of rocks hitting the truck on the other side of the hill. Then they heard the sound of broken glass.

"There went the windshield," said Chigger.

"Goddam," Dexter said, "I had no idea."

"You shoulda used one stick instead of two."

"I think we leveled the top of the hill."

"I just hope Mr. Henderson didn't hear that. If he did we're in trouble."

Chigger remembered Grumpy's exact words this morning when he picked them up for work. He had said, passing the hill, "That's Mr. Henderson's favorite spot. On top of that hill. From the top of that hill he can see the whole spread. His kingdom, he calls it. He can see for miles around."

"It was Mr. Henderson's favorite spot too," Chigger said.

"We really messed it up this time," Dexter said. "I shoulda used one stick. Dammit. We're out of a job again. We shoulda not quit the Dairy Bee."

"You remember Grumpy said that this was Mr. Henderson's favorite spot? He could see his whole kingdom from the top of that hill."

"Well, maybe some of the rocks will fall back on top."

"What's fallen has fallen. There ain't no more, Dexter. I hate to think what the other side of the hill looks like. Where we parked the truck."

"You reckon that was the truck we heard getting all busted up?"

"With our luck it was the truck. I'm just hoping Mr. Henderson wasn't going by and we killed him. We could go to jail, you know?"

"Jail? Hell, prison. I wonder how long we'd get if we killed him?"

"Henderson? A lot of years. He's got money. Grumpy and those other hands? Not much. Maybe a year or two."

"They say prison's not too bad."

"I hear Skeeter Pucket is out."

"Yeah. He's out. Next time we see him we'll ask him about prison. Hell, he gained weight."

"I wonder what Mr. Henderson is going to say?"

"He'll be pissed off."

"Well, we knew that. He's always pissed off."

"Well, he'll be more pissed off than usual then."

"You reckon all the rocks have fallen out of the sky?"

"If they haven't then we're in a lot more trouble than I thought."

"They may be in orbit. You know that? Wouldn't it be something if some of the rocks were in orbit? Wouldn't it be something if one of the rocks landed on Mr. Henderson's roof?"

"Better him than me I always say."

The two got out from behind the large rock and stepped away from the hill. They could see the top flattened.

Dexter said, "I wonder what it would take to put the rocks back?"

"You're crazy, you know that? We'd better call it a day. Quit before they fire us. I don't like to be fired. Takes a lot out of a man's pride when he gets fired. I'd much rather quit. Like the Dairy Bee job."

"Hell, the Dairy Bee was hamburgers. This is serious."

"I'm quitting now."

"I'm quitting too," said Dexter. "You know, thinking about it . . . You know what tees me off?"

"No telling."

"That Grumpy gave us the dynamite. That's what tees me off. You know what would have happened if that damn stuff goes off in back of the truck?"

"We'd be off in orbit like the rocks."

"My head could have landed on Mr. Henderson's roof. That tees me off. For someone like Grumpy to give us the day job and not say anything about how dangerous the dynamite is."

"That tees me off too."

They walked around the hill to the road. They saw the truck shattered, a large boulder had landed on the hood. Smaller rocks, but still large enough to cause serious damage, had broken the windshield. The top of the truck was covered in rocks, the top collapsed. They could see Grumpy's pickup coming up the road.

Grumpy could hardly wait for the truck to stop. He jumped out. "What happened?" he yelled as he ran toward them.

"The damn hill exploded," Dexter said.

Grumpy stopped and said, "You're not telling me that the hill exploded all by itself?"

"No," Chigger said, "We had to dig a hole where you said

Mr. Henderson wanted it. It was solid rock. So we dig a small hole and put two sticks of dynamite in it and light the fuse."

Grumpy said, holding up his hands, "Wait a minute, boys. You're not telling me you put two sticks of dynamite to dig a posthole, are you?"

"That's exactly what we did," said Dexter.

Grumpy said, "Well, boys, let's go up to see what it looks like, but just looking at the hill I can tell you Mr. Henderson is not going to appreciate this."

At the top of the hill, looking down at the cavernous hole, Grumpy said, very seriously, "Mr. Henderson is not going to appreciate this, boys." He took out his snuff, placed a pinch under his lower lip and studied the damage some more. He said, "No, he ain't. No, sir." Then he did what the two brothers had not wanted him to do. Grumpy looked out over Mr. Henderson's domain. "And you boy's ruined the view for Mr. Henderson," he said. "Mr. Henderson likes to come here every day and sit and look over his kingdom. He can turn around and in any direction—as far as the eye can see—he can claim the land. He owns all of this, boys. You know that. You know how important this hill was to Mr. Henderson." He spat some tobacco juice into the hole. "I told you this morning. You remember me saying how important this hill was to the old man?"

Chigger said, "Yes. I remember it well, Grumpy. Dexter does too, I'm sure."

"Damn. You ruined his view. No, sir. Mr. Henderson is not going to appreciate this one bit." Grumpy looked down to the road and said, "And then the truck. You boys ruined a perfectly good truck. That's the best truck we had."

"That's why we quit," said Chigger.

"Chigger speaks for me too," said Dexter.

Grumpy said, "Now you boys know you can't just up and quit. Mr. Henderson won't allow it. Mr. Henderson has certain rules of the ranch. When you work for Mr. Henderson you follow those rules. And rule number one is nobody quits Mr. Henderson. Now, Mr. Henderson might fire you but you ain't quitting. No, sir . . . " He looked up at the flattened hill again and said, shaking his head, "Mr. Henderson is not going to appreciate this. No, he ain't. No, sir."

"This is a free country," said Chigger. "We can quit if we want to."

"Chigger is right," said Dexter. "Last I heard this is still a free country. Besides we could have gotten killed running around with that dynamite in back of the truck."

Grumpy said, "You boys go on home. You don't want to be around when Mr. Henderson sees what you done. No, sir. You don't want to be around when he sees this. You boys go on home. I'll have Cornelius take you home. Lay low for a while. Don't talk to Junior about this. If he asks what the explosion was about tell him we're blasting stumps. Mr. Henderson will contact you in due time, boys. Take my advice. Go on home right now before he wakes up from his nap. And don't be thinking about leaving town."

Palmer and Little Jake and Big Jake and Sweet Tooth, and Cornelius Whitaker arrived in Cornelius' truck.

"What the hell happened here?" they wanted to know.

"The Adams boys," Grumpy said, pointing at them. "They got carried away with the dynamite. Put two sticks in the rock on top of the hill and set them off."

"What for?" Little Jake asked.

Chigger said, "To make a fence pole hole, that's what for."

"And you used two sticks for that?" Big Jake asked.

"Yeah," said Dexter.

"Well, dip me in shit," said Palmer. "Two sticks in the right place could blow the whole damn hill out of sight."

"Well, look up and see," said Grumpy. "That's about what they done."

"Goddam. They blew the top off Mr. Henderson's hill,"

Cornelius said, looking up to the hill, shielding his eyes with his hand.

"That's Mr. Henderson's favorite spot," said Little Jake.

Sweet Tooth said, "Every day he goes to the top of the hill and looks around to see all his land. And you guys blew it up?"

"We didn't know," said Dexter.

"We can see that," said Big Jake. "Any person with any sense knows that two sticks of dynamite are going to blow the top off a damn hill."

"Well, we didn't," said Chigger.

"We know you didn't," said Grumpy. "I thought you boys had sense enough. I guess you don't."

Chigger said, "Mr. Henderson is going to blame you, Grumpy, for not telling us about the dynamite."

"I've been thinking that you might be right," said Grumpy. "Mr. Henderson is going to blame you boys but you boys are small potatoes. He can't get much satisfaction out of you two. You're Dairy Bee hamburger meat to him. You ain't got nothing to lose. Then he's going to have to punish someone else."

"You," said Dexter.

"I'm thinking you might have a point," said Grumpy.

Chigger said, "Why don't we just tell him that the whole damn truck exploded. The dynamite exploded in the hot sun and took the hill with it?"

"But he can see the truck ain't exploded," said Palmer.

"That's easy enough to fix," Grumpy said. He went over and moved rocks from the bed of the truck until he found the box of dynamite. The rest of them had followed Grumpy and were standing around the bed of the truck.

"Cornelius?" Grumpy said.

"Yeah?" Cornelius replied.

"Start your truck and point it in the direction of town."

Big Jake said, "You ain't going to do what I think you're going to do, are you?"

Grumpy said, "Now everyone get on the truck with Cornelius."

Dexter and Chigger and Little Jake and Big Jake and Palmer and Sweet Tooth went in the bed of the truck. Grumpy remained behind with the dynamite. He cut off a long fuse and stuck it into the box of dynamite and then lit it. He ran and got inside his truck and took off. Cornelius followed him close behind. About a mile from the hill they stopped to wait. Grumpy was out of his truck and was standing by Cornelius' truck. The men in the truck bed were sitting on the sides waiting for the explosion. Nothing happened. Grumpy took out his pocket watch and studied it. "Damn," he said. "Let's go back." He got in with Cornelius and left his truck behind.

Cornelius turned the truck around. Grumpy was complaining about the fuse. They came close enough to the truck that they could suddenly see the smoke from the fuse. Cornelius was going straight at the truck. Grumpy started yelling for Cornelius to turn the truck around. The fuse was working. The dynamite was going to go off. The men at the back started yelling. They had seen the smoke from the fuse too. Cornelius took a hard turn left, circled the pasture and as he did the dynamite exploded sending the truck parts tumbling high into the air. The main chassis was pushed down and then a second explosion underneath shot it upward and it took off tumbling end-to-end, skyward like an errant rocket and it came to land on top of the hill. The men in Cornelius' truck could see it all happen. The blast had hurt their ears. They were hunkered down in the bed of the truck. Cornelius and Grumpy were protected inside the cab. A large piece of the exploding truck, the hood and a front fender attached, landed on top of Cornelius' truck barely missing the men in the bed. The men then sensed that more debris might fall on them and they jumped out of the truck and scattered, running for safety.

At the end, when all the debris from the truck and the rocks had fallen, Grumpy and the men gathered to review the scene. Grumpy said, "Mr. Henderson is not going to appreciate this. No sir."

"Well, dip me in shit," said Palmer, studying the scene.

"The truck is on top of the hill," said Little Jake.

"We know," said Grumpy. "You don't have to tell us that. We can see it with our own eyes. Now we have to get the truck off the hill. Mr. Henderson would never appreciate one of his trucks being on top of the hill."

"Tell him it was the explosion," said Chigger.

Grumpy said, "Mr. Henderson is not going to allow the truck to stay on top of the hill. I can guarantee you that. He'll fire us all before he'll allow that truck to stay there."

Little Jake said, "Mr. Henderson had to have heard this explosion. Damn. How many sticks of dynamite was that?"

"Ten," said Grumpy. "There's twelve in a box. The Adams boys used two. That left ten."

"I thought it was the end of the world," Sweet Tooth said. "Man, I never heard anything as powerful as that. Ten sticks?"

Palmer was standing at the base of the hill looking straight up at the truck. He said, "Ain't no way we're going to get that truck down without dynamite."

Grumpy said, "Let's not talk about dynamite. Not at the present time. We need to go get one of the tractors. The one with the winch and the cable. We run the cable up the hill and drag the truck down."

"I'll go get the tractor," Big Jake said.

"Cornelius will take you," said Grumpy, "and then he can come back to take me to my truck."

Cornelius took Grumpy to go get his truck while Big Jake drove the tractor to the hill. By the time Big Jake came with the tractor the rest of the men had figured out how to tie the truck chassis. Grumpy arrived and informed them that he was going to see Mr. Henderson.

"I know it's crazy," he said, "but I got to tell him that we're dynamiting. Just kind of prepare him for what we done. Maybe he won't be as pissed off. I don't know. You boys got any ideas?"

Chigger said, "While you're gone we'll drag the truck down. By the time you get here we'll have it done."

Grumpy spat very seriously and said, "Don't nobody let the Adams boys have any say so. You hear? Big Jake is in charge while I'm gone."

Big Jake waved from the tractor. Little Jake and Cornelius and Palmer played out the cable from the winch. They took the cable around to the back of the hill and walked it up. Chigger and Dexter and Sweet Tooth were already on top. They found the truck partially stuck in a crevice made by the explosion. They tied the cable through the windows and over the top of the cab. They signaled Big Jake and he started the winch. Slowly the cable wound itself around the winch while the men on top of the hill kept it from snagging.

Grumpy got off the truck and knocked on the door of the main house. Mrs. Henderson answered. She wanted to know what all the explosions were. Grumpy told her that they were having to dynamite stumps.

"Well," she said, "be careful. You woke Mr. Henderson up from his nap and he doesn't feel good. He's got a splitting headache. So he went back to sleep. He said that if you came over to tell you that you were using entirely too much dynamite."

Grumpy said, "Yes, ma'am. You tell Mr. Henderson that that dynamite is not exploding right. It's a might more powerful than usual. But I had a talk with the boys about that."

He went to his truck and headed for the hill. He could see Big Jake on the tractor. The cable had stopped. It had stretched tight and the truck would not move. Big Jake began to turn the tractor away from the hill trying to yank the truck off. The men on top of the hill were yelling for him to stop. But he was determined. He pulled more and more and the truck slowly began to budge. As it did, it fell further into the crevice and with the pull from the tractor the thin sheet of rock that now made up the front of the hill began to give way. Big Jake pulled on it some more. The men were screaming for him to stop. He was going to tear off the side of the hill. When the side of the hill began to collapse the men ran down. Big Jake pulled a little bit more. Grumpy was running to him to tell him to stop. Grumpy jumped on the tractor but Big Jake shoved him off. The tractor pulled some more and the truck fell completely into the crevice, acting as a wedge. The side of the hill separated from the main body and came crashing down. The truck was left dangling by the side of the hill, caught on a piece of rock.

Grumpy said, "Go ahead and bring it down. It can't get any worse than this."

Big Jake pulled on the cable and the truck came sliding down the face of the hill taking some more of it down. The truck, only a chassis, landed on its side and bounced up and righted itself. By now the men had come around from the back of the hill to see what damage had been done.

Grumpy said, "Mr. Henderson is not going to appreciate this. No, sir. He ain't."

Palmer said, viewing the mess, "Dip me in shit. We might as well all quit."

"Knowing Mr. Henderson for as long as I have," said Cornelius, "I don't want to be around when he sees this. Hell, he's got less than half the hill he had this morning. And the top is so full of holes he couldn't walk on it, old as he is."

Sweet Tooth said, "Grumpy, let's quit. We ain't going to be working here no how. We're better off quitting."

Grumpy said, thinking, "What are we going to tell him about Cornelius' truck? That one is all messed up too."

"I know," said Chigger. "Take it and run it into the other

truck. Tell Mr. Henderson that the two trucks were parked side by side when the dynamite exploded."

"That's a good idea," Grumpy said. "Cornelius? Take your truck and ram it into the truck and we'll leave it there. I'll tell Mr. Henderson that the two trucks were together."

Little Jake said, "I still can't believe Mr. Henderson didn't hear the explosions."

"He heard them," Grumpy said.

"What did he say?" Palmer asked. "Was he pissed off?"

"Mr. Henderson is sick, boys. He's got a headache and he went back to bed. But he heard the explosions. Mrs. Henderson said he said for us not to be using so much dynamite."

"Now he tells us," said Dexter. "Where was he when we needed his advice?"

"Cornelius?" said Grumpy. "Get your truck. Get it up to speed and then jump off and ram it into the truck."

Cornelius went to his truck and started it. He gathered speed across the pasture. He bounced the truck across the dirt road and then, when he was about fifty feet from the truck, he jumped off. His truck plowed into the chassis of the truck. The crunch of metal against metal made a horrible sound. Grumpy went over and checked out the wreckage. The other men followed him. The front of Cornelius' truck was destroyed. The truck had tipped forward when it imbedded itself into the chassis of the other truck and the rear tires were sticking up in the air. They were spinning and the brake pads were throwing off sparks. Big Jake was the first to smell the gasoline fumes from the ruptured gas tank. He began to scream to the other men. When they all got a whiff of the problem they all ran. They had sprinted about a hundred yards when the fumes caught on fire from the sparks. The fire started under the truck around the gas tank. The first explosion, the gas tank, created a whorl of fire and black smoke that completely engulfed both trucks. But that was minor compared to what followed. This time all twelve sticks of dynamite in back of Cornelius' truck exploded sending truck parts and rock spiraling into the air. The two trucks were now crashing as one, tumbling around the base of the hill. At the same time about one half of what remained of the hill shot up its rocks and they rained on the ground.

"I quit," said Grumpy. "I've been working for Mr. Henderson for some twenty years. He's seen me through some rough times and he's helped me and my family a lot. I never once lacked for anything working for Mr. Henderson. But I tell you boys one thing for sure. Mr. Henderson is not going to appreciate this. No, sir."

Sweet Tooth said, "Now, don't be hasty, Grumpy. You need to think this over. You know the old saying about haste."

"Sweet Tooth is right," said Palmer. "Don't be making any hasty decisions right now, Grumpy. You may be able to make Mr. Henderson understand that you used twenty-four sticks of dynamite to dig his fence. He might accept that. Although it would seem to me you depleted his inventory of dynamite in very few hours."

Dexter said, "I told you we ought to quit. It hurts a man's pride when he gets fired. Hell, no man has ever fired me."

Little Jake said, "Jack Johnson fired you from the Dairy Bee last month."

"He did not," said Chigger. "We quit. And that's a fact."

"That's not what Jack Johnson is saying," Big Jake said. "You screwed up the hamburgers so bad he had to fire you."

"That ain't true," said Chigger. "Me and Dexter made the best hamburgers in town."

"That's the only place that made hamburgers in town," said Sweet Tooth.

"Boys," said Grumpy, checking out the damage from afar, "let's not argue about hamburgers right now. You boys will have plenty of time to argue in jail."

"Jail?" said Cornelius. "What jail you talking about?"

"The one Mr. Henderson is going to put us all in," said Grumpy.

"What we need to do," said Big Jake, "is go into town, have us a couple of cold ones, think about what we've done and then confront Mr. Henderson."

"In a way that's a good idea," said Grumpy. "We need to get out of here before Mr. Henderson takes a look at this hill. That will give him a chance to cool off before he sees us again."

"Well, I can tell you one thing," Chigger said, "and I speak for my brother too . . . Mr. Henderson is not going to see me for a long, long time."

"Mr. Henderson will call for you," said Grumpy. "You can bet your last dollar on that. You'll face him and it won't be pretty, boys. I'm just hoping he takes all of this with a little sense of humor."

"Mr. Henderson?" said Sweet Tooth. "A sense of humor? You gotta be kidding."

Big Jake said, "He's going to kill us."

"Well," said Cornelius, "he can kill us but he sure as hell can't eat us."

Big Jake said, "Let's go sit down with a cold one and talk this thing over. I want to know how we got to this point."

"The Adams boys," said Grumpy, spitting his brown slime. "That's how we got to this point."

Indian Joe was selling cold ones behind the bar at the Belle Vania Saloon. The men walked in and sat at the table close to the door to catch the breeze. They ordered from Suzy, the waitress, and she brought them the beer. Grumpy took a long swallow and then wiped his mouth. He said, "Boys, this has been a day to remember. I don't think I've ever been through a day like this one."

Sweet Tooth said, "I think this is par for the Adams boys. Ain't that right?"

"That's right. Me and Dexter don't have too much luck," Chigger explained.

Little Jake said, "If it wasn't for bad luck you boys wouldn't have any luck at all."

"That's the truth," Dexter said. "And if I didn't fart I wouldn't have a scent in my pocket either."

Maribelle came in wearing a midriff and shorts and platform shoes. She was a skinny-legged lady in her late sixties, varicose veins bulging out on her legs like purple rope, well bathed, her bleached hair up in a beehive, her nails and cheeks and lips red as beets. It was her time to come in for her daily beers.

Big Jake called her over as she walked by the table. "Where's P.T.?" he asked her.

Maribelle said, "P.T.'s in jail."

"What did he do?" Little Jake asked.

"Oh," said Maribelle, lighting a cigarette, "he'd been misbehaving with me, giving me a hard time. You know how he can be. I finally got even with him."

"What happened?" Grumpy said.

Maribelle took a long drag from her cigarette and exhaled smoke from her mouth and nose at the same time. Suzy had brought her a bottle of beer. She sipped at the bottle. She said, "Well . . . Excuse me while I burp. I always do that on the first swallow." She held her hand up to her mouth for a very ladylike burp. "Well, as I was saying, we were driving down by the school and P.T. wasn't paying attention to his speed so Junior stopped him. So Junior says, 'P.T. you were driving over the speed limit for a school zone.' And P.T. says, 'I was not. I was driving twenty.' But then I say, 'You're lying P.T. You were going forty.' So he says to me, 'Can't you ever shut up your big mouth?' And he keeps cursing me, you know. So Junior says, 'And you ain't wearing your seat belt, P.T.' So P.T. says, 'I was wearing my seat belt but I took it off when you stopped me,' So I say, 'P.T. you're lying. You never wear your seat belt,' And P.T. says to me, 'Shut your mouth, bitch.' He calls me a bitch in front of Junior, you know. So Junior says, 'Does he always talk to you like that, Maribelle?' And I say 'No, Junior. Only when he's drunk.' So his ass is in jail for speeding in a school zone, driving without a seat belt, cursing in public, and drunk driving. I guess I fixed his boat, you know? He didn't have no proof of liability neither."

"Well, drink your beer then," Grumpy said. "You done good by him. I'm sure he appreciates all you did for him."

Maribelle said, crossing her thin, ugly legs, "Did you boys hear the explosions today? Seem to come from the west."

"We were doing some dynamiting," said Grumpy.

"Well," Maribelle said, "you must have done something cause the whole town shook. I know the ladies at the drugstore thought the plant at Amarillo had blown up. You know the plant. The atomic bomb plant?"

Grumpy said, "That was us. Working. Right boys?"

They were on their tenth beer when Skeeter Pucket came in. He was a fresh reminder of jail and prison. Chigger called him over and Skeeter came and shook hands with all the men and Maribelle. They invited Skeeter to pull up a chair. Maribelle had seen Big Mama and Shirleen and Pretty Julie sitting at the bar when she came in. Since the men invited Skeeter she took it on herself to invite the women to come to sit with them. They had to get another table together to fit everyone. Now they had the makings for a large party. Suzy brought another round of beer for everyone.

Before they could ask Skeeter about prison and how it was he said, "Did anyone hear the explosions? The first one was small and then they kept getting bigger and bigger. Wonder what it was?"

"It was them," said Maribelle, pointing her beer at the men.

"What the hell were you all doing?" Skeeter asked.

"Dynamiting," said Grumpy. "We didn't mean to disturb the town."

"Hell," said Skeeter, "Junior got in his car to go check it out but he came back and said he couldn't find anything."

"It was at the Henderson Ranch," said Grumpy. "Mr. Henderson don't allow Junior on his property although he's the law. He never forgave Junior for killing his cow accidentally."

"It was an accident," said Big Jake, "that could have happened to anybody. I tell you. Anyone can mistake a cow for a deer at night."

"But you see, boys, like I'm telling you," said Grumpy, "Mr. Henderson doesn't forgive anyone. How long's it been since Junior killed the cow accidentally? Ten years? Fifteen years?"

"Well," said Cornelius, "he wasn't the law then."

Dexter said to Skeeter, "How was prison? Hear you gained weight."

Skeeter played with the wet label on the beer bottle, scratching it with his nail. He said, "I just sat in my cell all day. You know they don't let us work like they used to. The judge says that that is cruel and unusual punishment. I ate like a hog."

Little Jake said, "We heard you ran over a lady in Dallas. Was that true?"

"Yeah. I ran over a black lady. Ran over her twice, as a matter of fact. Ran over her going forward then I backed up to see what it was. I was drunk as a skunk. I never saw her."

Palmer said, "Well, dip me in shit."

"I still can't believe you escaped," said Grumpy. "How'd you do that?"

"Easy," said Skeeter. "I just walked off one day. Nobody asked me nothing. I just acted like I didn't belong in prison. Just walked out."

"Where'd you go from there?" Chigger asked him.

"Europe. I had some money stashed away from work. I got a

plane to Europe. Then I got tired of those people. You know how they are. I couldn't understand them. So I went to Australia. Then I got homesick and turned myself in. The embassy in Australia didn't know what to do with me. So they put me up in a hotel."

"A hotel? What did you do then?" Maribelle asked.

"Threw the biggest party you've ever seen. Champagne. Caviar. All kinds of food. Charged it to the room. What were they going to do? Put me in jail?"

"You know," Dexter said, "you're pretty smart. I never figured you being so smart."

"Well," said Skeeter, "you learn a lot of things in prison. It's quite an education."

The women were beginning to get giddy and the men were flirting with them. Big Mama stood up and went over and sat on Grumpy's lap. This caused quite a stir around the table. There were whistles and catcalls. Then Pretty Julie went to sit on Dexter's lap. More laughter. Maribelle got brave and she went to sit on Big Jake's lap. This caused a lot of thigh slapping and hoots and hollers. The men had their minds off the dynamite and were having a good time. Cornelius had sneaked off to go to the bathroom and when he came back he was running. He had been urinating when he had looked out through the window and he had seen Beatrice and Nellie come out of a car in the parking lot. Beatrice and Nellie were Grumpy's wife and Big Jake's wife.

Cornelius cried out, "It's Nellie and Beatrice. They're coming in."

Everyone took off. The ones who could not wait to go through the rear door jumped out through the windows. Even Indian Joe disappeared. Beatrice and Nellie walked in and both said, "Where is the sonofabitch?" meaning Grumpy and Big Jake.

The place was deserted so they looked around for a while and then left. The men were hiding in the woods nearby and when the two women left they returned. They had not been there a minute when Indian Joe came in quietly. He said, "That was a close call. You men ought to go on home."

"Are you crazy?" said Grumpy.

"You saw how much love is lost between us," said Big Jake.

Junior drove up to the front door and got out. He was a big, strapping young man. The only policeman in town. He walked in looking for Grumpy. Grumpy, shy from what had happened to him so far today, didn't want any part of him.

"I know," Grumpy said to Junior, "Mr. Henderson called you. He won't let you on his property but he called you to tell me he wants to see me so he can fire me and everyone else."

"Mrs. Henderson let me in the property. As a matter of fact I just came from there."

"What did the old man say? That I was fired? That he don't want to ever see me or anyone of his hands again?"

"No," Junior said, "that's why I came to tell you boys. Mr. Henderson died this afternoon. That's why Mrs. Henderson called me. He'd been dead about an hour by the time I got there. Mr. Henderson wanted to be buried on top of the hill. But I drove by there this afternoon and it looks like the hill is gone."

"There's a reason for that," said Little Jake.

Grumpy said, "Let me talk. Junior, you don't know this but Mr. Henderson knew he was going to die."

Junior said, "How'd he know?"

"He just knew," said Cornelius. "He knew everything."

"Well," said Grumpy, "Mr. Henderson wanted the hill that way. He wanted to be buried on top of the hill but he didn't want to be so high that Mrs. Henderson couldn't go see him. You know she suffers from artheritis."

Junior said, "So you leveled the hill with dynamite? That was all those explosions we heard in town?"

"That's exactly it," said Grumpy. "That was Mr. Henderson's request."

"What about the two charred pickup trucks?" Junior asked.

Grumpy was quick. He said, "Two pieces of junk. We threw those in like a statue to honor his memory. You know he was always in a pickup truck."

"Mrs. Henderson said she wanted you to dig the grave," Junior said.

"Oh, the grave's already been dug," said Chigger.

Cornelius said, "She's got plenty of holes to chose from."

Grumpy took out his handkerchief and blew his nose. He said, "You know, boys, Mr. Henderson was the finest man I ever knew. I'm going to miss him."

"He was a fine man," said Big Jake. "I don't fault Grumpy for crying over him either. I would cry but I didn't know him as well as Grumpy. Mr. Henderson never took the time to talk to me."

Junior said, "He used to go on top of that hill every day to view his kingdom. He called it his kingdom. You boys remember that, don't you? I remember that about him. He loved that. It must have taken quite a bit out of him to see the hill gone."

"What do you mean?" Grumpy asked.

"Well, I mean that Mrs. Henderson went in to check on him and he'd gotten up from his nap and it looked like he went to the window to watch you boys work. That last explosion must have been too much for his old heart. Mrs. Henderson found him dead by the window. Just toppled over. Straight on his back like a chicken, stiff as a board, his legs straight up pointing at the ceiling. She had heard him get up and then she thought he was trying to open up the gun cabinet. She ran, thinking he might be contemplating suicide. You know how old Mr. Henderson was."

"And forgetful," said Sweet Tooth.

Junior gave him an ugly stare for interrupting. He continued,

"She found the rifle by his side. Maybe wanted to commit suicide. Who knows? He was in that much pain seeing the hill go down. Then she heard him fall. That's when she managed to get in his room. He was gone. Bluer than ink."

There was a thoughtful silence around the table. The men took sips of beer, avoiding each other's looks.

Finally Grumpy said, "I told the boys. I said, 'Mr. Henderson loves this hill, boys.' I just knew it was going to take a lot out of him. I kept telling the boys, 'Mr. Henderson is not going to appreciate this. No sir. He sure ain't.'"

"Well," said Junior as he left, "got to get to work. He's gone now. The county has lost its favorite son." To Maribelle he said, "P.T. is doing fine in jail. I'll just keep his ass there until the judge shows up."

Maribelle said, "You keep his fat ass there for a while. Maybe he'll learn how to respect me."

Grumpy said, "We'll be there shortly. After we finish this cold one. We'll make sure he gets his proper burial."

There was a general silence around the table again as the men thought out what old man Henderson was trying to do when he died.

After a minute or two, or so it seemed, Palmer said, "Well, dip me in shit."

Little Jake said, "He was trying to kill us."

Grumpy said, "I told you boys but you didn't want to believe me. I knew Mr. Henderson was not going to appreciate this one bit."

Sweet Tooth said, "The sumbitch tried to kill us."

"That old Mr. Henderson," said Grumpy, "he was a mean old fart."

Palmer said, after some personal reflection, "You can dip me in shit all you want but I ain't going to bury the sumbitch."

"Well," said Grumpy, "I don't hold no personal grudges. I figure burying him is the least we can do."

"After what we did to his kingdom, I agree," said Dexter.

The Sergeant

anuel Laberón, the sergeant, was with a group of men at the corner of Navigation and 37th Street waiting to be picked up for the day's work. Already several employers in pickups had come by looking for concrete workers. He was not a concrete worker. He was a plumber. And he would rather wait for a plumbing call than work concrete. If he got desperate he would work concrete, though. It was still early. He could wait. But if it had to be concrete it would be concrete. It would only be for a day. He was thinking that tomorrow would be different when the man drove up to the vacant lot at the intersection and got off.

"Plumbers," he yelled and that cleared out the crowd. There just wasn't too much call for the grime and foulness of plumbing.

———•———

Manuel Laberón kept going toward the man. "Are you a plumber?" he asked.

"Yes," replied Manuel Laberón.

"Are you a journeyman?"

"Yes," he said without knowing what that meant. He was not about to say no.

"Get on the truck," the man said, pointing to the pickup.

Manuel's new friend, Esteban, climbed in with him. The man asked, "Is he a plumber too?"

Esteban was pushing Manuel Laberón to the back of the truck. Manuel Laberón said, "Yes. My assistant."

Manuel Laberón had arrived in Houston from El Salvador last night. He had come to the Texas border on foot. From there he had contracted with someone to drive him into Texas. He had met Esteban at the house where the coyote had dropped him off. Esteban had come on his own and had not had shelter so Manuel invited him to stay in his room where they shared the mattress on the floor. Esteban was from Mexico. Esteban was surprised Manuel Laberón could speak English so well so he would use Manuel's gift for himself until he learned enough to get by. There was no rush to learn. Everyone around him spoke Spanish. All the stores on that side of Houston did business in Spanish. If anyone asked him something in English he could point to Manuel Laberón.

They were the only two on the truck for a while and then a man named Porfirio joined them although he admitted he didn't know anything about plumbing. He would be used as a mole to dig holes, get under structures, squeeze into narrow spaces. And he was chosen because he was right for the job. He was about five feet three at the most and weighed about seventy pounds.

After mingling with the workers for a while, the truck driver came back, got in the truck and took off with the three men. He went south on Navigation, toward the ship channel, and then got on the South Loop. Traffic was heavy. Then traffic came to a stop. The men stood up and looked over the cab. Porfirio had to stand on the sideboard in order to see. There had been a wreck and they could see the ambulances and police cars up ahead. The traffic moved slowly, by jerks, until they went by the wreckage. They saw the blood on the freeway before they saw a body on the ground covered with a sheet. An elderly man was sitting inside an ambulance, his head wrapped in gauze. A woman was crying inside a police car. The police were trying to hurry the traffic along. Manuel Laberón sat down behind the cab and both Porfirio and Esteban sat alongside him. The truck accelerated. They could see the wreckage behind them. Soon it would be forgotten. On the way home tonight there would only remain small tell-tale signs—a piece of glass not picked up, parts of a tire beside the guardrail, a small blue cloth, perhaps used by the victim to clean his glasses, wrapped by the wind around a rail post, a few drops of blood covered by the daily, unrelenting traffic—forgotten, as soon there would be another one, not necessarily at the same spot but close enough and often enough that it dulled the senses, that it made no sense to linger on the pain that someone else felt. It was enough to feel your own pain without taking on others'.

Manuel Laberón covered himself with his coat. He never slept well the first night. He lowered his head and in a few moments he fell asleep with the movement of the truck and the sounds of traffic.

He was Sergeant Manuel Laberón, El Salvador Army, Serial Number FSS-937-5493. *Soldado razo.* He stood at attention at the airport guarding the planes going out and coming in. His was the most important job at the airport. No one superseded him in importance, except for the officer of the day and he was never to be found. So it fell on Manuel Laberón to see to it that every airplane be inspected at arrival and be made ready for departure. Under him was a crew of ten men, all *razos* like him and, of course, younger.

He knew some English and at the moments that he had free he would read, especially the newspapers from the United States. Ah, the United States. Their planes were the best, the shiniest, the cleanest. Their pilots the best. The stewardesses were the most beautiful—blonde, brunette, redhead, any color or description—long-legged, carefree, a bounce to their step, made-up. The toasts of the world. They were the best. The newspaper? *The New York Times.* The best. And on Sunday he would scour the planes from America for the *Book Review* magazine. Well, what can I tell you. He was enamored with the *Americanos.*

His uniform, pressed and neat as it was, was never as good as what he could read about in America. In the first place the color was all wrong, a sort of slimy green which he saw only around the rim of the toilet during his work as a plumber. The cloth was cotton like in the United States but coarser, as though the fiber had not been refined to the point that it had in America. Or perhaps cotton did not grow as well in El Salvador as it did in the United States. His boots were rough and not shiny like the U. S. Marines, the leather obviously inferior and poorly cured. And they fit poorly too. His feet ached by the time he got home and his wife would have to spend several hours soaking his feet in warm lime water before he could walk again. His rifle, a Mauser that thank God he had never had to use, was old and rusty and would serve him as a bayonet-holder rather than a rifle in a time of crisis. He carried two bullets in his pocket. In the United States, he bet his fellow soldiers, they would have gondoliers upon gondoliers of ammunition readily at hand.

"In America," he said to his men, "you can afford to fire a hundred warning shots."

As a young man, Manuel Laberón had been somewhat of a writer but again, like his military career, he had tasted only the outside, the rind of success. The sweet core had escaped him. In a literary contest, he had won not first place but third. Regardless, he was elated and so was his family. His story, a small vignette about visiting his grandmother in the hills of El Salvador, was published along with the other winners and he was the hero of the neighborhood at least until the next issue. He regarded himself an author, walking the narrow streets with a pencil in his pocket asking neighbors if they wanted his autograph. He began his studies at the *Secondaria*. He was fascinated by English but very confused by its usage. He tried very hard to learn but there were words like maintain and mountain, and certain and train, lead and lead, laughter and daughter, etc.

But soon, like all fame which ebbs and flows, he became tiresome. People shunned him. His family advised him to stop the charade. Then the end came. His father, to teach him a lesson, forced him to work alongside him as a plumber where he had to, like his father, stick his hands into the grime and foulness of the job. He became ill but his father took him to work nonetheless. He roamed the streets chanting for work, for more grime and foulness, until he collapsed one day and had to be dragged home.

His life took a turn for the better while convalescing. The militia came one day to the neighborhood knocking on doors looking for young men. When they found Manuel Laberón in bed they asked him why he had not been conscripted and he answered that he was an author and authors aren't supposed to work. Authors lived from the largesse of the people, like politicians. He was informed that so did the soldiers and as soon as he was able he was sent to the jungle for military training.

He hated his regimen at first but soon he came to realize that being a soldier was a lot like being an author. Both had a lot of useless, unproductive time on their hands. He began to write once more. At that time he was not obsessed with the United States so most of his work was about his native land. At least weekly he sent off material for publication but nothing was ever published. In time, like any sane man would react, he gave it up and was left with nothing but the military and he came to love it. The military took the place of writing and in all instances gave him at least a sense of worth, which he was beginning to lose from the constant rejection of his writing. Soon, he took to the military as obsessively as he had writing. He became the ideal soldier. He followed orders so precisely that his commanders used him as a field guide, an example of what can be accomplished if one puts his whole mind and heart and soul to it. Some days, at the end, his uniform would still be without a wrinkle. While his fellow soldiers went on a spree during the night, he remained in the barracks and shaved.

One weekend while visiting his parents he saw the neighbor's daughter whom he had not seen in years and he fell in love with her and she with him. In one month they were married and he moved out of the military compound to live with her parents who adored him.

In two years he was a sergeant assigned to the presidential guard. He marched in front of the president during all functions, willingly exposing himself to any bullets directed the president's way. In other words, he was a shield, a human shield.

On one of the many assassination attempts he was wounded and his spleen had to be removed along with parts of his kidney, liver and pancreas. The president himself came to the hospital to visit him frequently and once again he was a celebrity. The president, in front of national television, awarded him the *Medalla de Protección Presidencial,* or the MPP, with clusters and fringes and tin doodads. His parents were proud of him as were his in-laws, not to mention his wife, who by now was pregnant. His father took a moment of the occasion to forgive him for not being a plumber, living in the grime and foulness.

After his recovery the president placed him at the airport not realizing that Manuel Laberón was not a person to be exposed to new things. And the airport, of course, where something new is happening every moment, was the worst place for someone like Manuel Laberón.

On his first day on the job, when he saw the shiny Delta plane up close he was stunned. He had never seen anything as beautiful in his life. All the planes he had seen up close before had been the old United States surplus, dull, grimy green military and presidential planes in military airports. Inside, he saw the captain and the second officer and the third officer and the stewardesses. It was a magical day for him. There on the first seat was *The New York Times, The New York Times Book Review*. It was his to take and read. To practice his English.

It was after a year of airport duty that Sergeant Manuel Laberón took a turn for the worse, the real beginning of the end which ended in his being banned from military service:

He was soaking his feet in warm limewater and reading *The New York Times* when he saw an article which made his mind reel. Was it possible? Was his English good enough to read the true meaning of this story? It was hard to believe but there it was in the most trusted paper in America, *The New York Times*. There, in those little, horrible black-and-white pictures *The New York Times* uses, was the picture of President John F. Kennedy and his sister Eunice. The article he had stumbled on and had read three or four times mentioned Eunice's husband: Sargent Shriver. The sister of the president of the United States was married to a sergeant just like him. In what other country could you find such democracy?

The screams his wife and child heard coming from the bathroom were screams of joy not of pain. And when his wife and child ran to his aid they found him with the bowl of warm limewater poured over his head and his body drenched.

"Do you understand," he told his wife, "that the president of the United States has a sister married to a sergeant like me? Do you realize the significance of this? How important that makes me? How important that makes you and our child?"

It was not hard to convince his wife. She, also, could hardly contain her excitement. Both went sleepless that night. In the morning, after Sergeant Manuel Laberón had gone to the airport, *The New York Times* in his hand, the wife walked with the child to her parents' house to spread the good news. More honors had come Manuel Laberón's way. The news spread through the neighborhood. People came to see Manuel Laberón's parents and in-laws to congratulate them. Manuel Laberón's father began to think of changing jobs, getting away from the grime and foulness. He could be a civil servant. That same day he went to the neighborhood municipal building and applied for the job of building inspector. By now word had reached the municipal judge. He saw to it that Manuel Laberón's father was given the job.

From here it is an easy task to explain how a man such as Manuel Laberón became obsessed with the United States of America. He scoured the airplanes for news of the great country. He would read different newspapers and very often he found stories that mentioned Sargent Shriver but curiously he could never find a photograph of the man. He longed to see Sargent Shriver in uniform. What military bearing did he have? How much starch did he use? How did he salute?

Not having a photograph, he began to fantasize about Sargent Shriver. One day he was tall. The other day he was short. His hair was wavy and dark. His hair was blonde and short, like the crewcut the U.S. Marines loved to wear. His fantasy began to take the shape of an enigma that he could not resolve.

His mind became so preoccupied with Sargent Shriver that one day, without exercising the slightest degree of reason, he decided to stow away in the rest room on a jet headed for Washington. He was found, of course, and was taken off the plane, placed in the embarrassing position of having to arrest himself. Being the good soldier that he was he did so and interrogated himself for a while, until he convinced himself that he was not trying to leave but had been trapped inside the rest room while inspecting the plane. Like any good writer, he had learned to lie so well that his story seemed plausible to him although he knew it was false. In other words, his illusions had melted his reality and he was able to conjure up any scenario his mind desired. By the end of the day he had expanded his story and he considered himself the hero for having saved the passengers from the grime and foulness he had found in the toilet. His plumberness had come in handy.

His superiors were leery though. Manuel Laberón could bear watching. By now he had spread word of Sargent Shriver at the airport. His men questioned his stability.

The frustration grew in Manuel Laberón. By now the compulsion to write had him overwhelmed. He decided to write a story about Sargent Shriver. He began to learn the names of the characters, from the matriarchal Rose Kennedy to the lowly Peter Lawford. He knew he could not write the story in English but he could write it in Spanish, the most florid Spanish he knew. Here is the translation:

The extremely likeable matriarchal Rose Kennedy waltzed into Eunice's room. Eunice was sitting at the dresser in front of the mirror primping her hair before the usual most elegant dinner.

"How lovely you look, my dear," Rose Kennedy said.

Eunice, without taking her eyes off herself in the mirror said, "Thank you, dear Mama."

Rose Kennedy went to the window and looked past the expansive yard, past the Joseph Promontory named after her husband and stared for a long time at the Atlantic Ocean. Her contentment was so much in evidence that Eunice took a moment to study her mother and could not remember when she had seen her so happy.

"A penny for your thoughts," said Eunice.

Unknown to Eunice, Rose Kennedy had been watching Sargent Shriver running in the freshly mowed lawn, the whippets running with him, jumping with glee. Against the sheer granite cliffs reminiscent of the Acropolis, Sargent Shriver looked like a pubescent Adonis running in his fatigues and combat boots in ancient Greece. The whippets loved him so. They would not have gone anywhere without their Sargent. Earlier, Rose Kennedy and the pres-

ident had tried to take the whippets for a walk but nothing would budge the whippets until Sargent Shriver appeared. When Sargent Shriver walked off with Rose Kennedy and the president the whippets followed. "You have such a way with animals," Rose Kennedy had marveled. "And with people," said the president. Secretly the president longed to be Sargent Shriver but there could only be one of him.

The whippets caught up with Sargent Shriver and nipped ever so gently at his heels. Finally Sargent Shriver tripped and the whippets were all over him, licking him, pawing him gently. Never had Rose Kennedy seen such love of animals for a human. Never had she loved someone outside the family as she did Sargent Shriver.

"My contentment," said Rose Kennedy, taking the sights below on the lawn, "is for you, Eunice. I never thought it possible we could love someone outside the family as much as we love Sargent Shriver."

Eunice laid her hairbrush down, took a tissue and wiped a tear of happiness from her eyes. She said, her voice breaking, "I know. I am so lucky, Mama. I simply don't know what I did in my life to deserve this." It was too much, too much emotion. She sniffled.

"Life is hard to explain," said Rose. "I wish I had married as well. But in this life you cannot have everything. Look at the Cabot Lodges."

"Oh, mother," said Eunice, "forget about them. Let bygones be bygones. Look at how enormously happy we are. How unhappy they are."

"I suppose you're right," said Rose Kennedy. "I know we are the envy of Hyannisport having Sargent Shriver in the family. . . ." A quick look down to the lawn and she said, "Oh, my dear. Look at him run. Like a Greek god. How could you be so fortunate?"

Sargent Shriver had run off the lawn and into the clump of salt cedars which bordered the property. The whippets disappeared with him.

Rose Kennedy said, coming to sit by Eunice, "I wish Sargent

Shriver would speak to Bobby and Teddy. Maybe he could guide them. Show them how a man should behave."

"What about Jack?" asked Eunice.

"Oh," said Rose Kennedy, "Jack is Jack and he's the president. We're past telling him what to do. If only all my sons were the caliber of Sargent Shriver."

"God only makes one of those every five generations," said Eunice, smugly. "And I have him. He's mine."

"If we could only get rid of Peter Lawford," said Rose Kennedy.

"Mama!" cried out Eunice. "Shame on you."

"It's true, Eunice. I cannot possibly see what got into your sister to marry him. An actor? In this family? I thank God your father is dead."

"I think you're being unduly harsh," said Eunice.

Rose Kennedy said, "I suppose it's hard for us to compare when we have Sargent Shriver in the family."

"You shouldn't compare, Mama," Eunice said.

Rose Kennedy went to stand at the window. Sargent Shriver appeared on the run from behind the clump of salt cedars. The whippets were close behind. On the lawn now she could see Jack and Ted and Bobby trying to catch Sargent Shriver. Sargent Shriver had the football in his right hand as one would carry a loaf of bread. He reminded her so much of John Heisman, E. F. Hutton, Smith Barney, Henry Wallace.

Rose Kennedy opened the window and said to them below, "Enough of the football. It's time to get ready for dinner. Sargent Shriver?"

"Yes?" came the husky, masculine voice from the lawn.

"I have spoken to Eunice. We insist you wear your uniform."

"I shall, then," the voice said. "Class A."

The dinner was dull until Sargent Shriver and Eunice appeared. Sargent Shriver was in his Class A uniform. He took breaths away, both male and female. Rose Kennedy stood to propose a toast.

"For Sargent Shriver," she said, "may he protect us from the evils of the world for all the days to come."

"Yes. Yes," said Jack.

Jackie smiled her practiced smile without saying anything. Then she lowered her eyes and looked about in that way of hers where one could not tell if she knew what was going on or not and one had to assume she did since Jack had married her.

Everyone stood. Although the crowd was small, the applause was deafening. The president of the United States proposed a toast. "To Sargent Shriver," he said in a booming voice, "the protector of our liberty. May I always have him at my side to protect me from harm."

Scowls spread over the faces of Robert and Edward like clouds slowly covering the moon. Of course they were jealous. How could one not help but be jealous? How could one not envy the beauty of the sun, the moon, the stars?

"Come," said Rose Kennedy, "sit by me. Make me joyful as you do Eunice."

Sargent Shriver took his seat but not before arranging the chair for his wife. Then he proceeded to take out his mess kit, as clean as the clouds overhanging Hyannisport, which he laid out in front of him.

Rose Kennedy took an interest in the mess kit and said, "I wish I had one of those."

"You can't, mother," Eunice said. "Those are army issue."

"But surely . . . " Rose said without thinking.

Jack interrupted her. "Now, mother," he said, "don't be asking things of the president that I cannot do."

Jackie smiled again and kept quiet.

Just then, as the meal progressed, an alarm was sounded throughout the compound. Sargent Shriver quickly rose from his seat and sped off in a flash, leaving everyone else seated. Dogs were heard to bark. There were voices outside. Gunfire. The crashing of bullets against the outside wall of the dining room. What could it *be? The Kennedy clan cowered under the table while Sargent Shriver protected them from the forces of evil.*

Then there was silence as they heard Sargent Shriver's heavy, booted footsteps outside. Closer and closer they came until the door to the patio opened and Sargent Shriver stood in his magnificent presence, the smoking Mauser at his side. "It was the Cabot Lodges," he said, "rifling through the garbage. Looking for dirt to use against us."

"And E. F. Hutton?" asked the timid Rose.

"He was the instigator," said Sargent Shriver.

"In politics," said John Kennedy, "one never knows from one day to the next who your enemy will be. Two hours ago we were playing football with them."

"Yes," said Jackie.

"Well, one of them won't be playing for a while," said Sargent Shriver. He showed them the blood on the palm of his hand. "I got him good."

"Sargent Shriver," said Rose Kennedy, "I don't know what our family would do without you."

"Another toast," said John Kennedy, getting out from under the table. He raised his glass. "To Sargent Shriver—our protector—the most honest, most intelligent man I have ever known."

Tears came to Eunice's eyes as she sipped her toast. She could barely say it but she managed to get the words out. "My husband," she said.

"Our leader and protector," said Rose.

———•———

Every night he worked on his story. Not only did he bother his wife with it, he was a nuisance at the airport. His fellow workers ran when they saw him coming. Soon, though, even a man like Manuel Laberón takes notice and he began to say less and less of his literary works.

But on the story went. Sargent Shriver saved the Kennedys every night. Every night a new episode, more trash raids by the

Cabot Lodges, the E. F. Huttons, the Smith Barneys, Pierre Salinger. It was always Sargent Shriver to the rescue.

Then came the first blow. He had just finished inspecting a plane headed for New York when he heard the stewardess scream. Then the plane seemed to be in a state of chaos, people running about, crying, screaming. He could understand that someone had died. But who? He began to ask questions. The first officer told him: "The president of the United States has been assassinated."

Manuel Laberón let out his scream of anguish, the long forgotten one, his mind in the worst possible turmoil. It was incomprehensible that such a thing could happen in the United States. Where was the military? The human shield, the man walking in front of the president? No, where was Sargent Shriver? Why had he not protected the president?

These questions flooded his mind like the water harboring all the grime and foulness in which he and his father had soaked their hands. Why had not the Kennedys insisted that an armed Sargent Shriver walk in front of the president? Why had Sargent Shriver not been allowed to protect the president? Why had Sargent Shriver not been assigned to the president night and day? What was the conspiracy? There had to be a conspiracy.

He began to read *The New York Times* even more, the entire newspaper, page to page. He studied the conspiracy. This time he had learned his lesson. He did not tell anyone, not even his wife. As soon as he got home from work he would eat by the mouthful, like a pig, and then he would hurry to his room to review his newspapers over and over again. Finally, after weeks and weeks of study he came upon a name: Lyndon Johnson, a Texan. And everyone knew Texans carried guns and shot at people they didn't like. Here was a man capable of having John Kennedy killed in Texas in order to become president himself.

Johnson had lured John Kennedy into Texas and had him killed. Of this he came to be sure.

"What should we ever do?" Rose Kennedy asked, bewildered and confused by the tragedy. "Where is Sargent Shriver?"

"Away," said Eunice. "Trying to find answers so that we can go on with our lives."

"Has he come to any conclusions?" Ted asked. He was sitting alone, a drink in his hands. Would he be next?

"He is about to come to several conclusions," said Eunice, "but we mustn't hurry him. His investigation is exhaustive and thorough. All of us know how he is."

"And a good thing too," said Rose Kennedy. "We wouldn't want to blame anyone who is innocent."

"Like the Cabot Lodges," said Robert. He was sitting opposite of Ted. He also had a drink in his hands. He puffed on his cigar.

"I wish you wouldn't smoke," said Rose Kennedy to Robert. "You're fouling the air."

"Let's all be patient and wait for Sargent Shriver," Eunice said, softly, trying to defuse the occasion.

"Has anyone seen Jackie?" asked Rose.

Sargent Shriver's heavy, booted footsteps could be heard outside. The whippets could not deny loving him and they were heard to squeal their joy at seeing him. The jingle and jangle of their rabies tags could be heard as the tags bounced off their choke collars when they jumped for joy. Presently Sargent Shriver opened the living room door, coming in from the patio. He looked distraught, having had little sleep the last few weeks. His eyes, sparkling beauties normally, were red and swollen from crying. In his hands he carried a large portfolio. He walked to the table between Ted and Robert and threw the portfolio on it.

"There," he said. "It's finished."

"Who was it?" asked Robert.

Sargent Shriver licked his parched lips. He said, "Lyndon Johnson."

"My God," said Rose Kennedy, "who's he?"

"The vice-president, Mother," Ted replied.

"When did that happen?" Rose wanted to know. "Since when did John need a vice-president? I know he was always into vices but was he that much into vices?"

"No, Mother," said Eunice. "You just don't remember. Every president has a vice-president."

"Whatever for?" Rose asked.

"To make the president look good," said Robert.

"This Johnson man must be horrible," said Rose Kennedy.

"He is," said Ted.

"And he did it?" Rose inquired.

Sargent Shriver pointed at the large portfolio on the table. "He didn't do it personally but there it is," he said. "It's all in there."

"Goodness gracious," said Rose Kennedy. "What are we to do?"

Manuel Laberón's mind wasn't into the story. He felt a deep sense of loss with the death of John Kennedy. What had happened to the United States? He could understand assassinations in Latin America but in the United States? Had the moral degeneration of his country and others like it reached the United States? If so what would Sargent Shriver's role be? Should he work for the preservation of the Kennedys or his country? The dilemma of the career military man. Would Caesar's generals be loyal to him or to the Roman Empire? Nothing had changed through the years. In the end he knew what Sargent Shriver would choose.

His despondency extended to his family. His wife, usually vibrant and expressive, was sullen and morose, dragging herself around in her housecoat all day long. The young boy, now six and an excellent student, became a problem in school. He would not finish his assignments, did not follow directions, did not go out for recess. He barely ate his taco at noon.

But the human spirit is resilient and for every stumble that life gave Manuel Laberón he found a way to keep from falling. After a few years he was his old self again and his wife was vibrant and expressive once more. His son took to school again like a hog to mud. Once more the obsession with Sargent Shriver returned. Where was Sargent Shriver? Never, never, in all the photographs of the funeral had the face of Sargent Shriver been shown.

It was at this time that Manuel Laberón came to feel that the distance between him and Sargent Shriver had been exaggerated by the horrible events in Dallas. Simply put, he needed to know more about Sargent Shiver. So he turned to that most horrible part of *The New York Times Book Review*—the query letter.

He wrote: "For information on Sargent Shriver, brother-in-law of the late president John F. Kennedy, and husband of Eunice Kennedy Shriver, information on his whereabouts, his military stations, decorations, exploits in the field of battle, personal remembrances, Kennedy files and conspiracy theories, conversations remembered, family life, pictures, etc. Will pay. Send to: Sgto. Manuel Laberón, Military Post, El Salvador International Airport, San Salvador.

And he mailed it to *The New York Times*.

If his obsessive behavior was the beginning of the end for Manuel Laberón, this query letter sealed his doom.

"What are we to do?" Sargent Shriver repeated Rose Kennedy's question. "What do you think we should do?"

"Release the information," said Robert and Ted agreed.

Sargent Shriver said, "And what about our country? What would become of it?"

"This country can endure," said Rose Kennedy. "The important thing is for the world to know."

Sargent Shriver stood as tall as he could and disagreed. He said, "This country cannot endure such a blow and recover to its past greatness. This information must be withheld from the people. The country is far above more important than the individual."

The argument continued into the night. With the passing of each moment, Sargent Shriver began to feel the building of animosity toward him by Ted and Robert. Finally, Rose Kennedy joined them and Sargent Shriver was left alone to fight the fight for his country. Eunice was torn between the two factions. Sargent Shriver, gentleman that he was, allowed her to stay with her family while he moved his things out. Not only had the Kennedys lost the presidency but now they had lost their most honorable member. In a matter of days, with John Kennedy gone, Robert and Ted had poisoned Rose Kennedy's mind. The portfolio was released to the Warren Commission who took it under advisement. Lyndon Johnson himself was allowed to go through it. The Warren Commission filed it along with all other conspiracy theories and nothing more was heard from it again. Lyndon Johnson had seized power. All the Kennedy people in Washington were replaced. The Kennedys had lost all power in a matter of weeks. The orders were cut for Sergeant Shriver, a persona non grata both among the Kennedys and the new administration.

Manuel Laberón had lost all power in the Kennedy administration. No longer did his colleague rule the family. These were again troubled times. But they would get worse:

A few weeks after the query letter was received by *The New York Times,* Manuel Laberón was in bed having a difficult time going to sleep. He had tossed for several hours trying to will himself to dream of the good times. He first heard the military helicopters around his house. He got up to see what it could be, standing at the picture window looking out into the illuminated patio. The voice was powerful over the loudspeaker. The helicopter spotlight was on him. He was being instructed to hold his arms above his head and not move. By this time the army had arrived on foot. Manuel Laberón heard the front door collapse under the weight of the tank. Soon the house was filled with soldiers. He was held against the bedroom wall, his feet spread out. His wife was taken by military females out of the house. His son, crying in fear, was taken by juvenile authorities.

His interrogation began at the army headquarters he knew so well. Leading the questioners was the CIA, followed by the FBI, the Secret Service, and lastly, the El Salvadorean Military Police. Interpol was there strictly as a European observer. What did he know of conspiracies to kill the president of the United States? What was his connection to Sargent Shriver? Over and over he told them what he knew. He spoke eloquently of the camaraderie between him and Sargent Shriver, between his wife and Eunice. He told them of Lyndon Johnson, the Texan. Most importantly, his story never varied. He was convinced he was telling the truth.

If the interrogation began at the army headquarters it ended several days later in the Manicomio Central on Avenida M—the hated and notorious Central Insane Asylum on M Avenue, the usual place for political prisoners. From here he was moved to the United States for further study at the super-secret Center for Propaganda Studies in Houston, Texas.

He experienced the second assassination, Robert Kennedy's, under heavy interrogation. Under the stress of his captors, with the loss of his family, unable to sleep or eat, he began the slow realization of the truth.

"And there is no Sargent Shriver?" he asked. "And if not why would *The New York Times,* the world's most trusted paper, publish his existence?"

The CIA operative, a Mr. Fendersen, said, "There is a Sargent Shriver but he is not a sergeant like in the army."

"Where is he a sergeant then? In an elite force not known to any of us?"

"No," Fendersen replied quickly, "that is his name. Sargent Shriver. It is not sergeant. It is Sargent."

Manuel Laberón asked, "Why would anyone name a person sergeant if not to confuse the general population into thinking he was a sergeant? Is this the American way? To fool the general population?"

"Let me show you," said Fendersen. He snapped his fingers and a blackboard and chalk was produced. He wrote the words and pointed out the difference. "Sergeant," he read off the board. "Then, Sargent," he said. "Do you see the difference?"

"I do now," said Manuel Laberón. "It is the same with threw and through. Here and hear. Fare and fair. Pray and prey."

His interrogators were finally able to convince him of his foolishness. His mind completely gone, his world lost, he began to write:

The matriarchal Rose Kennedy stood at the window looking down at the freshly mowed lawn. In the room with her was Eunice, preoccupied with her marriage, despondent over having to leave Hyannisport for some remote place. It was always the same when she had to follow her husband—despondency, fear of the unknown, a feeling of helplessness.

"And where are you and he going this time?" Rose asked. Eunice could plainly see the grimace on her face.

"Yokohama," replied Eunice, tears flowing freely down her overblown cheeks. She was tired of apologizing for her husband.

"My God," said Rose Kennedy, reeling from the information. "What God-awful place is that?"

"In Asia."

"Asia? Where is Asia? Will we ever see you and him again?"

"Hopefully, we can return in ten years. If things straighten out here. By then Lyndon Johnson should be gone. He has a bad heart, you know."

"*Lyndon Johnson does not have a heart,*" Rose Kennedy said. "*His anus pumps blood through his body.*"

"*I have to go. He is my husband.*"

"*Why did you ever marry him? A sergeant? Why could you not have married a general? A colonel, at least? Why bring something like that into the family? Wasn't Peter Lawford enough of an embarrassment to the family without you dragging this . . . this sergeant person into it? Tell me again. Where did you meet this creature?*"

"*At the carnival. Pitching baseballs.*"

"*And you had to bring him home like a lost dog.*"

As Rose Kennedy said this she could see the whippets chasing Sargent Shriver, trying to bite him, nipping at his Achilles tendons.

"*He runs like an albatross,*" Rose Kennedy said. "*Why go out into the yard if the dogs hate you? What reasonable person would do such a thing? And the tattoos? He did not get rid of them. The pubic hair one is absolutely horrible, Eunice. It aggravates me to no end. It's an embarrassment. Thank God the Cabot Lodges have not seen it. We will be the talk of Hyannisport if they do. Not that we aren't already. With a sergeant in the family and all that.*"

"*The pubic hairs shooting out like lightning from the crotch are symbolic, Mother.*"

"*Symbolic of what?*"

"*They are like lightning strikes. They symbolize how fast his unit can be at any location in the world.*"

"*I don't care. The tattoo comes off or you and he are not allowed in this house again.*"

"*I will tell him,*" Eunice said, crying some more.

"*I suppose you need money for food too? Is that why you're crying? The man cannot even afford food for the you and the children . . . But beer? Beer is another thing. He would die without his beer, right?*"

"*You can be so cruel, Mother,*" said Eunice, crying some more.

Down below, Ted and Robert were playing football against the Cabot Lodges, the E. F. Huttons, the Smith Barneys, Pierre Salinger. John had the ball, running with it, zigzagging, cutting across the grain, everyone running after him. He crossed the goal line and everyone heaped on top of him laughing. Even the Rockefeller girls were there on top of John. Across the way, in the shadows of the salt cedars, Rose Kennedy could see the hated Sargent Shriver, poking his unshaven face, trying to see if he could be included in the celebration.

"The tattoo goes," she said, rushing out of the room. "And your supper will be served over the garage. I want your things out of here tonight."

"Sargent Shriver is not a bad person," Eunice said. "He cannot help being what he is. His father was a plumber, sticking his hands into the grime and foulness of toilets and sewers. What do you expect? His mother ironed for a living."

"Please, Eunice," said Rose Kennedy, "we have been through this so many times. It's useless. The man is incorrigible. He will never amount to anything and neither will you while married to him. I only hope the children will reject him and his horrible ways before they become contaminated with his so-called morals. . . . I will have the servant bring you the food. Please don't bother showing up at the formal table."

"We leave for Yokohama tomorrow," said Eunice.

"God," said Rose Kennedy, placing her hand up to her forehead, "must you mention that perfectly horrible name again? I swear it gives me vertigo. I suppose the least I can do is send you money for clothes and food."

"That was what I was going to beg for," said Eunice.

One could not fail to see the hatred in Rose Kennedy's face as she left the room. Immediately, Eunice began to cry some more. What a mistake this had all been.

———•———

Manuel Laberón was returned to El Salvador and released from the insane asylum in time, when the authorities felt he would not be of any harm. He was discharged from the military without pension. His wife, although living with her parents next door, would have nothing to do with him. You can understand why his son did not speak to him. He spent the days soliciting work for his father, who had been fired as the building inspector and had returned to plumbing. On occasion, when Manuel Laberón felt sane enough, he would help his father, sticking his hands into the grime and foulness of the waters.

One day, while Manuel Laberón was gone a letter arrived having been forwarded from the airport. It was the answer to the query letter. It read:

> Concerning Sargent Shriver: I have information on his whereabouts, military posts, decorations, assassination theories, old pictures, life with Eunice and the Kennedys. Please send one thousand dollars to:
> Reginald Farley, Editor
> *The New York Times*
> P.O. Box 329
> Grand Central Station, N. Y. 10001
> P.S. I also have all the inside information on Peter Lawford. That's another story.

Manuel Laberón's mother could only thank God that he had not read the letter. She burned it along with Manuel Laberón's latest literary efforts.

Eladio Comes Home

The large mahogany upright piano stood at the wall opposite from the entrance, a door to either side. The left door led into a hallway with several bedrooms. The right door went into the large elongated kitchen that ran from approximately halfway to the end of the house. On both sides of the room were seated women all dressed in black with black shawls. At the entrance wall were but a few chairs placed on either side of the door. The rest of the wall was taken over by the two large windows where the canaries lived. The woman who had raised Eladio sat to the right at the middle of the wall. She was a rather stout, short lady, with a large head with lots of dark hair with a white streak at the center combed severely back and pinned with a black ornamental comb. Her upper arms were pendulous and her dress, black also, was wet under her arms from perspiration although the two women on either side of her fanned her continuously for fear she may faint. Everyone knew her as Chata or Tía Chata. A black veil draped over the top of her head covered her face so that no one could see her cry or see the wrinkles of her face or see the forlorn look in her eyes. At that instant the priest across the street rang *la primera* for rosary. Outside, the children who had come with their parents were playing. Some had gone across the street to the parochial school playground to play to get away from parental, critically watchful eyes. The men who had come were scattered throughout the porch which ran completely around the house. They were talking in soft tones. Occasionally there was a short burst of laughter but then the solemnness of the occasion set in and all was muffled again. They had before spoken with the brothers and had gone through the dreaded chore of greeting all the women inside.

"How old was Eladio?" one of the men, the mayor, asked as he approached the brothers. He was a small penguinlike man, larger across the middle than he was tall. He took off his hat and wiped the inside with his handkerchief. He wore a wrinkled light grey suit, a white shirt with a bad collar and an old solid black mourning tie.

"Eladio was nineteen," his brother replied.

The mayor had parked his car on the side street and had come from almost behind the house. It was getting dark and the mayor offered his condolences when he realized it was the brother. The brother was dressed in an army uniform, as were his other three brothers who walked over behind him. One of them was smoking. He had a flask in his hip pocket.

The mayor said, shaking his head, "Too young. Too, too young."

The brothers did not answer but waited for the mayor to continue. The mayor, not one to be at a loss for words, said, "I tell you, this war is going to be the end of the young men of this town. How many have died?"

"I heard fourteen," said the brother who was smoking and drinking.

"Much. Much, too much," said the mayor and he excused himself to go inside.

The brothers watched him waddle his way to the front of the house and he disappeared from the porch by turning to his right. Then they could see him through the windows, through the canaries, going across the front of the house. They assumed he entered because in a short while they heard the women began to cry again.

A man, the tailor in town who had lost a son in the war, came to where the brothers were standing against the wall and shook hands. *"Les acompaño sus sentimientos,"* he said. "My son," he said, "was killed in Normandy. He is buried there. One day I hope to go see his grave. If God wants it and He gives me life." And with that, as if he had announced something unimportant, he apologized for taking their time and left to go inside to pay his respects to Chata. The mayor was on his way out through the front gate. He was on his way to the rosary when the priest rang *la segunda*. When the tailor entered, the women, realizing who he was, that he had lost a son in the war, wailed again. The tailor's wife had been there since morning and had taken her turn next to Chata, fanning her. The tailor shook Chata's hand and embraced her lightly and went around the room shaking hands, even his wife's. He stood by the piano momentarily. By now the wailing had reached a high pitch and the tailor excused himself. He stepped out and put his hat back on. He followed the mayor and went through the front gate. The cars were beginning to arrive at the church.

At the same time a car drove up to the front of the house and stopped. The driver, a thin young man in his twenties, got out quickly and came around and opened the passenger door. Mrs. Gonzales, the school principal, got off and walked slowly on her ponderous legs to the front gate with the help of the driver. This was her son, Robertito. She was a widow, a heavy woman with thick legs and a dark moustache and thick eyebrows. She had been born with a large chocolate-colored mole on her forehead from which thick, coarse white hairs grew. She had the look of perpetual disgust—the corners of her mouth turned down, her eyes fixed at some point beyond reason—as one would find in a school administrator-teacher who had been at it too long, seen it all, heard it all and didn't care anymore. The town was scared of her. She wore a black shawl over her head like the other women. The son opened the gate for her and escorted her to the front door. He knocked lightly and one of the women asked them to enter. Mrs. Gonzales caused even more wailing than the mayor and the tailor. She had brought with her the memories of Eladio and his school days. The son took her by the arm to where Chata was seated and she bent down to embrace Chata. She went slowly around the room shaking everyone's hand, exchanging greetings, fixing everyone with her stare. Her son followed meekly. She finally came all the way around and the son was asked to go into the kitchen to get an extra chair. In the kitchen he saw the women he knew, his mother's friends, who were cooking and preparing coffee for the wake. He noticed Carolina there and he smiled but she was busy and she returned his smile with a look of indifference. He came back, set the chair by the piano and stepped behind his mother.

Mrs. Gonzales looked back over her shoulder at her son and said, "I imagine the boys are outside. Why don't you go offer your condolences to them?"

The son excused himself, went to the door, and left.

"What a beautiful son," the tailor's wife said.

"God keep him from going to the war," said the mayor's wife.

Mrs. Gonzales said, "Fortunately, he has a heart condition."

Chata's cat came out from behind the piano, stretched, and went around the room rubbing itself against the women's legs.

"They say a cat is bad luck," the butcher's wife said.

"Not true," Mrs. Gonzales, a cat lover, said very sternly. Everyone remembered she was the principal and that she was above the butcher's wife and that ended the conversation. The butcher's wife looked blankly at the wall, as if she had not said what she said.

Chata, behind her veil, was lost in thought. She was thinking that perhaps this was a dream, a bad dream, and that she would awaken before long and she would tell her canaries what she had dreamed. The canaries would make such a sound that she knew they were laughing. And then someday she would be laughing, playing the piano, singing with her canaries and Eladio would come in. He would be in uniform. A sergeant at such a young age. She would embrace him so tightly and then she would say that she would never let him go. How much love she had for him and the others. They had been very young when their mother died and they had come to live with her. She couldn't remember the time and it bothered her enough that her lower lip trembled. How foolish and sacrilegious of her, their aunt, not to remember when her sister had died.

"Chata hasn't been herself since this happened," whispered the mayor's wife.

"Of course not. She's stunned," Mrs. Gonzales replied, again killing the conversation.

The mayor's wife pursed her lips as though she would cry and then bit her tongue.

It was time for the canaries to sing and they filled the room with whistles. Chata did not hear them. Mrs. Gonzales stood and went to the windows and unfurled the drapes held to one side by a hook. In doing so she covered the windows and the canaries slowly quieted down.

At that moment the priest sounded *la tercera* and Chata awoke from her thoughts and began to wail and talk at the same time. The others did not lose the opportunity to cry out also. Only a few of Chata's words could be understood: church, bells, rosary, priest. They were incoherent enough to trigger even more cries from the collection of women. Ultimately the sound reverberated through the house with so much force that it appeared the house would burst with the intensity of so much sorrow. The weakest part of the house was the chimney. The top fell harmlessly at the rear of the house where no one could see it.

Mrs. Gonzales had the presence of mind to get up and tiptoe into the kitchen where she noticed the dust coming from the hearth. She looked up the chimney and saw the empty night sky. The other women were so preoccupied that they had not noticed. Carolina, whom Mrs. Gonzales hated, caught her eye kneading dough for biscuits. She would be sure that Carolina did not speak to Robertito. She left the chimney as though nothing had happened. She did not want to say that the top of the chimney had fallen. There was enough pain in the house as it was. Instead she poured herself some tea and one for Chata, which she carried into the parlor but not before turning her nose up at Carolina.

The tea satisfied Chata as she drank it under her veil. The others took the opportunity to rest and go into the kitchen to eat and drink. Chata was left alone with Mrs. Gonzales.

"You know that Mr. Gonzales would have been heartbroken over this," Mrs. Gonzales said.

Chata nodded her head.

"This would have been a horrible blow for him to take," she added. "You know how much he admired the boys. Well, you know how much Robertito admires the boys."

Chata put her cup down, rested it on her lap and looked over to the canaries and Mrs. Gonzales, her gaze following, saw the five stars on the window over the cage. She got up and removed one of the stars and handed it to Chata.

Robertito had found the brothers on the porch at the east side of the house. He approached them slowly, timidly, hoping they would not move before he got to them. Most of the men who had been outside had gone to the church for the rosary.

"What time does the body arrive?" Robertito asked. He could not help but feel a sense of guilt not being in uniform.

"Eight," said one of the brothers.

"In one hour," said Robertito checking his watch. "I can't begin to tell you guys how sorry I feel that Eladio was killed. I heard it was Iwo Jima?"

Three of the brothers excused themselves and went into the kitchen by the porch door. The remaining brother, the one with the flask and cigarettes, said, "He was killed in Iwo Jima."

Robertito said, "Maybe I can go with you to get the body."

"We already have enough men," the brother said.

"Maybe, if you would allow me, I can stand guard over the casket."

"No. It's not necessary," said he. "Listen, we don't want too much for him. You understand?"

"I understand. It was just that I felt that I could help in some way by guarding the casket."

"No."

"Whatever you say. I was just volunteering in case you needed someone to guard the casket."

"No, we don't need anyone."

"I just thought I'd ask. You know that if you don't ask then you don't find out. Now I know how you feel."

"Would you just leave me alone? Please?"

"All right. I was only trying to help."

"I know. I appreciate it. We all do. You want a drink? A cigarette?"

"No. I don't drink or smoke. Eladio drank, didn't he?"

"Yes. Eladio drank and he smoked. We all drink and smoke. What else is there to do?"

"I've never had a drink in my life. Never had a cigarette."

"You ought to drink. You ought to smoke. How can you stand it?"

"I just can. I don't even have the desire. I'm not even curious."

"What about women?"

"What about them?"

"I saw you making eyes at Carolina in the kitchen. I could see from here inside through the window."

"She's just a friend."

"You don't love her?"

"No. I don't love anyone. I'm not like Eladio. Eladio loved all the women."

"He sure did. He loved women and women loved him."

"But Eladio was handsome."

"Yes. He was handsome. You sure you don't want a drink?"

"No."

"I hate to end this but I'm going inside to eat something now that the crowd has thinned out. About you guarding the casket, you can do it if you want to. I've changed my mind."

"And your other brothers?"

"They won't mind."

"I can just sit by the casket. That's what I meant. I don't have a uniform or anything like that. I'll sit by the casket."

"That's good of you."

"Thank you for letting me. I was feeling real down. You don't know what it feels not to be going to the war. Staying behind."

"Keeping all the women satisfied."

"Oh, no. Nothing like that."

"Why didn't you go?"

"I went but they turned me down. I have a bad heart."

"Well, you're lucky. Having a bad heart. I sometimes wish I had something wrong with me."

"I wish I could have gone. But my mother was glad I came back. I was only gone for one night. She missed me so much you would have thought I had been gone for a year."

"You don't have to be telling me all this."

"I'm sorry. If I don't tell it to someone, then who's to know?"

"Tell it to somebody else. Carolina. Some woman. This is woman talk. I want to know if you want a drink."

"No. Thank you.

The mayor left the rosary early. He was at the front of the house waiting for the delegation of men to accompany him and the brothers to go get the body at the depot. He was standing by the front gate smoking a cigarette when he heard the train. He counted the number of men he had available. Now all they had to do was wait for the hearse.

The men were waiting when the priest left the rectory and crossed the street. The priest greeted them and went through the gate. At the sidewalk he greeted some of the men standing there and he kept on to the porch. He knocked on the door and was let in by the mayor's wife who had seen him at the porch. He embraced Chata and went around the circle as all the others had done. He shook hands and then said, "We will never understand the ways of our Lord Jesus Christ and God. Let us pray." He lowered his head and said, "Dear God, I know that at these times it is very hard to understand Your wisdom. But we must trust in You and Your plan for our lives. Bless Chata and the boys. May they be safe from now on. Protect them, dear God." The priest raised his head and looked around. He felt that his presence was an impedance to the whole affair so he proceeded into the kitchen where he saw Carolina at the table. She offered him some coffee but he chose tea. As he sipped, the smell of the old soot from the fallen chimney caught his senses. He went to the hearth and looked inside and up through the flue. He said, "I can see the sky. The chimney seems to have fallen. But that is the least of our worries."

The hearse arrived while the priest was contemplating the fallen chimney. Robertito came into the kitchen to get him to go with the men. Robertito saw Carolina again and went over and extended his hand. Carolina cleaned her hand before shaking. He tried to speak to Carolina but the priest hurried him along.

The men had collected at the front of the house and the mayor appointed who should go and who should stay. No one wanted to ride in the hearse so two cars were needed. The rest of the men, according to the mayor, would stay to move the piano into the kitchen. The casket would go where the piano now stood.

By the time the men arrived with the casket the piano had been moved and placed in the kitchen in front of the chimney.

As the men manhandled the casket into the parlor, the wails reached such a force that one would have thought the house could not take any more. The pitch, the noise—almost inhuman in its intensity—curdled the blood and made the hair stand on end. The frightened children playing outside and at the parochial school ran away. It would not have seemed unusual for one of the pallbearers to run out in fear of so much sorrow. The house bulged in pain. The canaries, used to more pleasant sounds and by now agitated from the previous wailing, were now all aflutter, flying desperately about, trying to hide from the noise the women were making. But there was no escape and the canaries were forced to hear, to be bombarded with the pitch and intensity of a sound so alien, an experience so bizarre, that it tore into their little hearts. They flew into the window sill, smashed into the windowpane and eventually, instead of reaching freedom, killed themselves from fright.

In the kitchen, the women began to hear the gradual song of the piano strings as the strings began to resonate with the cries. The piano had taken a life of its own. Now the mahogany wood reverberated along with the strings. It was a crescendo with its own lament, its own sorrowful story to play. And yet, Chata's voice could be heard above all else.

At the same time, as the casket was pushed against the wall, with the force of so much emotion, the rest of the chimney fell and the sound in the kitchen, along with the piano's cries, was unbearable. The people ran out, fearing the whole house would tumble.

Once outside, the priest, who had followed the gathering, circled them around him and began his own rosary, one eye on the missal and one eye on the house. Only Chata and the brothers and Robertito remained inside but the noise stayed in the house as though it could not leave and the people outside could hear their own voices trapped within. The piano, moved by the ever-increasing sounds of sorrow, reached a fortissimo that pierced the ears. The vibrating strings from the piano disturbed the soot from the downed chimney and the ashes came through the kitchen door as a dark cloud looking for relief and they spread slowly throughout the porch, completely surrounding the house, which finally let out a moan so full of pain and sorrow that the women and the men and the priest ran to the church to hide from the intensity of the moment. The house, they could see from across the street, had taken a pale color. Unknown to them, it had begun to die.

Parents

Ilook at my father and I hope to God, with some pain in conscience, that I don't grow to look like him when I get old. He has grown smaller, a miniature of the man he was. Sitting next to me he appears more like a weathered child than my father. His face has not changed in size, yet it is so much bigger than his body. The skin is coarse, the pores so large in some areas of his face, especially at the end of his nose, that I can see inside them. I can see the black, whatever it is, inside the huge pores. His ears have grown larger, like transparent pink caladium leaves with the morning sun shining through them. I swear that his ears go from almost the top of his head to his lower jaw and at their edges I can see the coarse curling hair against the same sunlight. And then I feel for him and I say to myself, what of it? How much are you going to care how you look when you get that old?

"I'm seventy-five," he tells me. He has caught me staring at him out of the corner of his eye. I try to concentrate on the road.

I don't say anything. I'm afraid that if I do, I'll get him talking again. It's just now been about one minute since he stopped talking. Not that he's been quiet for the minute. He's been humming something, no song at all, something without a tune.

He takes a damn note and repeats it again and again. My God, he gets on my nerves.

We are coming into the town of Alice, Texas. I look for and see the old, long-abandoned, white stucco building on the south side of the road, the building that will be forever etched in my mind. The sign over the torn door says, "We made mufflers." I laugh again. Over to the east I can see the rain clouds forming. He sees me looking at them and he takes it as a cue. He says, "It hasn't rained in a long time. I don't remember when it rained the last time." Then he stops and watches my driving and asks the same question again. "Has it rained in Houston?"

He has asked me if it has rained in Houston at least ten times since last night. I say, again, "Only a little bit. Not much."

"Well here . . . it hasn't rained at all. It never rains. But it looks like rain over there. See?" He points with his crooked arthritic finger at the clouds I was just noticing. His hand is almost touching my face. He lets his arm drop and it falls on my shoulder where he leaves it. He smiles at me and then squeezes my shoulder. He has dared to touch me against his better judgment. He is trying to tell me that we are father and son. He realizes that he has embarrassed both of us by showing emotion and he drops his arm and remains silent.

I nod my head to mean that I have ignored him and that I see the clouds and I look over to see him, the seat belt firmly buckled against his belly, wearing a lime-green double-knit shirt that my ex-wife sent him some ten birthdays ago, but he thinks that he honors me if he wears it. His trousers are the eternal deep green polyesters with the large grease stain on the right thigh, the grease stain a symbol of my past life for I can remember exactly the barbecue when it came about, when I was still married. I remember the quarrel. He won't have the trousers cleaned because the cleaning costs more than he paid for them.

He tries to cross his leg. He keeps kicking the underside of the dashboard and he finally gives it up and then acts like he didn't want to do it in the first place.

"*Mugrero chinga'o,*" he says. And that seems to describe his present life.

I had often wondered what he would be like as an old man and here he is sitting next to me, looking not at all what I imagined him. I'm embarrassed with myself and I'm sure he is too.

I've only been here since last night, came in on the ten o'clock flight to Corpus and already things irritate me. He was there to meet me at the airport. He arrived four hours ahead of time, just in case something happened—a flat, an accident, burned motor, some natural disaster, war, any catastrophe that may fall on car or driver, any sudden inclement weather, whatever. "You can never be too far ahead on time," he says when he picks me up, which is to say one cannot trust life. He has grown to expect and believe the worst.

Now he has conned me into taking him to see his sister in Corpus Christi. So I am going back from where I came last night. He is excited because he wants me to see my aunt's house. She has remodeled. "Wait until you see it," he said last night. "You are not going to believe it. She got some money last year. . . . Her cousin died last year."

"Your aunt's daughter," my mother says from the sink where she is cleaning after supper. "You never met the family. They live in California. They moved to California during the Depression."

"A cousin," my father repeats to me. "Her cousin died last year. . . . Why did she leave her money?"

"Because," my mother says, "she wasn't married. *Era señorita.*" Which means that she was not married and a virgin. "She worked at the light office in Los Angeles all those years. She finally died of cancer. Female problems. She had money in the bank and she left some of it to your aunt."

"Your aunt didn't know what to do with it so she remodels the house."

"I don't know what's the matter with your mother," he says, looking out through the windshield. "Every day she gets worse." He loves to drag me into their problems. What he really wants is for me to side with him against my mother. He says, "You agree, don't you? She is getting worse. Now she wants me not to drink. Not one beer because the doctor said for me not to drink. You know I love to drink." He reaches under the seat and takes out a small bottle. He laughs and says, "You're not going to tell her that I hid the bottle under the seat, are you?"

"No," I say.

He opens it and takes a swallow. He goes, "Ahhhhhhhhhhhh," for the longest time. Then he makes a face and shakes his head with his head bent down and his eyes closed. He looks to be in agony. He throws his head back. "Ahhhhhhhhhhhh," he says again. Now his eyes are opened and he is following the road with me and he says, "That tastes good. Nothing tastes better than a drink of whiskey. You want one?"

I had better say yes because he will not leave me alone if I refuse. I know him. He wants a partner to share the blame when my mother smells his breath. "He drank too," he will say and my mother will have to quit because she is afraid I will get upset and leave. I have done it before and she has felt so bad for so long, until I return and then she tries to make it up to me by cooking all weekend long and she won't say a word about our drinking . . . not until we're at the airport and I'm ready to board the flight. "Don't drink so much," she will say, making the sign of the cross on my forehead. "It's bad for you. Look at your father. You don't want to be like him. Old and not worth anything. You'll have a stroke like him and you won't be able to do anything. Can't even cross his leg. Who'll take care of you?" Meaning that I'm divorced and with no one to take care of me but her. She feels I should be married. The fact that I don't want to be married does not matter to her.

My mom is different. She has grown smaller but her proportions are normal. Her skin is still very beautiful. Her hair abundant and shiny like I have always remembered her. The only thing I find that betrays her are her hands. Her fingers are bent.

When we arrive from the airport my mom is in bed taking a little nap so that she can stay up. She is happy to see me. She hugs me and says the same thing. "How time flies. I wish Frances was alive. She would be so happy to see you. I was remembering the day when you tried to milk the cow and she kicked over the milk bucket."

For some reason that has always stuck to her mind. And then, "I saw Cleo the other day. She came to visit her mother. She is still so beautiful. It's a shame the two of you could not work out your differences. Her mother says she still loves you."

"She or Cleo?" I ask, trying to confuse her.

"Cleo. And her mother. They both love you."

"It's good to know," I say.

"Wouldn't it be wonderful if the two of you would get together again? You could get married again. This time we would have the reception in our house. Do you like the potato salad? I made it especially for you . . . the way you like it."

And when my father walks out she says, "He thinks I don't know he's going for a drink. I don't know why he has to sneak around like a little boy. He's got bottles hidden all over the house, the workshed, the garage, even under the seat of the car. Everywhere. He's getting senile, you know. Did he drive from the airport?"

"Yes."

"Oh, no. In the dark? How could you let him?"

"I didn't know he wasn't supposed to drive."

"I told him to let you drive. He didn't offer to let you drive?"

"No."

"I can't believe he did it. He can't drive very well anymore. And then at night. The only time I let him drive at night is when I'm with him to help him. You know it kills him. He used to be the best driver in the world. Now he can't do it. He needs to change his glasses but if I tell him then he won't do it. He doesn't care what happens to him as long as he does the opposite of what I want. That's the way we live."

"And you want me to marry to live like that?"

"You and Cleo wouldn't be like that."

"But that's exactly the way we were."

"No, it wasn't. You're not like your father. You take after me. Very pleasant and caring. . . . You need to talk to him."

"What do you want me to tell him?"

"You tell him that he needs to get new glasses. And tell him not to drink. The doctor said for him not to drink. It's bad for him."

"What else do you want me to tell him?"

"Not to drive. To change his glasses. To not drink. Tell him to throw those trousers away. And the shirt. Tell him not to eat fat. He eats the chicken skin and I read where that's bad for your cholesterol."

"Mom, he's almost eighty years old."

"He wouldn't be alive if it weren't for me."

I swear that after only thirty minutes I want to go back to Houston.

"You need a place of your own," she says. "Too bad you and Cleo had to sell the house. What a beautiful house it was. And in such a good neighborhood. What a shame. Have you seen the old neighbors?"

"Yes. I went by the other day. The Wilsons invited me to a party."

"What a state you put them in when you and Cleo broke up. It was a shock to them."

"It was. But that's over, Mom. I have my life to live and that means without Cleo."

"The blows life hits us with. I often think that you and Cleo could have settled your differences if you two would not have been so stubborn. You can be as stubborn as your father."

"You just said I was like you. Pleasant and caring."

"Yes. But the stubbornness you take after your father."

The clouds are beginning to darken over the dry empty fields plowed to perfection in perfectly straight lines, perfectly placed row upon row waiting for the rain to germinate the seed into sorghum.

My father sees me looking at the fields and he says, "They planted hygeia." Which means sorghum to him. *"La siembran hoy y sale muy bajita con mucha espiga,"* he says. As opposed to the old days when the sorghum was tall and had a small head. *"Gringos chinga'os saben todo,"* he says. This time he leans down and picks up his leg by the ankle with his hands and helps it over the knee to complete the crossing of the leg. He shifts about and gets more comfortable. He has the bottle between his legs. "Another shot?" he asks me and I agree. He goes through the same routine with his "Ahhhhhhhhs" and grimaces until he tells me he loves it. "Your mother doesn't know I brought this," he says.

My mother stayed home. She does not like her sister-in-law. Many years ago her sister-in-law said things about her and my mother has never forgiven her for it. But my mother will not discuss the problem with me. She finds this to be another reason that I might not agree with her and she will then turn off the conversation and go to something else. But the minute I leave she will tear into me with my father for what I have done with my life. I know. My father tells me everything. Not that he particularly wants me to know everything but it's his way of getting me not to like my mother. He starts, "You know how mean your mother can be with me when you're not around. She talks about you and not too kindly. She loves Cleo more than you. She went to see Cleo the other day when she was here. Did she tell you that?"

"Yes," I answer.

"She did? I thought she wouldn't tell you because she knows she did the wrong thing. She's mean, I tell you. And now that she's getting old I don't know what to do. Maybe we ought to see about getting someone to take care of her. I can't take care of her, not in the condition I'm in."

"Me duele la pinche pierna," he says. "Your mother says it's the drinking but you know her. Everything is the drinking. The other day I had a little diarrhea and she said it was the drinking. I didn't tell her I ate chicken skin. That gives me diarrhea."

"Then why do you eat it?"

"I like it. You know, your mother doesn't want me to eat chicken skin. She watches her cholesterol. I like chicken skin."

"I'd rather not talk about it," I say. I wish he didn't tell me about his bowel movements. It's something I don't want to talk about.

"She doesn't want me to drink but drinking is the only thing that keeps me from going crazy around her."

He reminds me again about the speed limit at Agua Dulce. *"Los pinches polecías se esconden detrás de la casa de los bomberos. Ahí están los cabrones—sanavaviches—esperándote. Y tú pasas como un desgraciado—hecho madre—y te chingan. Te echan al bote los putos. Son puro shit cow."*

It is barely sprinkling and I don't know whether to start the windshield wipers or not. If I do it may make matters worse. Since it is his car he reaches across me and gets them going, thinking that I might not want to use them. It's all right if I use them but he won't. They wear out, you know. He adjusts them and now we have a muddy mess on the windshield. The topsoil blowing in the wind with the little sprinkle has turned the whole thing into mud. He pushes a small button and the windshield washer comes on. He smiles. *"Pinches gringos. De todo saben,"* he says.

He hasn't worked in eighteen years. He retired from the highway department where he worked like a mule—his nickname—all his adult life. His skin has turned an ashen color where at one time, in his working days, he was dark. *"No salgo al sol. Aquí estoy como un joto adentro de la casa."* He reflects for a moment and I know he is trying to capture some incident from long ago. His lip begins to tremble. He is rubbing his fingertips against his thumb over and over again. He says, "Then they wouldn't call me. Remember?"

I remember and I tell him. He was old. He had lost all respect from the road crews. At night, when the roads were icing over, he would not be called on to help. He would find out about it in the morning.

"It was Oscar," he says. "He never liked me. And the reason is that I knew he couldn't do the work. I could do the work of two men. The Mule, they called me. And for good reason. And Oscar was jealous. He always was. The other men would tell me. When he got to be foreman he tried to break me. He tried to make me quit by giving me more work than anyone else. I never gave in. There wasn't a job I wouldn't do. That's why they called me The Mule."

"Is Oscar dead?" I ask.

"No," my father says, "the sanavaviche is alive. Retired. Doesn't go out anymore. Remember he used to be at the pool hall drinking beer every night. You used to hate him for what he did to me, remember?"

"Yes. We all hated him."

"You wanted to break a cue stick over his head when he was drunk. Remember?"

"Yes."

It has begun to rain hard. The familiar smell of wet soil is in the air. How many thoughts come back to me with the smell of wet soil. I am in the fields following a team of mules. I am on horseback behind my grandfather going into town for supplies. We have taken the mare in heat to be bred close to Freer and we have been on horseback for a day. I am at the top of the hill where the little house stood, helping my grandfather cut the clouds with a knife to keep the storms away. My grandmother is suddenly by my side. I can feel her warmth. My mother is bathing me in the old tub, pitching ladles of warm water over my head, singing a song to make me sleepy. I am in my mother's arms in the rocking chair. My father, young and robust, has come from work and he is outside cleaning himself with soap and water from the outside spigot.

"*Qué piensas?*" my father asks.

Grudgingly I return to the present. "*De nada,*" I reply.

The smell of wet soil has turned me. Now I feel a part of the land and I don't want to leave. My senses have filled me with nostalgia, with a *querencia,* and driven me back home.

We got through Agua Dulce without a speeding ticket. The patrolman was not hiding behind the fire station as he has told me. He takes out his bottle and takes a swig. He offers me some and I take it and have a small nip just to satisfy him.

His sister is widowed and she is not expecting us, which is the typical way in South Texas of dropping in uninvited and unannounced. Although we have all day, he wants to be in Corpus at ten in the morning. I check the car clock and we are on time, maybe a little ahead. But not enough to satisfy my father. We should have left earlier. "You never know when something might happen. A flat. What if we have a flat and don't have a spare?"

"You don't have a spare?"

"Sure I have a spare. You think I'm crazy? Driving without a spare? I've got two spares."

"So we have a spare."

"We have two spares."

"Why are you worried about not having a spare?"

"I say, 'What if we didn't have a spare?'"

"But you have a spare."

"I know I have a spare. I always have a spare. Two spares. Why are you shaking your head?"

"Nothing. Forget it."

We pass Banquete and I don't remember going through it. Last night I noticed that it has become even smaller than what it used to be, like my father and mother. The whole of the main street is abandoned. The traffic light has been disconnected. The two or three silos for sorghum have been abandoned. Now the sorghum is going direct to the ship channel in Corpus.

Robstown is next and we go through the new cutoff, turn south on 77 and then get off at the 44 exit.

My father says, "Here in Robstown is where they killed your mother's nephew. Do you remember?"

"Yes," I say.

"They say he was one of the other ones. You know what I mean?"

"Yes, I know what you mean."

"Poor boy. He was young. Got in with the wrong crowd. There are a lot of bad people in Robstown. And Corpus too. Yes, sir. You see that abandoned store over there?" He points out of the window to his right.

"That big one?"

"Yes. That used to be a Wal-Mart. They had to close it down."

"I've never heard of Wal-Mart closing. What happened?"

"The employees stealing. They stole so much they had to close it down. Now they don't have a job. Crazy, isn't it? *Están locos. . . . Ni tan locos. Están todos en welfare.* The whole town is on welfare. Why should they work? The government gives them food, houses to live in, spending money. Same way in our town. Nobody is working anymore. I wonder where the government gets all that money?"

"From the people that work."

"How long can it go on? It can't go on forever."

"It will stop one of these days. You'll hear a lot of crying."

"So they killed the poor boy. They slit his throat. Took him to a dirt road out of town and killed him. They say all of them were on marijuana. Be careful with marijuana, son. Marijuana kills you. . . . I'll never forget that your mother's cousin was on marijuana. Used to sell it. He tried to sell it to me one time and I told him to leave me alone. If my father would have found me with marijuana he would have killed me. But this man, he sold it. Always carried it in a case in his car. He smoked it all the time. . . .Well, that's why they killed the young boy. He was one of the other kind and he smoked marijuana so they killed him. A lot of people don't like people of the other kind. You know what I mean? Me? I don't care. Two of my nephews are of the other kind and I like them. Your cousins. You know who they are."

"I know who they are," I say. This is common knowledge.

"One of them came to work with me one time. Your uncle wanted to make a man out of him. He thought if he worked on the highway in the sun with a pick and axe he would become a man. But he spent the day under the shade of the truck trying to get out of the sun. So the next day we leave him behind at the warehouse and when we come back he has cleaned the warehouse and set up pictures on the walls and made places for us to sit. He has picked flowers and put them in water inside hubcaps. It was nice. He did a good job. But his father came for him. Why do you think they're that way? He never became a man. Do you think if he had worked with me that he would have become a man?"

"No. Not the way you think of a man."

"No?"

"No. They are born that way. They can't change."

"That's what I believe too. This boy never changed. Never became a man. His father tried to make him a man but he never did. Your mother says that the boy's mother pinched him in church all the time and that's why he turned out the way he did."

We are on the outskirts of Corpus Christi. We pass by the airport, the same one my father picked me up from last night. It has stopped raining and the smell of wet soil is gone. The sight of the airport has changed my mind again. Now I wish it were Sunday, tomorrow, and that I would be turning into the airport road and that I would be leaving.

My father knows his way around the new Corpus Christi freeway and he tells me where to get off. After a while I recognize the streets but I let him tell me where to turn. Then he says, "There. Right there is the house. Stop. Stop. Go into the driveway. What do you think of the house?"

His sister has painted the house pink and trimmed it in a dark green, greener than his trousers. She has had the composition roof painted the same green. The house stands out, to say the least, but in this neighborhood not as much as one would think.

"Beautiful house," my dad says. "How do you like the colors?"

It bothers me to think that if I had stayed to live in South Texas that I would have approved of those colors. It's hard for me to believe but it's very possibly true. I don't know what gods to thank but I have escaped and I am so glad. Now my senses have me on the airplane and on the way home. I wish the flight were in the morning instead of the afternoon. I know I will try not to come back for a long time.

"She chose the colors herself," my father says.

I could say something but I feel it better to leave things alone. I get out of the car and go around to open the door for my father. He needs help getting out. His legs have not moved in a while and they are numb. I take his legs and turn them out, toward me. They are dangling above the driveway. I take him by the shoulders and pull him toward me. He is standing but not very steady. He needs help for the first few steps and then he gathers momentum and he is on his own, unsteady, but on his own. He stops at the sidewalk and says, "Isn't the house beautiful? Didn't she do a good job?"

"Beautiful," I say. "It should be in *House Beautiful.*"

"How's that?"

"The magazine. It should be in a magazine."

"Well," my father says, "don't get carried away. It's not that beautiful. But for the neighborhood? Look around you. It's the brightest house in the neighborhood."

My aunt has spared no expense. She has gone to the junkyard and gotten several large tractor tires and has painted them different pastels. She has laid them flat on the ground, filled them with soil and she has planted vines in them. I walk as cautiously up the stairs as my father in front of me. I am anticipating the mean dog to come out from under the porch. I don't have long to wait. The dog is out and climbing the stair right behind me. He is growling and barking. My father is trying to get on as fast as he can so that he can reach the door before the dog does. But we are not fast enough. The dog, a large brown beast with a dark muzzle, has placed himself on the door and is not going to let us knock. My father is trying to kick the dog but his efforts are so feeble that the dog won't even notice him. The dog is biting at the air. My father comes around to hide behind me.

"Tell him to leave," my father says.

"Leave," I say.

The dog growls at me.

My father says, "You've got to say it with authority. In a big voice."

"Well, you do it," I say.

"Like this," my father says and he lowers his voice to gain some authority to it. "Go!" he shouts.

The dog will not move. My father says, *"Sanavaviche. Perro hijo de su chingada madre."* Next he yells for his sister. No one is home. The next noise we hear is the crunching of oyster shell under someone's feet. It is the neighbor who is coming from the next house to see who we are. She says that my aunt is in the hospital. She was taken earlier this morning. The dog must belong to her. She talks to the dog and the dog goes to sit by her side. My aunt is at Memorial Hospital. The neighbor tells us how to get to the hospital and we leave.

I am feeling bad about the house, about my aunt. But I hate that she likes pink and green for house colors and that my father approves because this is what the Anglo will showcase as being Hispanic. Why do we make ourselves so vulnerable? So I go from hating my aunt to hating the Anglo for using the ignorant and showcasing them as the best we have to offer. If I know the Anglo press they will find an excuse to put this house in the newspaper. Now I see the low-rider, the pachuco, the poorly educated, their children dancing in costumes like freaks being thrown at us as being the true Hispanic, as if all that we can do is dance. I see the low-rider exhibit in the Houston Museum of Fine Arts. What an insult. Let's compare like to like: The low-rider and the toothless hillbilly. Let's have the toothless hillbilly and his rusty car in the Houston Museum of Fine Arts. Let's say he represents the Anglo culture. Let's see his children dance barefooted in the dung infested yard. Let's compare the ignorant against the ignorant. The good against the good.

I realize that I am engaging in an internal argument set off by house colors but sometimes that is enough to set me off. My father is watching me mouthing words.

"What's the matter?" he says. "Are you worried about your aunt?"

"No," I say. "I was just thinking."

"What did you think about the house?" he asks.

"It looks like hell," I reply. "Why can't she paint the damn house white?"

"She wanted it to be colorful," he says.

"If you are in the majority you can be colorful. If you are in the minority you paint it white."

"You're angry. Why?"

"Because," I say.

"Because why?"

"You wouldn't understand."

We arrive at Memorial Hospital. We have to park far away from the entrance and it takes us forever to get there. I check with the office and my aunt is not there. I ask them to call around and they are nice to do so. We locate her at Doctors' Hospital. The woman there gives us directions and we go off again.

Doctors' Hospital is new and is on the way out of town, on the way to the airport. So I am back where I started from again. This time I drop off my father at the entrance and go park. We locate my aunt and she is on the fifth floor. When we enter the room she is sitting up watching television. She is watching the president on the news. She loves Clinton, which makes me hate her even more. Whoever said that all of us should vote should have his head examined. By now I have devised a plan where her vote counts for one tenth of mine. The ignorance factor. She turns the television off and she and my father embrace. She shakes my hand. The doctors have not figured out what her problem is. Her doctor is out of town and the doctor covering for him has come. He asked her name, looked at her tongue and was gone. He will not return until tomorrow afternoon. There have been six other doctors to see her, none of which she could understand. Two were from India. Two were from Pakistan and two were from the Philippines. The nurse comes in and asks us to step out into the hallway. Presently she comes out with some samples and walks past us. She tells us we can go back in. It will be tomorrow before the results will be known. My aunt is not in pain. She feels good. She looks like she could be in a motel watching television. Her problem, she says, is that she is on Medicare and the doctor wants her in a hospital two or three times a year.

"But your neighbor said you almost fainted," my dad says.

"What does she know," my aunt says with a wave of the hand.

I answer the usual questions and we visit for a while before I tell them that we must leave. I have to stop at Alice to buy groceries, a ritual that my father enjoys. My aunt seems relieved that we are leaving so that she can return to her television.

She says, "Don't worry about me. I'm OK. I'll be out on Monday or Tuesday. He only keeps me here a few days."

"Remember I was in the hospital last month," my dad says and it surprises me. This is the first time I've heard about it.

"You were in the hospital?" I ask.

"Just a checkup," he says. "Nothing serious. We didn't want for you to know. I had a cold. Medicare pays for everything."

"I think I have a cold too," says my aunt. "I think I'll have them check for that while I'm here."

I go for the car and leave my dad standing outside at the entrance. Our trip to Corpus was for nothing but my father is very satisfied that he has done something for today. Once he gets in the car he curses and I ask him if he has a problem. He has forgotten to urinate. I help him out of the car. I watch as he gets out slowly and walks to the front door. He has the wrong door, the exit door, and it won't open. He stomps on the mat in front of the door to see if it will open but it doesn't. I tell him to try the other door and he steps over to the other door and it opens. I watch him go in, still unsteady on his feet. The door closes behind him and I lose sight of him. I drive around the parking lot slowly, trying to time his exit. After a long time I see him come out and I go and pick him up. He has urinated all over the front of his trousers. I get out and open the door and help him in. He notices the urine on his trousers and he tells me it is water from the faucet where he washed his hands.

Finally, night comes. I am thankful. We have talked ourselves full. We ate earlier. My mother fixed her usual when I come and my father and I barbecued some ribs. We drank beer and sneaked a shot once in a while. My mother has fallen asleep during the news. My father can hardly keep his eyes open. I can go to bed, to sleep. I think of myself awake in the morning. I will stay in bed late, rise, shower, and then eat a late breakfast. My mother and father will have eaten and the eggs will be in a plate by the stove ready to be fried. For how many years has my mother been doing that? When did it all begin and what made it a habit from which she never deviated? By the time I eat breakfast and read the paper my father will be pestering me to get packed so that he can take me to the airport. My mother will go with us. She wants to help him drive at night. The day will be over and I will be on the plane, very thankful that the weekend has come to an end.

———·———

In the morning I stay in bed till ten. I am thinking. Then I go down for breakfast. The eggs are on the saucer where I knew they would be. My mother is in the next room watching television. My father is with her reading the paper. They come into the kitchen and Mom serves me coffee and then goes to fry my eggs. I sit down.

"Did you sleep well?" my mom asks.

"The mattress is getting old," my father says. "We need to buy a new one as soon as we can afford it."

"I slept very well," I say.

My father doesn't know how to please me so he hands over the newspaper.

I say, "No, Dad. You read it first."

Mom says, "I'll have your eggs done in a second."

"Remember," my dad says, "that we have to take off early for the airport. Your mom is going with us."

I am home.

Always Verbena

He felt a mantle of dread as he looked from the cab window down from the freeway at the old neighborhood—the nondescript streets, the sameness of the housetops, the evenness of the equilaterally fenced yards—proof he had not outlived the despondency which had accompanied him when he fled. And when the cab took the freeway exit he was raked through the emotions of still another pain: He began to be overcome with nostalgia.

The cab driver looked at him through the rearview mirror and noticed the change, the quiet discomfort in his face. "Are you okay?" he asked, adjusting the mirror.

"Yes," he replied, thinking he did not need to explain anything to any stranger.

The cab driver said, "You still want me to pick you up in an hour?"

"Yes," he replied.

"The old neighborhood?" the cab driver correctly guessed.

"Yes."

"You don't get by often?"

"No," he said.

At the intersection of the feeder road and Main Street, on the northeast corner, he saw the old drugstore. Somehow the business had survived the freeway. The building had grown gritty and blue. The stucco overhang above the front door, which had supported the sign, was gone.

When he had left, in the dark of night, the drugstore was the last building in the neighborhood he had seen, the last testimonial of his heartache on that fateful night. Now there were other buildings on the corner, a pawn shop next to the drugstore. Across the street was a hardware store. That was new. Across the freeway he could see a hamburger place. Across from it was a taquería next to a gas station.

The cab driver turned right and all of a sudden he could see Main Street, not the real Main Street, the one downtown, but the Main Street of the barrio.

Nothing much had changed. The street was the same, the same noise, the same smells, what looked like the same type of people, all enhancing his nostalgia. The buildings were still there. Only the store signs had changed. Where he remembered the bakery to be was a laundromat. Next to the laundromat he remembered was the bicycle shop. That was gone. In its place was a pizza delivery store. A few blocks down the street he saw the new place for the bakery. It was now where the tire shop had been. And so it went, on and on, his memory being erased by the new storefronts.

He remembered little Beatrice had fallen down on the side-walk in front of the big department store and had skinned her knees. What an insignificant episode to be so etched in his memory, insignificant compared to what had happened after-wards.

The cab driver said, "Over here," and he pointed to his right at a vacant lot, "they're going to build a new grocery store."

Across the street was the old Vincent's Grocery Store. A few cars were in the parking lot. Next to the grocery store was the large parking lot for the hospital. Little Beatrice and Roberto had been born there. He could remember exactly the events. How time had passed him by.

Today was Friday. Everything seemed to happen on Friday. He was born on a Friday. Both his parents had died on Friday. He had married Beatrice on a Friday. He had left that night on a Friday. His daughter, little Beatrice, had died on a Friday, injured on Monday but died on Friday. In one week he was gone.

"Where are you from?" the cab driver asked.

"Texas," he answered.

"What part?"

"Houston."

"Did you have a good flight?"

"Yes. A little bumpy at times but a good flight."

The cab driver looked at him through the mirror and said, "I always ask about the flight. Makes good conversation. A guy told me once that he was almost killed in a flight. He had a strange story. . . . I've been to Houston. Most people hate the weather in Houston but I liked it. I mean, what can you say? Sure, it's humid. But so are other towns. Lots of jobs in Houston. I heard a man can make twenty dollars an hour just sweeping in one of those refineries."

"Yeah," he said, not interested in the conversation. His mind was taking in so much he could hardly keep up with the cab driver.

The cab driver sensed his dilemma and said, "I'm sorry. I didn't mean to bother you. I won't talk anymore. . . . Let me say one thing though. Here at this intersection is going to be a bowling alley."

The cab driver had stopped at the traffic light and he was tapping his fingers on the steering wheel. "A bowling alley," he repeated softly to himself and then whistled.

He had not forgotten the city blocks. Ten. And then the cab turned to the right, went two blocks and then turned left. He looked through the window at the street sign and read: Second Street. The old street.

There on the corner, little Beatrice, five years old, waited for him, sitting at the curb. In her hands was her favorite doll. She appeared to have been crying. Fighting, he figured, with Roberto, ten. Fighting about something. Soon he would be told.

He had to stop the car in front of little Beatrice and he leaned across and opened the door. She was still sitting on the curb, sulking. She was rubbing her doll against her cheek. He asked her to climb in and she did but with so much reluctance that he felt she would be angry with him.

"What happened?" he asked.

"I'm angry," she replied.

"What did Roberto do now?"

"I'm not angry at Roberto," she said.

"Then who?"

"You," she said. "I'm angry at you."

The cab driver heard him speaking to himself and said, "You okay?"

"I'm okay," he said.

"You got relatives here?"

"Yes. In a way. I have relatives here."

"This a business trip or pleasure?"

"Neither," he said.

"Just messing around?"

"No. Not really. I have come for my son's funeral," he said.

The cab driver glued his eyes nervously to the road and said, "Sorry about that."

"That's all right," he said. "How could you have known?"

"If it means anything to you, I lost a son in Vietnam. So I know how you feel. I loved that boy. I've never been the same since. The old lady? Well, what can I tell you. She won't ever be the same either." The cab driver looked both ways at the intersection before crossing. "It's just not the same. . . . Anyway, I'm sorry to hear that. . . . You need to forgive me for asking so many questions. It's just that driving a cab is a lonely business. You kind of want to hear what the other guy is thinking . . . what he's up to. What his problems are. You know what I mean?"

"Yes. I understand," he said.

A block had gone by and little Beatrice was sitting in the front seat still angry with him. He was trying to explain what had happened. How he had felt. Why he had left. But little Beatrice was shaking her head so that she could not hear. And then Roberto appeared on the sidewalk running alongside the car. He told Roberto not to run. He might fall.

He gave out a small cry but he was able to stifle it with his palm. Then, as much as he fought it, he had a tear in his eye.

The cab driver looked at him through the rearview mirror. "It's all right to cry," he said. "The doctor told us it was good to cry."

He knew to the day how many years it had been. Those things one never forgets. Those things one always remembers. Those things cling to the memory like maggots that feed on the soul.

Next Friday it would be nineteen years. Roberto then was twenty-nine when he died. He could not remember Roberto's birthday. Little Beatrice, yes. January twenty-second. It seemed that Roberto had been born in August because he remembered that all his birthdays were hot.

Little Beatrice was crying. Outside, Roberto continued to run alongside the car even though he had told him not to. He tried to comfort little Beatrice by stroking the top of her head but she shoved his hand away. He was hurting her, she said.

The taxi driver said, stopping, "Well, this looks like the house. Am I right?" He looked down at the pad by his side. He had written the address at the airport. He looked up and matched the house number. "Yep, this is it," he said.

Antonio looked out through the open window. He knew Beatrice had painted the house several times by now but always white and always with the red trim. He knew she was not about to change. It was the old house, small, but neat with the porch in front. He had added the porch to give the house a better facade, to improve the blocklike appearance of the front. It still leaked where he had connected the porch to the front wall. He could see the streaks of rainwater. Beatrice had the flower garden on either side of the porch steps. She had put the flower garden in as he worked on the porch. Verbena. That's what she planted. Always verbena. The sidewalk leading to the house had cracked long ago.

"Is this the residence of Antonio García?"

The voice on the phone had appeared familiar. It was the feeling of a familiar voice changed by time. The familiarity was there but he could not be sure.

"Yes," he said into the phone.

"Is this Antonio García?"

Now he recognized the voice. It was Beatrice. "Beatrice?" he said. "Is that you?"

There was a momentary silence and he could hear her sobbing. "It's me," she said, finally.

"Why are you crying?"

"It's Roberto," she said. "He died early this morning. I thought you ought to know. You don't have to come."

"I want to come," he said. "How did he die?"

"He died of AIDS," she said. "I wanted to tell you in case you didn't want to come. I know how you used to be about those things."

"I want to come."

"I thought that if I told you he died of AIDS that you wouldn't want to come."

"I've told you that I want to come. Did he suffer?"

"Yes. Very much. He spoke about you. In his last days—for some reason—he wanted you to come see him. For some reason he remembered things the two of you had done years ago."

"You should have called me. I would have come."

He could hear her sniffling. She said, "Well, I never know what to do. I never know who is forgiven and who is not."

"So you still want me to pick you up in an hour?" the cab driver said.

Antonio could not take his eyes off the house. "Yes," he said. "If you don't mind?"

"No, sir," said the cab driver, "I don't mind. But it may be another driver. You never know. I might get a fare to the airport again."

"As long as I get someone to pick me up in an hour I'll be fine," Antonio said. He hesitated to open the door.

The cab driver said, "It's hard, I know. When my son died that was the hardest thing . . . to tell someone he had died. It was hardest that first day."

"She knows he died. She was the one who told me."

"Then it won't be so hard," the cab driver said. He opened the door and went to the trunk and opened it to get his luggage.

Antonio opened the door and stepped out. His luggage was on the sidewalk. He looked into the cab to read the meter. He paid the cab driver and the cab driver shook his hand.

"Good luck," the cab driver said, taking the fare and folding it into the wad of money he had removed from his pocket.

Antonio nodded and turned toward the house. The cab driver drove off, waving. Antonio picked up his suitcase and suit bag and walked to the gate. He opened the gate and stepped into the yard. He walked slowly, as if expecting something to happen, someone to shout at him, someone to tell him to go away. He climbed the porch steps and knocked on the door. He could hear Beatrice coming toward the door. And then, typical of her, she stopped to rearrange something. The figurine on the table-top was not centered. The magazines were out of order. She turned on the last lamp. There had not been enough light. Finally she came to the door and opened it.

He had not known what to expect after all these years. She had aged well. How old was she? Fifty-nine. She had to be fifty-nine. The numbers came to his head to interfere with the sight of her and then he threw the numbers out of his mind in order to concentrate on that moment. The two were momentarily stunned. To her he appeared to have aged well also. He was sixty. She remembered his birth date—May seventh. She still had it on her calendar.

"Beatrice?" he said. "Is this you?"

"Yes," she said. "I'm assuming it's you, Antonio?"

"Yes, it's me," he answered. "May I come in?"

"Yes . . . of course," she said. "Come in. You are at your house."

He began to go through the door when she noticed his luggage. "Here," she said, "I'll take that."

"No need to," he said, stopping her, "I can leave it out here. I only plan to stay for an hour. You see, I need to go see Roberto and then I will find a place to stay. If you would be kind enough to tell me where the funeral home is."

She picked up the suitcase and suit bag and said, "Roberto has been cremated. That was his wish. And you will stay here . . . in Roberto's old room. And I won't hear anything to the contrary. I won't have you spending good money on hotels when I have room."

"That's very good of you," Antonio said. "It's just that . . ."

"I know," Beatrice said. "I know how you must feel."

"I'm lost," he said.

Antonio helped Beatrice with the luggage and she directed him to Roberto's room. Antonio felt Roberto's presence as he walked in. He felt Roberto's laughter, his joy for life. He said, "Maybe I should stay somewhere else," he said.

"I said," Beatrice said, "that I would not let you stay anywhere but here. In Roberto's room. I'll give you time to freshen up."

She walked out of the room leaving him alone with his demons. Next door was little Beatrice's room. He did not know if he could stand to go there. He could hear Beatrice in the kitchen moving pots and pans around.

"Sit at the table," Beatrice said to him when he came out of Roberto's room. "What do you want? I have milk. Coffee. Soft drinks. The neighbors have brought over all kinds of food. We will never be able to finish all of this. Maybe tomorrow after the services Roberto's friends can eat it all."

He sat down at the table filled with food. "When did Roberto find out he had AIDS?" he asked.

"Two years ago. Then is when he set out to track you. He found out where you lived. Your telephone. He wanted you to come see him but I did not want him to call you. I felt that you would not want to come and then he would have had his heart broken over that. He had enough worries and pain that I didn't think he should add to them."

"I told you I would have come."

She said, "The Antonio I knew would not have come."

"I'm a different Antonio now."

"You have grown?"

"I have changed. The years change us all."

"Roberto did not last long. Poor Roberto. I told you he suffered a lot. His death—when it finally came—was a blessing."

"You seem to be taking it well."

"I let go of him a long time ago. I had no more to give. So at the end, when he was suffering so much, I prayed that he die. I was tired of seeing my son go through what he did. . . . What did you say you wanted?"

"A soda, please."

"Well, then a soda you will have."

"On the phone you said the funeral was tomorrow at ten?"

"Tomorrow," she said. "Ten o'clock."

Beatrice opened the refrigerator and took out a soda and opened it and placed it with a glass full of ice in front of him. She took a soda and ice for herself and she sat across the table.

"So," she said, "how have you been?"

"You've changed," he said.

"We have all changed. Like you say . . . the years change us all."

"You have changed a lot, I mean. I didn't know what to expect. How you would be."

"And?"

"I find you very strong."

"I hope you mean that as a compliment."

"I do. I really do. I also find you very beautiful. I did not . . . "

"Know what to expect? A wrinkled old woman?"

Antonio gave out a little laugh. "I'm so nervous I don't know what I'm saying. Forgive me," he said.

She leaned forward on the table and said, "Tell me about yourself. Did you ever get married? Did you have a family? Do you have grandchildren?"

"No," he said. "I never got married. I went out like everyone else but I never got married."

"You never found the right woman," Beatrice said.

"No. I guess I didn't. I never . . . . " He shrugged to say that he would rather not complete his thoughts.

"You never what?" Beatrice asked.

"Nothing. It's just thoughts that remained with me . . . that I still have, by the way. And you? Did you get married?"

"No."

"Why not?"

"I don't know . . . well, actually I do."

"I never felt I was worth another try."

"Poor you, Antonio. You will not forgive yourself."

"No. . . . I can't seem to."

"For my part, I came to realize that I could not bring little Beatrice back. I wanted to so badly. How many times I would have died for her. But I couldn't. It just couldn't be. I asked God to take me a hundred times and he wouldn't. In the end God was of no use. And if God is of no use what chance do I have? I let go."

"You are a lot stronger than I. I don't know what to say."

"Oh, there are a lot of things one could say."

"I know what you mean but I'm not the one to say them."

"So what are you going to do? Go to the funeral and then run away again? Are those your plans? Or are you keeping them a secret?"

Antonio was taken aback. He said, "If you want I can leave. I didn't want to stay here."

Beatrice sat back on her chair and said, "I'm sorry. I didn't mean to attack you. But there is some anger here in my heart. You know that."

"I could not blame you," Antonio said. "It's just that if we are going to bring back everything again I am not staying. You may be stronger than I am but I can always walk out. . . . I guess that's what I'm the best at doing."

Beatrice said, "Let's not talk of that again. Today is a new day. Did you notice I planted verbenas?"

"Yes. Very beautiful. I smelled them on the way up the stairs."

Beatrice stood up, a smile on her face. She said, "You would never guess who helped me plant verbenas."

He was surprised to see her smile so suddenly. He said, "I could never guess."

Beatrice went to him and took him by the hand. "Come, I have something to show you," she said. "Come with me."

Beatrice took him down the hallway, past Roberto's room. She noticed Antonio's hesitation when she stopped at little Beatrice's bedroom door. "Don't be afraid," she said. "I wouldn't hurt you."

Beatrice opened the door slightly and had him take a peek inside the room. It had been repainted. The furniture had been changed. Toys were strewn all over the floor. And on the bed he was startled to see a little girl asleep, curled up with a teddy bear. She had black hair and a very fine, delicate, face like little Beatrice. He felt his mind reel as if he could not sort out the reality of the moment. Or had he been taken back in time? He stepped back into the hallway to catch his breath.

"Who is she?" he asked Beatrice.

Beatrice said, "It's your granddaughter. Roberto's daughter."

"Roberto?" he asked, confused.

"Roberto was married briefly," Beatrice said. "She is Roberto's daughter."

"And his wife?"

"His ex-wife. A beautiful person," Beatrice said. "She is busy with the arrangements so I'm keeping her today. Oh, she stays with me often. She loves to come over."

"And what is her name?"

"Beatrice, after me."

"Could I touch her?"

"Sure you can touch her," Beatrice said. "She's tough, like me."

Antonio tiptoed into the room and went to the little girl's

bed. He ran his hand over her forehead and she moved slightly. He moved back and backed out of the room.

"She's beautiful," he whispered.

"That she is," Beatrice said. "What a surprise, huh?"

"What a beautiful surprise," he said. "I had no idea. No idea in the world."

They heard a car honking up front.

"Who could that be?" Beatrice said.

Antonio said, "The cab driver probably. He was supposed to come for me in an hour."

Antonio and Beatrice went to the front door and it was the cab driver. He was sitting inside the cab smoking a cigarette. When he saw Antonio and Beatrice on the porch he came out of the cab and walked to the front gate.

He said, "I didn't get a long fare. Are you ready?"

Antonio said, "No. I have changed my mind. I'm staying. I thank you just the same."

The cab driver scratched his head and said, "Then there's been a change in plans?"

"Yes," said Beatrice, "there's been a change in plans. And don't be so nosy."

"It's my job being nosy," the cab driver said. Then, as an afterthought, he said, "You want me to come to take you to the airport?"

"Yes," said Antonio. "If you don't mind."

"When and what time?"

"Tomorrow. My flight leaves at five."

"I'll pick you up at three-thirty. It may not be me," the cab driver said, "but if it's not me I'll get someone else to pick you up. I'll call it in. Again, I'd like to say that I'm sorry about your son."

"Thank you," said Antonio.

The cab driver went into the cab, started it and sped off.

When the little girl woke up she was introduced to her grandfather. She was apprehensive of him, staying close to her grandmother, peering at him from behind Beatrice's skirt. Antonio decided that he would just let matters be. She could come to him whenever she was ready. She reminded him of Roberto. She was self-reliant, very strong, and had an opinion on everything. She dominated Beatrice, had her waiting on her every wish.

Finally her curiosity got the best of her and she asked him, "And who are you?"

Antonio said, "I am your father's father. Your grandfather."

"Where have you been? Were you hiding?"

"Yes," Antonio replied.

She said, "I am four years old and I have never seen you before in my life. You just come once in a long time?"

Beatrice saved him from further embarrassment when she sent the child to her room to read. "Your mother will be here soon," Beatrice said. "Remember you promised to read a book before she got here."

Little Beatrice said, looking at Antonio, "I don't want him here."

Beatrice said, "Shame on you for saying something like that to your grandfather."

"He is not my grandfather. I have a grandfather."

"But you have two. Now say you're sorry."

The child smiled at Antonio and said, "I'm sorry."

Antonio said, "I accept your apologies."

The child sulked for a while but she returned to her room and closed the door. Beatrice said, "She minds very well. I hope you didn't take her too seriously. She's just jealous. She runs her mother off. She hates to have to share me with anyone."

"I can tell," said Antonio. "I can tell she is very smart."

"Oh, the things she says and does," Beatrice said. "You wouldn't believe me if I told you. I have a lot of fun with her.

She keeps me entertained. Whenever I'm sad I call Janie to bring her over. I think she wants to spend the night. That's her problem. She is planning on how she's going to ask her mother."

"Was she close to Roberto?" he asked.

"No," Beatrice said. "Roberto was in another world. Children were not in that world. He saw her once in a while but that was it. He remembered her birthday, Christmas, things like that, but close? No. When he died she didn't ask anything about it."

Antonio was sitting at the kitchen table and Beatrice was busy putting up dishes. He noticed the silence for the first time and he felt awkward, dispossessed. He felt a little better when Beatrice looked at him and said, "We are having company for dinner at seven. It's almost five. You must be tired. Why don't you take a nap. I'll wake you up at six . . . six-thirty."

Once back in Roberto's room he felt the presence of demons again which he knew he had to exorcize. Rather than flee, this time he would stay. He lay in bed and heard the sounds of the car, the movement of the wheels, the sudden stop. He saw Beatrice run from the house screaming, her face contorted into the most painful expression he had ever seen.

Roberto was sitting at the edge of the bed. He was smiling at him. Little Beatrice was on the floor playing with her teddy bear. "Where have you been?" asked Roberto and Antonio fell asleep before he could answer.

At six-thirty Beatrice knocked on the door and woke him. He took a shower and put on another suit. When he came out to the kitchen Beatrice admired his new shirt and tie and even little Beatrice smiled at him. Shortly, they heard a noise at the front door and heard it open. It was Janie, Roberto's ex-wife, who Beatrice introduced to Antonio. She had heard about him from Roberto. The two neighbors from either side and the one from across the street, all widows, came over also. They were delighted to meet Antonio. They were not living in the neighborhood when Antonio had left. The neighbor across the street, a lady named Maria, had lived there the longest and she and her husband had moved in ten years ago. Her husband had died last year.

"We're getting old," Maria said and everyone agreed and laughed.

By nine the party was over. Antonio had not had a chance to talk to Beatrice alone. After the party Janie stayed to help clean. Little Beatrice had her plan in place and she was able to finagle her way into spending the night. Antonio excused himself and went to bed at nine-thirty. He heard Janie leave at ten.

Shortly thereafter there was a stillness in the house which bothered him. The demons had returned to torment him. All around his bed he could see devils and spirits dancing about, making his night miserable. He tossed and turned and covered his face with the sheets but he kept going over that horrible day when he had accidentally killed his daughter. Slowly he fought back. He was crying as he tossed around. He became drenched in perspiration from the sheer movements of his body, the tremors, the thrashing, almost like seizures. And still the demons persisted. He had killed his daughter. He was about to get up and get dressed when he heard the knock on the door.

It was Beatrice. "Are you all right?" she asked.

How could he answer what he couldn't hear?

"Antonio?" Beatrice asked again. "Are you all right? Can I help you?"

She opened the door and found him in a state of shock. His eyes were open but he could not see. "How long have you been like this?" she said. He could not hear her words. She sat him up in bed. By this time little Beatrice was up with the commotion and she too was in the room. She wanted to know what had happened? Beatrice asked for her help. They both took Antonio and walked him into the living room and sat him on the sofa. Beatrice sat next to him and very gently lowered his head on to her lap where his tremors gradually subsided and he fell asleep while she stroked his head. Little Beatrice went to sleep at her feet.

"How long have you been like this?" she asked as he slept. She was crying.

There were many of Roberto's friends at the funeral as well as Beatrice's neighbors. Beatrice's sister had driven from Santa Monica with her husband. She did not speak to Antonio. Her husband did. He came over and shook his hand. They had not seen each other in many years. They spoke briefly and Antonio realized that Beatrice's sister did not want her husband to talk to him so he cut the conversation short. Beatrice's brother and his wife were there also and he did not speak to Antonio. He was more resentful, his stare full of hate.

One of Roberto's friends spoke about him briefly and that was all of the service. Afterwards, Beatrice took Antonio to little Beatrice's grave. They both cried and little Beatrice, the granddaughter, wanted to know why they were crying. From there they all went to the house.

By three o'clock in the afternoon the people had all left and Beatrice and Antonio were alone. He was in Roberto's room getting his things together while Beatrice sat on the porch in one of the chairs waiting for him. Presently he came out with his luggage.

"Come sit with me," said Beatrice. "You have some time. We have not spoken in a while."

Antonio sat next to Beatrice. He said, "It's been good to see you."

"Antonio," said Beatrice, "why didn't you ever call? Why didn't you tell me where you were? Why didn't you tell me you had suffered so much? Every night?"

"Every night, it seems," he said. "I was afraid to call."

"Afraid? Afraid of what?"

"Afraid of you."

Beatrice let out a little laugh. She said, "That's odd."

"Why do you say that?"

"Because I was afraid of you."

"Is that why you didn't call me? You were afraid?"

"I didn't want to find out where you were. I was afraid you would turn me down again. I couldn't take that. I loved you too much to be hurt again."

"I felt the same way."

"Antonio?" she said and then hesitated with a sigh. "We don't have much time. We're not young anymore. We can't be saying things we don't mean. Don't you agree?"

"Yes, I agree," said Antonio.

"Antonio, we don't have time for demons. Those things are in the past . . . If you want to know the truth, I love you. I have always loved you. That is why I never married again. There was no room in my heart for anyone else but you . . . I realize that in saying all of this you may turn me down. You may hurt me again. But that is the chance I have to take. You understand that this is my last time? There is no more time, Antonio."

Antonio felt the warmth of the love he had for her. He said, "You are a brave woman. Very brave. More brave than I could ever be. . . . I could never have said what you said. I could have never exposed myself to rejection. I was prepared to walk out silently. But now that it is out in the open I have to tell you that I love you more than anything else in the world. I have missed you more than I could ever say. . . . What I did was a foolish and immature thing. I thought I would have to live with you and the daily rejection. I could not have lived."

Beatrice took his hand and kissed it. She said, "I could not have been mean to you. It was not your fault. You have to understand that. It was not your fault."

Antonio wiped a tear from his eye and said, "You are a wonderful woman. Look at how much I have lost being without you."

"Your demons will be gone," Beatrice said. She too was crying.

The same cab driver drove up and stopped in front of the house. He got out and opened the trunk. He looked to the porch and saw Beatrice and Antonio. He said, "Are you ready, mister? You see I didn't get a long fare again."

Antonio got up from his chair and helped Beatrice up from hers. He carried his suitcase, Beatrice his suit bag. As they walked down the porch stairs they were met with the smell of verbena. When he reached the walkway Antonio bent down and took a bloom and gave it to Beatrice.

"Here," he said. "Your favorite flower."

"Verbena," said Beatrice, smelling the flower. "Always verbena."

And they both laughed.

They walked to the cab. The driver took the luggage and threw it in the trunk and slammed it shut.   He took a long look at the both of them and said, "You notice I'm not saying anything. I'm not being nosy."

Antonio stood in front of Beatrice and hesitated. Beatrice understood his indecision and she leaned toward him to show him she wanted to be held. He took her in his arms and hugged her. She gave him a small peck on the cheek and rearranged his tie. She said, smiling, "When will I see you again?"

Antonio released her, opened the cab door and said, "My dear lady, first, I've got things to do. Things to take care of. But I will be here Friday."

"With more luggage?" she asked.

"With more luggage," he said.

"That will be fine," she said. "I will be expecting you. I'll have your favorite meal."

"And I will bring the wine."

"Oh, my," she said, blushing, "I've never had wine."

"Friday you will have wine for the first time."

"How romantic it sounds."

"The most romantic evening you have ever had. . . . Do you realize," Antonio continued, "that everything seems to happen to me on Fridays?"

He gave Beatrice another hug and a kiss. He said, "Maybe start all over again?"

"I would love that," she said.

He stepped into the cab and he was gone. Beatrice stood at the sidewalk and watched as the taxi went the half block and turned left and disappeared. She stood for a while trying to see if she could spot the taxi on the freeway.

He could make out the house from the freeway. He thought he could see Beatrice standing in front, waving.

When he turned the corner he saw little Beatrice and Roberto skating on the sidewalk. They saw his car and began to wave excitedly. They were so happy to see him. They were making every effort to skate as fast as the car. He slowed down to allow them to keep up with him. He reached across the seat and rolled the window down.

"Hi, Dad," they yelled.

"Be careful," he said to them. They were waving at him, laughing, perfectly content and happy.

"Be careful," he said again.

The car driver heard him and said, "You okay?"

"Yes," he said. "I'm okay."

"Everything seemed to go okay?" the cab driver asked.

"Yes," Antonio replied. "Everything went fine."

Delivering Meat

Panchito was standing on the manhole cover while the rest of the boys counted slowly. Four. Five. Six. On they counted and Panchito stood on the fiery metal cover in the middle of August at twelve o'clock noon at one hundred and twelve degrees. The children slowed down as they reached sixty, taking two or three seconds in between numbers. Panchito could hardly stand the heat on his feet. He was perspiring. The heat was going up his feet, through his body and up to his head. But Panchito endured. In the end he stepped off the manhole cover and collected a penny from everyone. He had won the bet, had stayed put on the manhole cover for one minute, although the way his opposition counted made for a long minute. He stepped around on the hot sand as if his feet did not hurt him but he was in pain. As soon as the children were gone he would run home and run water from the outside faucet over his feet.

But good news arrived as he was collecting his money. One of the boys came running shouting that the butcher had fired his delivery boy for being late every morning this week. The butcher was looking for a new man. They did not give the messenger time to rest. They all ran for the butcher shop.

Amando, the butcher, was cutting meat on a wooden block when the whole party arrived. They all wanted the job. Amando looked them over and said, "Wait a while. We'll see who is man enough for this job."

Amando finished cutting his meat for the afternoon and placed it in the display cooler, arranging each piece of meat to enhance it's salability. He wiped his hands on his large apron and then he went to the rear of the butcher shop followed by the children. He stepped off a hundred yards. He said, "You boys are going to run from this line to the finish line. Whoever wins gets the job."

The boys lined up at the starting line and Amando made like the starter. "On your marks, get set . . . go!" There were so many runners that a few stumbled at the start. One of them was Panchito but he managed to gather speed and pass the runners along the way. He finished first. Amando gave him the job. One quarter a day. Work for six days a week. Sunday was a day of rest and church. He was to be available in an instant. He was to run, deliver the meat, get his money and return. If there were no deliveries to be made he was to sit at the front of the store and yell out that meat was available, that Amando had slaughtered a cow. He was not to fraternize with friends in front of the butcher shop. He was not to horseplay with friends that went by. He was to be respectful and alert at all times. He was to wear shoes in front of the butcher shop. It was up to him if he wore shoes when he ran his deliveries. He had to wear a hat that Amando would provide. It was a butcher's cap made of paper with the name of the butcher shop imprinted. It said, "Amando's Butcher Shop." If he lost the cap he would be docked a nickel. He would get a new cap once a week, on Monday. He would have to bathe every Saturday and he would be expected to wear decent clothes and that meant a long-sleeved shirt and long pants.

The heat on the day he began his career as a meat delivery boy was 116 degrees. It was 110 in the shade, if shade could be found.

He was sitting outside, telling everyone that Amando had slaughtered a cow that morning and that meat was available. He heard the phone ring and then he heard Amando's gruff voice. It sounded like an order. He was on his way. Amando came to the screen door and called him in.

"The widow Garcia needs a delivery," he said. "Do you know where she lives?"

Panchito said, "There are many widows Garcia."

Amando slapped him across the face. He said, "That's for being disrespectful to me. And there's more where that came from. The widow Garcia lives across the railroad tracks in the big house. That one."

Panchito said, rubbing his face, "I know who she is."

Amando said, "Let me fix her order. You wait here."

Panchito sat on the wooden barrel and took off his shoes. He watched as Amando reached into the cooler and grabbed a handful of hamburger meat. In the other hand he had a piece of transparent paper that he placed on the scale. He placed the meat on the paper and waited for the scale to settle. Then he read the magnified numbers on the scale cylinder. He opened the case again and grabbed a small amount and placed it on top of the meat on the scale. He said, peering through his half glasses at the scale, "With this lady you have to give her a little bit more than a pound. She weighs the meat, you know." He tore a piece of butcher paper off the roll and wrapped the meat. "Here," he said, handing the meat over to Panchito. "This is your life blood. Your job. Your reason for living. This is not meat. This is your life in a small container."

"Yes, sir," said Panchito.

Amando took a piece of pencil and marked the price on the outside: Twenty-five cents. "You see, Panchito? You see what I wrote?" he said.

"Yes, sir," said Panchito.

"Twenty-five cents. You must bring back twenty-five cents.

You see, Panchito, you must charge for what you sell. If you don't, you might as well get out of business. We are not into this business as a recreation. We are here to make money. Do you understand?"

"Yes," replied Panchito.

"Now go and don't let me see you again without twenty-five cents in your hand. And don't put the money in your pocket like it belongs to you. There is too much temptation for you if you put money in your pocket. Place it in your hand so that you understand that the money you carry is not yours. Do you understand?"

"Yes," said Panchito.

"Yes, what?" Amando inquired.

"Yes, sir."

Amando said, "Come over here," and Panchito went to stand in front of him. Amando backhanded him. "That's for being disrespectful," he said. "And there's plenty more where that came from."

"Yes, sir," said Panchito. Now the other side of his face was red.

"Go," said Amando. "I've given you enough advice to last you a lifetime."

Panchito started for the front door when Amando stopped him. He said, "All deliveries start from the back door, Panchito. You don't see the cook in the restaurant up front walking through the front door, do you?"

"No, sir," said Panchito.

"All employees start business through the back door. The front door is reserved for our customers, Panchito. Do you know what a customer is?"

"Yes, sir," said Panchito.

"Now leave," said Amando and this time Panchito took off through the back door.

He felt the immediate heat of the ground. His feet ached for a second and then he got used to the heat. He ran directly out and across the vacant yard behind the butcher shop. He jumped down the incline and down to the sidewalk and he found the concrete to be hotter than the ground. He poured on the speed. He went one block, two blocks south toward the railroad tracks. At the railroad tracks he turned west and went one more block. He could see the widow's house and he turned right, south again. He slowed to a walk in front of the house and he opened the gate and walked up the sidewalk to the porch and knocked. He heard the widow inside and then he heard her say something. He held the package of meat against his side.

The widow opened the screen door and looked over his head as though she had not seen him. She looked about and finally she looked down to him and asked for the meat. "What piece of garbage did Amando send me now?" she said, making a face at Panchito.

Panchito handed her the meat and said, "One pound of hamburger meat. A little over a pound to be exact. Amando says you weigh the meat."

"He does, does he? Well, why would you think I do that? Not because I enjoy it, young man. It is because he is dishonest. You wait here."

Panchito waited outside while the widow went inside. He could hear her taking out pots and pans, looking for her scale. Presently she came to the door and invited Panchito in. "I want you to see something," she said. Panchito followed her in.

The room was dark and cool. The widow had an oscillating fan on top of a table. Panchito followed her into the kitchen. The widow had the hamburger meat on the scale.

"See for yourself," she said, pointing at the scale.

Panchito went to the scale and read it. It was well short of a pound on her scale.

"You see what I mean?" she said. "The man is completely dishonest. You take that package of meat back and you tell Amando that if he has to cheat an old widow to make a living he ought to close his shop and go pray for his soul because if anyone is going to go to hell it is him. You tell him that. Do you understand, young man?"

"Yes, ma'am," said Panchito.

"And who are you, young man? From what family?"

Panchito said, "My mother is Isabel Garcia. My father is dead."

"You are the grandchild of Gabriel and Maria Garcia?"

"Yes, ma'am," said Panchito.

"Your father is not dead, young man," the widow said. "You have been lied to. Your father lives in San Antonio. He left your mother."

"My father is dead," Panchito said.

"You have been told that so many times that you actually believe it. Your father is not dead. Take my word for it. Now go and take the meat back and tell Amando that when I order a pound of hamburger meat I expect to get a pound of hamburger meat."

Panchito took the meat off the scale and said, "Yes, ma'am."

He ran as fast as he could back to the meat market. He went in through the back door and Amando was sitting on the wooden barrel. He had placed Panchito's shoes against the wall. As soon as he saw Panchito he noticed the package in Panchito's hands.

"What happened?" Amando said, standing up and glaring at Panchito.

Panchito was out of breath. The ground had gotten hotter. He had stumbled on the railroad tracks and the package of meat had fallen out of his hand and rolled in the grit of the railroad ties. He said, "The widow weighed the meat and she said that it was not a pound. She said you cheated her."

Amando jumped at Panchito and slapped him. "That's for being disrespectful," he said. "And there's plenty more where that came from."

"That's what she said," Panchito said, rubbing his face.

"Damn widow," Amando said, taking the package away from Panchito. He noticed the grit on the outside of the package and assumed the widow had thrown it on the floor. Panchito was not about to confess that he had fallen down at the railroad tracks.

"There's only one thing to do," said Amando and he opened the package and threw in some more hamburger meat. "Here," he said. "Take it back. Let her weigh it."

He handed the package over to Panchito and Panchito took off running through the back door. He was crossing the empty yard in back of the butcher shop when he heard Amando yelling at him not to put the quarter in his pocket, "It's too much temptation," he heard him say. Panchito jumped down the incline and landed on the sidewalk. The concrete was hotter. It was late morning. It would get hotter. He was at full speed in no time. He headed south then turned at the railroad tracks and then he went south again. He knocked at the widow's door and she came and opened the screen. She showed him in this time without letting him wait outside. The room felt cooler and Panchito paused for an instant in front of the fan. The widow looked at him like she did not appreciate him enjoying her fan. Panchito walked into the kitchen and placed the package on the scale. The widow looked at the package and made her face again.

"Why is this package so dirty?" she said.

"I dropped it," said Panchito.

"You dropped it?" the widow said.

"Yes," said Panchito. "I fell at the railroad tracks."

"Never mind the story," the widow said. She looked at Panchito and said, "Young man, do you know who the butcher is?"

"Amando," said Panchito.

"Yes. We all know he's Amando. But do you really know who he is?"

Panchito said, "All I know is that he is Amando the butcher."

"You have no idea who he is?"

"No, ma'am."

"You have no idea what he is to you? What relation he is to you?"

"No, ma'am."

"You've never been told?"

"No, ma'am."

"Who do you think he is?"

"Amando, the butcher," said Panchito.

"You are so green," the widow said. "I'll just leave you like that. Leave you not knowing. You didn't know your father was alive in San Antonio? And you don't know who Amando is?"

"No, ma'am. My mother has told me that my father died in the war. He was a hero."

"Son, don't make me laugh. You are so green. So, so green. . . . And now about the so-called meat you deliver. All in concert with the dishonest Amando. Are you two together on this?"

"No, ma'am. Amando added some more meat. He said for you to weigh it."

"That is what I'm doing, young man. If you notice, the scale is pointing at the one-pound mark. If I had not weighed this package do you know that I would have paid for something I did not get? Do you believe in taking an old widow? Has your family come to this?"

"No, ma'am."

The widow then took the package off the scale and opened it. But before doing so she said, "Look at all this filth on the package. You claim to have fallen down?"

Panchito said, "Yes, ma'am. I fell at the railroad tracks."

"Can't Amando get a more reliable person to deliver meat?"

"No, ma'am," said Panchito.

"And when did you fall down? Coming or going?"

"Going," said Panchito.

"Do you mean to say, young man, that you took this filthy wrapping back to Amando and he did not have the courtesy to use a clean piece of paper? He did not think enough of me to use clean paper? Is this what you are saying?"

"I don't know," said Panchito.

"You take this filthy package back and you tell Amando that I consider this to be an insult to me. To send such a filthy package. So unappetizing. I could not bear to eat the meat inside this package as filthy as it is. Take it. Take it away from my sight."

Amando was cutting meat when Panchito arrived exhausted and his feet aching with the heat of the ground. He saw the package in Panchito's hand and he said, "What have we here? The package of meat? Come back again? Returned again? For what reason? Tell me. Tell me, Panchito."

Panchito leaned against the wooden barrel and eyed his shoes. He said, "The widow says that the package is filthy. She said it was an insult to her for you to send such a filthy package."

Amando said, "She's the one that made it filthy. She threw it on the floor. Didn't she?"

Panchito said, "No, sir."

"No, sir? What do you mean, no sir?"

"She did not throw it on the floor. I dropped it on the railroad tracks."

"Damn you, young man," said Amando. "I ought to whip you right here with a butcher knife. Come here."

Panchito said, "No, sir. You're going to slap me. You hit me twice today. That is enough."

"You are being very disrespectful," said Amando. "I will deal with you in another way. I will find a way. You wait and see."

Amando took the package and undid it. He tore off another piece of butcher paper and wrapped the meat again. He said, handing over the package to Panchito, "Take this and don't come back without the quarter. Do you understand? That quarter is your pay for the day."

"Yes, sir," said Panchito and he took off running through the back door.

He arrived at the widow's house and this time she was waiting for him. She said, through the screen door, "You will not set foot inside this house until I see the package."

Panchito showed the widow the clean paper and the widow said, "That, my green young man, is better. You can come in and we will weigh the package together."

Panchito stopped by the fan for a moment again and again the widow gave him a stern look. He followed her into the kitchen where she placed the package on the scale. It was a pound on her scale.

"So far so good," the widow said. "Before I open this package," she continued, "I want to know if you truly don't know who Amando is?"

"Amando is the butcher," he said.

"And you don't know what relation he is to you? Is that right?"

"Yes, ma'am."

"And you believe your father is dead?"

"Yes, ma'am."

"And you believe this with all your heart to be true?"

"Yes, ma'am."

"How thoroughly green you are, young man. . . . And now for the meat. We shall open it together."

She took the package off the scale and laid it on the counter by the sink where the sunlight shone the brightest. She opened the package and made her face again.

"This is what Amando calls meat?" she said. "This? This is meat? Come look at this. Do you consider this meat? Do you?"

Panchito said, "I don't know. I just deliver the meat."

"But aren't you responsible for the product you deliver? Aren't you as dishonest as Amando? Aren't you two birds of a feather? Both dishonest. Running about town waving your meat at the public knowing that what you have inside the package is nothing but gristle? Is this the respect you and Amando have for the people of this town?"

"No ma'am," said Panchito.

"Take this meat," the widow said, "and tell Amando that this is out of the question. I will not buy meat from him again. Wrap the meat and take it back. I will not touch it. Gristle makes me break out. Take it. Take it. Take it away from here, young man."

Amando saw Panchito running through the vacant lot behind the butcher shop with the package in his hand. Amando cursed under his breath. "Damn widow," he said.

When Panchito ran inside to keep his feet from burning up, Amando said, "What now? What problem do you have now?"

"The widow," said Panchito, "she did not want the meat. She said it was gristle and gristle makes her break out. She said she would not buy meat from you again."

"Well, where else is she going to buy meat?" Amando asked.

Panchito said, "I don't know, sir."

Amando was sitting on the wooden barrel. He buried his face in his hands. He was shaking his head slowly. With his head still buried in his hands he said, "You have not earned your salary today and here it is almost twelve noon. Put your shoes on. Go stand outside and tell the people that we have meat to sell. Go. Go on. Put on your shoes."

Panchito was sitting outside in his chair, his paper cap on when Amando came out. He had two soft drinks in his hand and some lunch meat and bread. He spread the meat and bread on top of a wooden barrel he had outside and he said to Panchito, "Come. Come over and let us eat."

They ate several fold-over sandwiches and drank the soft drinks watching the few people go by. When they were through eating Amando sat by Panchito and he said, "How do you like the job so far?"

Panchito said, "So far, I don't like it very much."

Amando slapped Panchito and said, "That's for being disrespectful. And there's plenty more where that came from."

"Yes, sir," said Panchito, rubbing his face again.

Amando said, "That's the redeeming part of the meat business. No one likes it but someone has to sacrifice to do it."

The widow's words rang in Panchito's mind. As he had run off the last time she had said, "Ask Amando who he is. Maybe he will have the decency to tell you."